Royal Rising

LOVE IN LAANDIA
SWEET ROYAL ROMANCE

HOLLY KERR

Also By Holly Kerr

Royal Rumble

Royal Retelling

Royal Rising

Royal Reluctance

Royal Rebel

Royal Replacement

plus

Suitor Science series

Love & Alliteration series

Don't series

Charlotte Dodd series

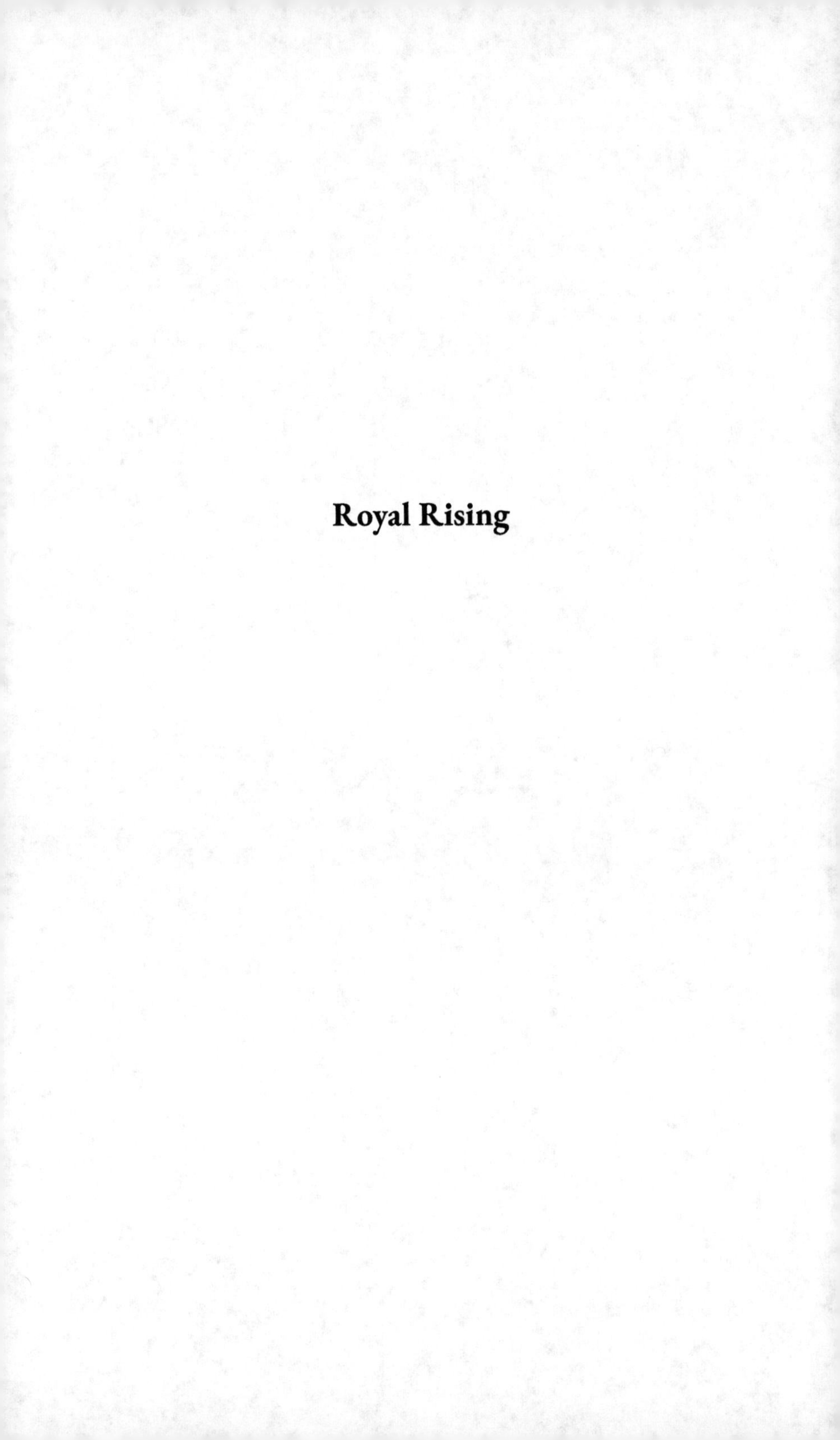

Royal Rising

Dedication

To Dad – my Bob.

And all the other dads out there

Prologue

Sixteen years ago...

Once upon a time, a prince attempted to learn to drive.

This would be a strange sort of fairy tale because, in all the stories of far-off kingdoms, brave knights defeating dragons and fair maidens locked in towers, no Prince Charming had ever failed a driving test.

Twice.

And even though he finally managed to get his license, Prince Kalle Llewellyn Anton George, firstborn and heir apparent of King Magnus of Laandia, is still having trouble driving.

"Clutch, now gas," I instruct, pedalling with my hands to show Kalle how to work his feet. "You've got it."

Two days ago, Kalle finally passed his driver's exam; but instead of setting out in the beat-up pick-up the king had assigned for his use, Kalle decided he also needed to learn to drive on a standard transmission. I don't know if it was because of FOMO, some girl, or his little brother Gunnar's new fascination with everything with a motor, but the prince is determined to master the stick shift.

And since the only standard vehicle at the castle belongs to my father, Royal Groundskeeper and Man of the Lawn—that's what my sisters and I call him, not any official title—Dad was tasked to teach Kalle how to drive with a clutch.

Apparently, that one lesson was more successful than his four months of in-car lessons by the king's security team because, after only a day, Dad gives Kalle the keys to practice on the quieter roads around the castle.

And he sends me with him.

Kalle and I are three weeks, and four days apart in age—I'm older. We're acquaintances, but I wouldn't call us friends, mainly because Kalle rarely spends his energy on anything that isn't re-lated to sports. I enjoy watching sports on occasion but anything ball-puck-or-racquet-related is not my friend.

I like numbers. And books.

My childhood bookshelves were full of fairy tales. As I got old-er, these were replaced by retellings of fairy tales, with an emphasis on the more PG-plus versions. I read romance novels, royal ro-mances being a personal favourite, which is ironic since the chances of me having a royal romance are slim to none. Even with me hanging out at the castle, the home of the royal family of Laandia.

Every summer since I was nine, I spent my days helping my father in the gardens at the castle. That doesn't mean I hung out with Kalle, his brothers and his little sister, though; I may have a first-hand view of the comings and goings of a real royal family but Dad put me to work. I learned about annuals and perennials, how to spot a weed, what weeds are not our friends, and the best time to prune.

I was a good pruner. I still am, finding quiet satisfaction in clipping each branch at just the right spot.

My mother has high hopes for a royal romance. She has four daughters; there are four princes. You don't need to be a numbers person to do the math. Unfortunately—for my mother—the closest any of the England girls have got to a royal romance was when Bo asked my sister Enid to dance at last year's Christmas party in Battle Harbour. That kept Mom going for weeks.

I've long ago taken myself out of her dreams for a prince to fall for an England girl. I stopped being impressed by the brothers after I had the misfortune of seeing Prince Bo and Prince Gunnar light a fire with their flatulence.

And now this.

Kalle lets off the clutch, jamming his foot on the gas, which is not how I showed him, but at least my father's truck jerks forward without stalling. He picks up speed but the gears screech as he shifts into second.

I can't hide my grimace at the sound.

"Wasn't that bad," Kalle grunts, shifting into third a little too fast.

"Wasn't that good either." I've been shifting gears since I was twelve, and driving around the country roads surrounding my family's farm with my older sister since I was fourteen.

That's what you do in Battle Harbour when you're not born into the royal family. For us, it's just a small fishing village on the edge of Laandia, which is a tiny country smack dab between the provinces of Quebec and Newfoundland in Canada, and the Atlantic Ocean.

"Think you can do better?" Kalle asks, hitting eighty so he can shift into fourth.

"I know I'm better, and you shouldn't go so fast on this road. They just redid the shoulders and you'll spin out on the gravel if you hit it." He gives me a look—half grumpy, half confused. "I live out here," I tell him.

"I knew that."

"You have no idea where I live," I shoot back. Growing up in such close proximity, yet with such an insurmountable distance from the royal family, wipes out most of the reverence one might feel around them. I have respect for the monarchy, I like King Magnus, admire Queen Selene, but despite sitting in front of Kalle in every class we've been in—Edie England, Kalle Erickson— and the fervent hopes of my mother, we've never been close.

To my mother's dismay, I have to add.

"I know where you live." Kalle has an insolent arrogance that comes more from being the type of male who excels at every sport rather than being born a prince.

I say that because both Odin and Bo show better manners than their older brother.

"How could you know where I live?"

"I just do. You're not invisible, you know."

"What are you talking about?"

"You're in the garden all the time with your dad. You could come and say hi." Kalle gives me a sideways glance and I snap my mouth shut. It's been hanging open since he said he knows where I live.

"I... I'm working," I finally manage.

"I see you with your book. You're not working all the time."

This may be the first actual conversation I've had with Prince Kalle and I'm not holding up my end of it very well. "I... That's my break."

Kalle shrugs. "Just saying, you can come say hi on your break. We don't bite."

He downshifts as we approach a stop sign. He's still not great with the clutch but at least this time, he doesn't need a reminder from me. Which is good because I'm not sure I could get the words out.

Regardless of how I try to pretend I'm indifferent to him, this is *Prince Kalle of Laandia* talking to me like he wants me to... I don't know what. Hang out? Be friends?

I'm the daughter of the man who weeds his gardens. The royal family is not my friend.

"Ok," I manage.

"You can talk to Mom about flowers." Kalle makes a face like a man who doesn't understand the joy of putting hands in dirt.

"Yeah."

He turns at the stop sign, thankfully in the opposite direction from where I live. Kalle might think he knows where I live, but he doesn't need to see it. Not that there's anything wrong with the old farmhouse with the red-painted barn that's seen better days, but it's no castle.

The road is a straight stretch, clear and empty at this time of the morning. Kalle wanted early because he had some practice to go to, so I showed up before my shift at Mr. Frosty's ice cream shop. I help Dad in the gardens on my days off. It's a beautiful day, already warm and sunny, with a sky as blue as Kalle's eyes.

It's impossible not to make the comparison. It's also becoming difficult not to stare at the way he lounges in the seat like he's some professional driver, which he clearly is not. His right- hand rests on the gearshift, his forearm tanned and sprinkled with reddish-blond hair. The sleeve of his T-shirt is snug around his bicep. Kalle might only be sixteen but looks older, more like a man than most of the guys our age, with his height—still growing at six-two—and the width of his shoulders.

His arms are impressive.

I whip my attention away from his arm. From him, which is also difficult because the cab of my father's truck isn't very big and Kalle's hand is at an interesting distance from my bare knee.

I should not care about Prince Kalle's arm or any other of his appendages.

I should look out the window and do my best to ignore him, just like he's been doing for years.

Only... has he? *I see you with your book.*

I nibble on a hangnail and focus on an object on the shoulder of the road that is quickly approaching because Kalle is going pretty fast.

I squint into the sun. I think it might be— "Turtle—!" I cry.

"What?"

Kalle swerves—I have no idea why. It happens so fast; one moment, we're (speeding) down a deserted road, and the next, he jerks the wheel to the left, the tire catching on the newly laid gravel shoulder. He jerks it to the right, horribly over-correcting, so now we're aiming for the opposite shoulder and the huge turtle trying to cross the road.

"Don't hit it!"

He misses the turtle but heads straight into the ditch.

It's a shallow ditch, more of a dip with overgrown grasses and the occasional shrub. We hit two of the shrubs and leave a path of flattened grasses before Kalle comes to a stop only inches in front of a patch of barbed-wire fence.

A herd of black-and-white cows munch placidly on the other side.

"What did you yell for?" Kalle demands, both hands now clutching the wheel.

"There was a turtle. I just pointed it out."

"You made it sound like I was going to hit it." He bangs his forehead against the steering wheel. "Jesus. My parents are never going to let me drive again."

"It's not that bad."

"I almost killed a cow. And a turtle. And you."

It's the "And you" that melts something inside me, something I never even knew was meltable.

"You didn't kill anything," I soothe. "It's not a big deal."

Still leaning his forehead on the steering wheel, Kalle looks over at me with his really blue eyes. I can't help but notice his lashes are long and thick and there's a tiny pimple on his chin.

Why have I never let myself realize how cute Prince Kalle is? Of course, I *knew*—all the princes are attractive, even ten-year-old Gunnar with his white-blond hair and mischievous smile—but it's only now that I've let myself *see*.

Not the best timing, Edie.

"It feels like a big deal," he grumbles. "I drove us into a ditch. There's no way I can get out of this."

"But I can. Switch spots," I tell him. "I'll get us out and it'll be like nothing happened."

I managed to back the truck out without any more damage, except for the small dent from a shrub that was more the size of a small tree, and get us back on the road. Kalle is even persuaded to carry the turtle across the road—luckily it isn't a snapping turtle.

It also takes a bit of convincing, but Kalle finally agrees to drive back. Get right back on the horse, my father always says. But I can tell he's worried about what his parents, and my father, will say.

It's an easy decision to make. "I'll say I was driving," I announce as we pull up to the castle. "That I was trying to see what the turtle was and hit the shoulder."

"I'm not letting you do that."

"You don't have a choice. It's my father's truck, and he'll believe me. No one will ever know, and you won't have to worry about the king not letting you drive."

Kalle is still arguing when we get out of the truck, but keeps his mouth shut when I confess, except to praise me on how I got the truck out of the ditch.

That afternoon, Kalle stops by Mr. Frosty's with a group of friends and takes me aside to thank me.

The next time I help Dad in the garden, I stop in to say hi.

1

Edie

I T FEELS LIKE I'VE been hit in the stomach with a taser.

And I know what a taser feels like, thanks to my father's insistence that I take a self-defence/security course when I started working at The King's Hat pub. He set it up with my younger sisters, Enid and Eloise, because both had recently been the recipient of bad breakups and Dad thought knowing how to take a man down would be beneficial for all. One of the lessons involved using a taser on each other, to Enid's everlasting joy, and I can still remember the jittery, nervous sensation with exact clarity.

I feel the same way as I get ready for this date.

It's just a date. I shouldn't be this nervous. And it's not like I haven't been on dates—I'm thirty-two. I've *been* on *dates*.

But this one is different.

"*I* am dating a prince."

I speak the words aloud to my reflection to make it more believable.

It doesn't help, and only brings Ernie, my cat, off the bed to weave between my legs. I like to think it's his way of showing support, but he probably only wants to be fed.

"I am dating a *prince*," I tell Ernie, who heads to his food bowl in the kitchen.

It took me three days to agree to go for dinner with him.

It's not like there is a lack of princes in Battle Harbour—we've got four, and one of those is my boss at The King's Hat. Kalle, the prince in question, likes to call me his partner when there's a nasty task that he doesn't want to do, like filling the lady basket in the women's room or cutting up limes for the bar.

He says the juice squirts in his eyes, but that's because he's never bothered to learn to cut them up properly.

Kalle is not the prince I'm going on a date with.

It still seems surreal. That I, Edie England, born and bred in Battle Harbour, Laandia, daughter of Bob and Martha and second eldest of four daughters, have accepted an invitation to dine with a prince. I shake my hair out of my customary ponytail, apply makeup to highlight my brown eyes—my best feature—and try to decrease the size of my nose—my worst.

I look okay. Good enough for dinner with a prince? I have no idea.

I'm still critiquing my reflection when the chime of FaceTime interrupts my playlist. I expect the call is from one of my sisters but my smile widens when the face of Stella Laz fills the screen.

"You're dating a prince," she greets me, speaking loudly over the barking of dogs.

"So are you," I counter.

The flash of her smile is instant but quickly vanishes as a series of texts light up my screen.

"Is everything okay?" she asks.

My shoulders slump. "Sisters. I'll deal with it later. What's new with your Prince Charming?"

Stella and Prince Gunnar are a new thing, still trundling along on wobbly legs like a newborn calf. My friendship with Stella is also quite new, but already more secure, brought about by the shared experience of being bridesmaids in the first royal wedding of Laandia. Lady Camille of Saint Pierre married Prince Odin, and since Camille didn't have a wide circle of friends able to make up the wedding party, Stella and I were recruited.

Actually, Stella's stepsister was supposed to go with Prince Gunnar, but she bailed at the last minute and Stella stepped in.

It's a long story.

Stella's always had a reputation as being difficult. She's sharp-tongued and bad-tempered, but when you get past the crusty surface, there's a soft, squishy centre right there waiting for you.

Unlike in *Cinderella*, in this reality, Prince Charming fell for the wicked stepsister instead of the boring blonde. Not that Cinderella is boring— Okay, maybe she's a little boring. In my opinion, there are better fairy-tale princesses out there.

"We're not talking about me and Gunnar," Stella points out, her sharp tone softening more every day.

"And we shouldn't say I'm dating a prince because it's a *date*," I counter. "One date, not plural. I'm going on *one* date with a prince. Prince Mathias."

And then what?

But I don't say that out loud.

Prince Mathias is the nephew of King Magnus of Laandia. Beside the four princes and the princess, there is another royal family living on the side of Laandia by the Quebec border, and I met them at Odin's wedding.

I suspect I would have gotten an invitation to Prince Odin's wedding even without Kalle bringing me as a date, but I definitely wouldn't have been a member of the wedding party.

Along with Mathias's interest, it still blows my mind that I, daughter of the former groundskeeper of the king of Laandia's castle, got to be a bridesmaid for the new Princess Camille, soon to be prefect of Saint Pierre.

And if I hadn't been one of the bridesmaids, I doubt Prince Mathias would have asked me to dance. And then invited me to have coffee with him the next day.

And now dinner.

I'm going to dinner with a prince.

It sounds strange, even to me. Yes, I work with Prince Kalle every day and we have shared plenty of meals together, he is *Kalle*, not *Prince*. There's a difference.

"You went for coffee with him yesterday," Stella reminds me. Not that I need reminding. "The entire town noticed, so I think that can be considered a date."

When you live in a town as small as Battle Harbour, everyone knows your name and your business, especially if you have a close association with the royal family. And when you're seen out and about with one of the Peace River royal family... "You should get used to that," I warn Stella. "Having the entire town notice things. Gunnar makes a splash wherever he goes."

It's better to talk about Stella than acknowledge how nervous I was just walking through the town square with Mathias. I—who has been called bubbly too many times to count—could barely string a sentence together. And *still*, Mathias invited me to dinner!

"We're leaving next week. Six weeks in Southeast Asia." Stella tries for cool but excitement tints her every word. "So no one here will notice anything." There's the smile again. "But I didn't call to talk about that."

"What did you call for then?" But I grin at the screen to take away any sting.

"To give moral support because that's what friends do. You look nice," she adds.

I check my reflection for the sixteenth time, pushing a wayward strand of dark hair behind my ear.

I miss my ponytail.

I'm not used to lipstick.

I'm wearing high heels.

But I have to admit that I do look nice. "Thanks."

"Good luck," Stella sings. "You can let me know how it goes if you want."

"I'll call you tomorrow with all the dirty details," I promise. "Not that they'll be dirty."

Stella laughs as she says goodbye.

I'm going out for dinner with a prince. My reflection shows a nervous/excited/slightly crazed grin with too many teeth.

I point at the mirror. "Get it together," I tell myself in my best end-of-night-voice when I have to tell those holding up the bar it's time to go home. "He's just a prince."

The laugh bubbles up because... Mathias is a prince.

Reluctantly, I check my texts.

Enid: You ready to wow him?

Ella: A PRINCE! Mom is FREAKING!

Eloise: He's so cute. Looks just like Odin.

Ella: When are you going to get that P O is so out of your league.

Enid: Plus married

Eloise: A girl can still dream

Enid: Mom does that enough for all of us

And then on a separate text string, there is a text from my mother.

Mom: I am so proud of you! Even if this goes nowhere, know that you have fulfilled my dream to have a prince fall for one of my girls.

And my mother is not joking.

When I told her I had not only met Prince Mathias at the wedding but danced with him several times, she clapped so much her palms were tomato red. And there were real tears in her eyes.

It's a good thing I'm not part of Laandia "society," like in Bridgerton or my mother would be one of the mamas who terrorize the season's bachelors in their attempts to marry one of their daughters to a prince.

She'd focused her attentions on King Magnus's sons and completely forgot about the royal cousins. Lucky for them.

Mom has kept her hope alive that somehow Prince Kalle will look at me as more than just a friend someday, but I can't see that happening.

And I don't like to think about it because it's hard enough watching him date every single woman in town—and many more who are just visiting.

I've stopped watching.

I'm used to working with Kalle. I can keep it all business, with no longing looks or hesitant sighs when he walks out of the room. As far as Kalle is concerned, I feel nothing but friendship for him. There is friendly affection between us—we are friends. He's one of my best friends.

That's it.

But as I give Ernie one last pet and head out for a quick stop to check in at the bar before I meet Mathias, there's a strange sensation mixed with my excitement. There's a tug—a pretty strong one—for me to stay right where I am. To get out of this dress and into my jeans.

Because as heady it is to be going on a date with a prince, there's that something in the pit of my stomach that's telling me it's wrong. That it's not Mathias I'm supposed to be with.

I do my best to ignore it.

2

Kalle

COLLECTING DIRTY DISHES IS up top of the list of things I never expected to do with my life.

But I'm not the type of business owner who never pitches in: I show up at The King's Hat when it opens and I'm usually here when it closes. If I'm not, Edie is. I pay her well to put in the hours and take on the responsibility, but there's the little voice inside me that makes sure I'm seen helping out when things need getting done, like clearing the pint glasses from the tables when my servers are getting slammed.

"Have you done Wordle today?"

I've never once tried Wordle, so I know Dillon, slumped on his stool at his usual spot at the end of the bar, isn't talking to me. I don't bother looking up from filling my bin with empty dessert plates, sticky with caramel sauce, from the table of the group who just left.

But my head jerks up when I hear the unmistakable click of high heels, plus a low wolf whistle from Dillon. "Jeez, woman, you look *good.*"

I glance up to see Edie. Only it's not Edie. I look again.

It's Edie, but it's not *my* Edie. This Edie is…

"Thanks, *man*, but I'm still not telling you what it is," Edie says to Dillon, fiddling with her ear. She's dressed in black, some shiny fabric that hugs her ass and... other areas, and leaves her arms bare. "I got it in four."

The bar area is quiet but the tables in the rest of the place are filled with the dinner crowd, with waitresses Leah and Bethie winding their way through with trays of plates and foaming pints. The special tonight is shepherd's pie and the scent curls in from the kitchen door and reminds me I haven't eaten yet. It's busy but not as chaotic as it will be later. Wednesday night is darts night, which means a good crowd.

But it's the dark clouds rolling in from the Atlantic, warning all of the storm blowing in, and it's going to fill up the place. A storm like that will keep in the boats in the harbour tomorrow, which means the fishermen will be looking for something to do tonight.

There are five drinking establishments in Battle Harbour, but mine always fills up first.

I make a mental note to check the kegs. Make sure Bethie gets her break after the supper rush is over. Give Tyler free rein on the bar.

It still doesn't distract me from Edie standing before me like she's waiting for my approval.

"Did you buy a dress?" I demand rudely because I can't find any other words. The words I should pull forth are *incredible* and *stunning* and *sexy as hell* but no go. Edie is good-looking on a regular day, long dark hair pulled back from her heart-shaped face and the constant quirk of a smile, but when she makes an effort like tonight, she's something else.

Edie's mouth twists into a frown and she's wearing *lipstick*. Who is this person?

Woman. This is a woman. Who is this *woman*?

"I borrowed this from my sister, but yes, I own a dress," Edie says in a calm voice. It takes a lot to get a rise out of her, even with me being rude. It's unbelievable how steady she is, regardless of what she's facing down, including bad-tempered me.

I don't mean to be rude but people are just so annoying. Not Edie. She never annoys me, but she's around so much that she gets rude Kalle more than anyone else.

"*U* is the first letter," Edie tells Dillon, twisting her hair so it hangs over her shoulder. Her eyes are big and brown, looking more like chocolate buttons than ever.

I lean the dirty dishes bin against the bar and give her a good look up and down—and then wish I hadn't because, damn, she looks good, and I don't need to be thinking that about my best friend. "Never seen you wear one," I grumble.

"A dress? Did you miss the fact I wore a turquoise bridesmaid's dress less than a week ago?" she asks, dark eyes narrowed like I'm an obnoxious patron after a few too many pints. "I was right beside you when we walked out of the church."

I don't want to think about Edie in *this* dress when my head is still cluttered from images of her in *that* dress. The dress shows off her little waist and the curve of her hips, creamy shoulders and a hint of cleavage—

She's got it going on in this dress too.

There's no way I can call what's going on in the front of Edie *cleavage.*

Intermammary cleft. That's better. Nothing sexy about *that.*

"*U* doesn't help," Dillon complains, studying his phone. "I have no idea what this word is and I've one guess left."

Dillon, the head of my four-man security detail, parks his butt at the bar when he's on duty, solving every puzzle he can get his hands on. A former Marine, pushing sixty with a bald head, grizzled beard, and shoulders that take up two spots at the bar, Dillon has a daily competition with Edie to see who can get the Wordle word of the day.

Edie usually wins. She's smart. Smarter than anyone gives her credit for.

Now she leans over Dillon's shoulder. "You smell good," he says with the appreciation of a man who hasn't gone on a date in however long he's been working for the castle. Or at least a date I know about. Chase, the second member of my team and currently washing dishes in the kitchen—his choice—is fairly vocal about his dating prowess but Dillon has never chimed in.

"What's your favourite bra size?" Edie asks him.

Dillon gives her a quizzical look before turning back to his phone. "Double D," he cries. "Udder."

Edie pats him on the shoulder. "Good boy."

I drift closer, not needing to get a sniff of her good scent, but... just because. "Where you off to?" I ask, trying to sound casual like Edie looked like this on a regular basis.

She rarely takes a night off unless I force her, so no, she doesn't look like this on a regular basis.

That I know of, I guess.

Usually, it's jeans and a T-shirt, with running shoes because she's always on her feet. Not those strappy things with the sky-high heels that make her legs look so—

Nope. Not looking at her legs.

"The woman has the evening off, so as far as I'm concerned, she doesn't have to answer to the likes of you, Maj." If Dillon used that tone on anyone else, they'd be backing down quicker than he can jump off that stool, which is pretty fast. And technically, he shouldn't call me Maj, because I'm not about to be king anytime soon.

"Last time I looked, I sign your paycheck," I remind him.

"Aye, but I like her better'n you." He winks at Edie, who smiles widely, dimples marring her cheeks like the indent of lips on a good head of stout.

I raise my eyes skyward. "There's no respect," I mutter.

Being the next in line to the throne of Laandia means I've had to put up with a security detail since I moved out of the castle. Dillon and Chase have been with me for about six years since I bought The King's Hat. They're the best of the bunch.

"All sorts of respect, *Your Highness,* but we still like Edie more than you. But still—*m'lady*—" Dillon drawls, bowing his head and using his nickname for Edie rather than his usual "woman." "Where you off to looking like a million bucks?"

"I have a date." Is it me or does Edie sound proud of the fact? "Dinner at Nonna's."

Nonna's Ristorante is one of two decent restaurants in town, the other being Daily Catch, the best seafood place in all of Laandia.

I say that because I became the owner last year.

There are other places to eat in Battle Harbour, but when I say decent, I mean a place to take a girl out for a good meal.

I really don't care where Edie is going—it's who she's going with that has my insides tangled into a knot no sailor is going to be able to undo. Because if this is a date, unless she met someone on her way back from getting coffee this morning, Edie's date is with Mathias Erickson.

I don't bother trying to hide my grimace. "With my cousin."

"Prince Mathias asked me to dinner, yes," she confirms, and I wish with all my being that she'd bumped into *anyone*—even her uber crush, Ryan Gosling—crossing the town square this morning.

"Prince Mathias, huh?" Dillon asks, glancing at me and back to Edie.

"Yes." She lifts her chin proudly. Edie is *proud* to be going out with Mathias Erickson, sixth in line to the throne of Laandia, and it's not because he's a prince.

She likes him.

The knot in my belly tightens even more.

"I always thought you and Maj..." Dillon begins.

Edie stops him with a hand. "Don't start."

Everyone says it and even more think it. The *why aren't Kalle and Edie together* has been a constant question since we started hanging out as friends, back when we were sixteen.

And it's one that is becoming more and more difficult to answer.

Edie gives the official response. "We're friends."

"Yeah, but friends... you know," Dillon points out.

"We don't," I growl. Even if we did, it'd be nobody's business but ours. But we haven't. Never. Ever. In the sixteen years of friendship, I haven't made a move on Edie. Not even when I found her crying after being dumped by Greg Kaan a week before the prom. Or that night when she studied for her mixology exam by lining up the cocktails on the bar for us to taste test.

And I was tempted that night. I'm not sure what exactly stopped me, only I did stop before I found out if Edie's lips were as soft as they looked.

She's got lipstick on tonight, a soft pink colour that shines in the bar lights. I can't look at it or I'm going to start thinking—

"You can't walk over to Nonna's looking like..." *Gorgeous.* The word pops into my mind, fully formed with a dozen descriptives following. Like *breath-taking.*

Beautiful.

"What's wrong with the way I look?" *Crap.* Now I've made her mad, difficult to do with Edie, even for me.

"Nothing," I growl. "Just—Mathias will expect you to be driven."

She frowns. "I told him I'd walk. How would you know what he expects? You said you don't even know him."

I turn away so she can't see my expression, which probably mirrors my face when I tried Chef's cabbage and sausage pie the other day. "I know enough," I tell her, not doing anything about the mulish tone in my voice.

"It might be nice to share some of that *enough.*"

I don't bother to answer because there's no point in telling Edie what I know about Mathias. I can only hope she'll figure it out for herself. "You'll turn an ankle on the cobblestones with those heels," I point out, taking another quick peek at Edie's bare legs in the process.

Other than the wedding, I think I've seen her in a dress maybe one other time; twice if you count my mother's funeral, but I wouldn't have noticed if half the town had come buck naked that day.

Edie has amazing legs; slim but strong with surprisingly delicate-looking ankles that would snap like a twig if she tripped wearing those shoes. The cobblestones through the square are a bit uneven, never fixed after the winter thaw and— "Dillon?"

"I'd be happy to escort you," Dillon supplies, sliding off his stool. "Since you helped me out with Wordle."

"I don't need…" But she stops herself with a shake of her head. She's worked at The King's Hat since we opened and she knows enough not to argue with me when I've got my mind set.

Only I'm a little confused as to why it's so set on Edie tonight.

3

Edie

MATHIAS SMILES AT ME from across the table.

I smile back.

It was nice of Dillon to drive me, saving my carefully straightened hair from frizzing in the drizzle of rain.

The storm is almost on us, giving off a holiday vibe along with rain and high winds.

The people of Battle Harbour react to storms in two ways—they either hunker down at home, as my dad says, or they hunker down someplace else.

Which is why every table at Nonna's is full. Everyone who decided they wanted somewhat authentic Italian for dinner during a storm looks up with undisguised interest as I walk in.

I smile, I wave, I call hello to a few. When I take the seat Mathias holds out for me, the whole place goes silent.

"You seem to be popular," Mathias murmurs with a half-smile after Renaldo brings bread and water and promises we'll love the juicy, jammy red he'll bring us.

He's extremely good looking.

Mathias, that is. Renaldo is five feet tall with a compact figure and old enough to be my grandfather. I've known him since I was a little girl and Dad used to bring us here for Mom's birthday.

I can't get my mind off Mathias's good looks, especially how his blue eyes are studying me from across the table. The *small table*, which means Mathias is close enough to touch.

His forearm especially—that appendage rests casually on the white tablecloth.

Unfortunately, his sleeves are long despite the summer heat and buttoned at the wrist.

I'm a sucker for a nice arm. Biceps, primarily, but I like a nicely muscled forearm as well. Hands, too; tanned and strong and slightly calloused to show they're no stranger to hard work.

I blame Kalle for my arm fetish.

Mathias's hands look soft and pale, suggesting he doesn't do much outside.

It's no matter; he's still very attractive with a jaw squarer than most houses. His hair looks bronze rather than blond in the warm lighting, and his eyes are as blue as the summer sky. And the breadth of his shoulders?

Smaller than Kalle's.

Not that Kalle is the man I compare other men to, but I do spend quite a lot of time with him and can't help but notice his shoulders.

The whispered comments are still flowing and I hope people in here have more to talk about than me. "Do you ever get used to the attention?" I ask Mathias, pleating the tablecloth.

"Am I getting the attention?" Mathias demands, hand pressed to his chest. "I think it's you who have caught their eye. You look amazing, by the way. My apologies for not telling you the moment you walked in."

I drop my gaze because as cheesy as the remark is, it hits the target. "Thank you. You don't need to apologize."

"I'm glad you agreed to dinner." Mathias's voice is radio-DJ deep.

"I'm glad you invited me. I have to eat, don't I?"

I slowly exhale as we study the menu. I don't know Mathias, so that's why this is awkward. I'm here to get to know him, like a fact-finding mission. If I look at it like that rather than a date witnessed by an entire restaurant, maybe I'll be able to relax and enjoy myself.

From the next table, Mrs. Powell catches my eye, gives me a big smile and doesn't even try to hide her thumbs-up.

Thankfully, Mathias is looking elsewhere than the vicinity of Mrs. Powell. "This seems like a nice place."

"They have really good pasta." I shake out my napkin and put it on my lap. "Not surprising, since it's an Italian restaurant and they must make a lot of pasta."

"Have you ever been to Italy?" he asks politely.

"I haven't been anywhere. Well, I've been to Canada twice, but that doesn't really count because it's right next door. My sister went to France for her honeymoon, and my girlfriend Kaia wanted me to go to New York City with her, but that was when my mom was sick and my other sister lost the baby and—" I come to a screeching stop. "I'll stop talking now."

To my surprise, Mathias doesn't seem fazed by my verbal diarrhea which only ever comes out when I'm out of my comfort zone. And this is very much out of my comfort zone. "Have you ever wanted to travel?" he asks.

"Wanting and actually doing it are two very different things. I guess I've always been content here in my little slice of Laandia."

Renaldo brings the wine but I have to wait for Mathias to do the smell and taste, commenting on the blackberry, which Renaldo loves and chimes in with a few other blackberry-like wines, before I can get a mouthful of the stuff.

And I really need a big mouthful.

"I would like to show you Italy," Mathias says after we give our order. "I have a friend with a place on Lake Como—"

"Near George?" I interrupt because George Clooney will now always be synonymous with the lake in Italy.

Mathias smiles. "It is quite close."

Taking a deep breath, I ask him where else he's been, and the first part of the evening passes with Mathias telling me about his favourite places.

I don't have a favourite place because Laandia, and Battle Harbour, is my favourite place. I know that even without leaving the country. It has everyone and everything I care about.

The only disadvantage is that, as a single thirty-two-year-old, I've pretty much depleted the dating pool.

The last date I had was three months ago with Angus Deeks. We went to Catch of the Day and he spent most of the time detailing his own catch, how much his fishing boat can hold, and what fish they catch.

To give Angus credit, he wooed me with tales of the pods of whales he's seen over the years. I love whales. I just wish I knew the extent of his conversations consists of more than talk the sea and what's in it.

The date I had a few weeks before Angus, had been a newly divorced friend of my sister's husband, and he took me to Spots and Stripes pool hall on a Sunday. Every screen had an American football game playing and that was all *he* talked about.

It was because of him that I agreed to go out with Angus.

So even if Mathias weren't a prince, he would still be a better date than those guys.

It's not until after our main course—penne pesto with chicken and a heaping spoon of parmesan for me, and beef ragu over tagliatelle for Mathias—that he realizes he's said enough about himself. "Tell me about yourself," he urges.

"You know the basics—born and raised in Battle Harbour," I say, swallowing the first bite of heaven followed by a mouthful of wine. "My father was the groundskeeper at the castle, he and my mother are still happily married, and I have three sisters."

"That's a lot of females in one place. I do better with just my one sister."

"Renee? I have to admit, I Googled you, so I know most of your basics. Father Dante, mother Emelia, you, younger brother Jonas, and Renee. You have a beautiful home in Peace River and a condo in Toronto, where Jonas and Renee spend most of their time."

Am I supposed to know all that? Should I have admitted it? Do I seem like some sort of stalker now?

When we met for coffee, we talked mostly about the wedding. Of course I Googled him; my father wanted to do a background check but my mother told him he was over-reacting because Mathias was a member of the royal family and everything about them could be found on the tabloids or internet sites.

Mom would be so happy to see a picture of me there having dinner with a prince.

Thankfully, Mathias smiles as I give him the rundown of his own family. "I would hope for nothing less, but you've put the ball back in your court because I know almost nothing about you."

"I know the basics but not the good stuff. Let's play Three Questions: we ask anything and the other has to answer."

Mathias does not look amused at my suggestion. "Is this something you do on all your dates?"

"Sometimes, but it's usually what I do with Kalle when he's had a bad day."

Kalle's name chimes between us, like a gong rung for dinner.

"I would think most would want to avoid my cousin when he's had a bad day." Mathias's tone is cool and I want to gulp my words back like that last mouthful of wine. "Working together must make that difficult. Do you spend much time together outside the pub?"

"Is that one of your questions? Because they should be really probing questions, where you ask a lot in only a few words," I offer. "Like, *what do you do in your spare time and who do you do it with,* which would cover interests and hobbies and friends in one shot."

What I want to know is *it's obvious you and Kalle don't get along, so what's up with that?* But I don't think the time is right for that, even though Mathias will undoubtedly give me more information than notoriously close-mouthed Kalle.

Mathias quirks a smile. "Thank you for the clarification. That was definitely not a question, since I'm limited to three. All right,

I need to make this a good one, so... What is your favourite thing about living in Battle Harbour?"

"The way the sun rises over the ocean," I answer automatically. "Where my parents live, it's on a ridge and the perfect spot to watch the sun rise. My sisters and I have a thing when we meet a few times a year and watch it."

"During the solstices and equinoxes?"

"Actually, yes."

"How very pagan of you." Mathias lifts his glass to me. "I've done research into my ancestors, and the Vikings were aggressive pagans. I'm not sure how one can be an aggressive pagan, though."

"Sounds blood-thirsty. Rituals and human sacrifices, maybe?"

"You must not think much of your Viking ancestors," he chides.

"You sound like Odin. He's always trying to promote Viking history."

The smile dims a bit. "Are you friendly with all my cousins, or just Kalle? Ah, but you must be, to be in the wedding party."

I was a bridesmaid purely because Camille didn't have the friends to fill the ranks, but I'm not about to tell Mathias that. "I don't know Camille too well, but what I do know, I like. And I've sort of grown up at the castle, helping my father when I could, so I know the boys and Lyra from afar rather than being close friends. Except for Kalle. We learned to drive together, and we've been friends ever since. What about you? Are you close with your siblings?"

"Honestly, Jonas is an insufferable bore, and Renee is too ob-sessed with her upcoming wedding to pay any attention to anyone other than her wedding planner. I used to wish I was closer to my cousins," he says with a wistful note in his deep voice.

"You don't spend much family time together?"

"That's my father's fault. He holds somewhat of a grudge against his brother."

"Against King Magnus?" The king of Laandia is always top of the world's list of most popular monarchies, and even in Battle Harbour, it's rare to hear a word spoken against him.

"Afraid so." He spins the tagliatelle around the tines of his fork and I have to wait until he finishes the mouthful for him to continue.

"Long ago," he begins, and I lean forward, expecting a variation of a fairy tale where two brothers fight over the love of a good woman. "When my grandfather Euan was still alive, my uncle promised to step down in the line of succession. My father was supposed to take the throne."

I pause because that seems... unlikely. I've never heard that before, but then again, I'm not privy to the inner workings of the monarchy. Still, I can't imagine Laandia without King Magnus. "I didn't know that."

"Not many do. Odin's abdication at his wedding was a sore spot for my father."

"I'm sure." My thoughts scrambling, I pull on a thread. "I had no idea. So if this had happened and Magnus had stepped down and your father had become king, then you would be the crown prince instead of Kalle?"

Mathias nods. "King Magnus would have stayed with his band. I'm sure a lot of things would be different."

From the clipped tone in Mathias's voice, I get the sense he thinks *different* equals *better*.

For the first time today, a little red flag is raised. Not entirely red—more like a dusty rose, but it makes me uneasy. Because of my father's position, as well as the fact King Magnus is just so *cool* to have ruling my country, my loyalty toward the royal family has always been a constant. To consider how things might have been different... I don't want to think about that.

Mathias must read my reluctance on my face. "There's no sense of discussing things which will never be. I shouldn't have mentioned it. I take it Kalle has never spoken of this?"

I shake my head. "Would you want to be king?" I have to ask. "If that's how it had turned out? Kalle..."

Kalle does not want to be king. Everyone knows that.

"I would consider it an honour and a privilege," Mathias says in a low voice. "Now, is there anything else you'd like to know about me, other than boring information about my family, or should I move on to questions for you?"

"Why me?" I blurt out. When Mathias frowns, I wave a hand between us. "I'm the daughter of a groundskeeper and I'm the manager of a pub. You date women who aren't managers of a pub. I have to admit, I'm curious—out of all the women at the wedding, why me?"

"Other than the fact you're a beautiful woman who seems very accomplished for living here?"

I think that's a slight on Battle Harbour but I let it go. "I don't paint or sing, and my French is passable at best. I like to garden and I'm really good at bookkeeping and making schedules. I would not consider me accomplished, but thank you for saying so."

"You sound like you read Jane Austen."

"And love Bridgerton, so my ideas might be a little skewed."

"Not at all. You know what really caught my interest when I met you?" Mathias leans forward. "You kept your shoes on for the entire wedding."

"My... shoes...?"

"Most of the other women your age danced in their bare feet, or those horrible sneakers. I like that you kept on your shoes."

I smile, like he's given me a compliment, only I don't really know if Mathias is joking or not. And under the table, I slip my feet back into my shoes.

4

Kalle

THE STORM BREWING OVER the Atlantic brings in the wind and the rain and the fishermen; it's never good to be on the water during a summer storm like the one moving into place over Battle Harbour. The warnings have gone out, so only a few of the most die-hard or idiotic will head out like usual at dawn in such weather. I hope not many, because if boats go out when it's like this, people die.

I don't like it when people die.

Having the bar filled like this on a Wednesday is both good and bad—it brings in money but often brings in trouble as well. There are generations of fishermen and women working from the docks in Battle Harbour and most are friendly with each other; a lot are related. There's a few that come from away, but there's a big group of local men whose families have been fishing and lobstering for longer than Laandia has been a country.

They may be friendly, but they see fishing as a competition. And with four or five pints in their belly, some of the unfriendly competition always rears its head.

The way Jubblie Mark and Ken McKibbon are trash-talking over the pool table has my fight radar on full alert.

And that's fine with me. In this mood, I'd like nothing more than to bounce some idiots out of here tonight.

Along with picking up dirty dishes, I never pictured myself as the owner of a bar.

I never really pictured myself as anything—I had the sports; the hockey first, moving on to a short career in baseball before my shoulder took me out, and then an attempt at curling that went so much better than I expected. I knew my sports career wouldn't last forever but I'm not a planner. I didn't have an idea of what to do after I gave up curling.

There was always a blank space between that and when I became king. The unknown; a fuzzy gray space of uncertainty.

And then I decided to buy a bar.

The King's Hat, pre-me, was a different sort of place.

Bruce, the former head of Dad's security team, opened it after he retired and had some idea for it to be some sort of upscale gentlemen's club. He reno-ed his house, a beautiful building right in the town square, and opened his club.

Unfortunately, there aren't a lot of upscale gentlemen in Battle Harbour because it's a fishing village.

A fishing town now, with a variety of small businesses. There's a solid middle class, unfortunately a spreading lower economic class, but not a lot of upscale.

Bruce floundered on with his vision, and people came because they liked him, and because Dad was a common visitor. He even provided the reason for the name; on the wall opposite of the bar are four of Dad's gold records, and in a glass case between them is the hat that he wore on the band's last tour, a gold-and-black checked newsboy cap, faded and worn.

When we lost Bruce, I swooped in and bought the place without thinking too much about it. The place meant a lot to me: I'd had my first legal drink here, the same for Odin and Bo, and spent hours playing pool and darts with Jonathan McKibbon. I lost a lot of money playing poker, but I got really good at the game.

I talked to a lot of women here; waitresses, customers. Mothers of customers. Just because it was called a gentleman's club doesn't mean women were excluded. Maybe there were some nights when Bruce set up the temporary stage and brought in dancers from the next town over, but they were for stags and birthday parties, and women weren't really invited those nights anyway.

I always showed up the nights when there were dancers. I talked to a lot of them, too.

But just because it meant a lot to me didn't mean I didn't want to change things up.

I once dated an interior decorator who complained that the bar didn't have a *theme*. I didn't think it needed one. Once it was mine, I gutted the place, taking out the smaller rooms that Bruce preferred, and made one big space, creating circular tables around the load-bearing beams. I added a second pool table in the back corner, put in a few dart boards, and updated the bar with a fourteen-foot mahogany L-shaped beauty.

I liked the wood-panelled walls but added mounted televisions. My old hockey stick is on the wall, the one I used when we won the World Juniors', as well as the bat that I used for my first home run. There's another glass box with three baseballs in it—my second year playing, I missed hitting for the cycle by a double and the team gave me the balls just to rub it in—and a curling rock that I acquired from a not-to-be-named club.

And I stuck framed pictures everywhere: Dad in the band, him and Mom on their wedding day, me and my teams, along with Odin sword-fighting, Bo when he won his first lumberjack competition, and so many of Gunnar doing his Gunnar things.

One of my favourites is one of Lyra in her first and only dance recital. I think she was twelve and the expression on her face is pure disgust.

I coach hockey in the winter, baseball in the summer, and every season, I take a picture of the kids and put it on the wall.

There's no theme—it's British gastropub mixed with sports bar with a family living room flair—but it's mine.

It's the first thing that I've had that is solely mine, something that will succeed or fail because of me. I took a big leap opening the place, and there were a lot of sleepless nights.

There were more conversations with Edie with her trying to convince me that I could do it. And I did it.

I do a great job running The King's Hat with Edie helping.

For now, it fills the hazy gray space until my future is set. If I am going to take over as king or not.

Until then, I have my bar.

I take a bag of garbage out to the alley around nine just for a breather. The rain is still a steady drizzle but thunder rumbles overhead with the odd flash of lightning over the Atlantic. The temperature has already dropped and I should send Dillon out to pick up Edie. I know she didn't take a coat. The storm is coming, and it's coming fast and I'd hate to see her stuck in it, especially in that dress.

But as I step out into the alley between the buildings, I see shadows.

Two people are in the alley, and one is wearing that dress.

I freeze, half in the kitchen and half in the cool, rain-soaked air, black plastic bag clutched in my hand.

Edie and Mathias are in the alley.

The King's Hat is next door to an Indian takeout place that makes great butter chicken but I suspect won't last the year. There's been four businesses there in the last five years, none able to get out of the red.

I know this because I bought the building next door.

Edie lives over the Indian place in one of the two apartments. I live over the pub, so I'm well aware of Edie's comings and goings.

I've never seen her coming in like this.

The door to her apartment is at the back of the alley, close enough for the light in the laneway to illuminate the couple. I get there just in time to see Mathias lean down and kiss her.

One hand at her waist, the other holding an umbrella, so at least there's that. He'll keep her dry as well as keep his hands to himself.

Edie kind of leans in and up, folding her hands against his jacket.

My finger stabs through the black plastic.

I know Edie dates; she's a good-looking woman and she meets men... wherever. And she'll go out with these men for a few dates now and again. For a few weeks. I'm sure she kisses them. There's been a couple she's been serious about, like thinking-of-the-future serious.

She got engaged once. It didn't work out.

I've never asked her why. Our friendship isn't like that. I can tell her just about anything except details of the women I date. She's the same way.

It's better that way.

But Mathias?

I get what she sees in him—what any woman would see in him. He's a prince, and he looks like a clone of Odin, so he's a good-looking one. Plus, he's polite and smiles instead of growls like me.

But Mathias?

They're still kissing. If I go back inside, they'll hear me. If I drop the bag into the bins, they'll definitely hear me. I sink into the shadows by the wall and wait because there's nothing else to do if I don't want them to know I've seen them.

It would be nice to interrupt though. Get Mathias's hands off her.

He probably smells like garlic if they went to Nonna's.

Is the cat out here watching?

After the mouse incident a month or so ago—which might have actually been a rat, but I'm not telling Edie that—I left out some cat-friendly food to persuade a few of the strays to stop and eradicate whatever rodents were out there. Now there's been no sign of anything but a skinny tabby that lurks even more than I am right now, waiting for his dinner of tuna and leftover fish pie.

It seems wrong to have the cat watching Edie kiss my cousin.

Or anyone at all.

Not that Edie kissing anyone is a problem for me. We're not friends like that. We're *friends*, nothing more.

I toss the bag of garbage before I think twice; broken glass tinkles as it lands with a soft *thud*. The door to the kitchen shuts behind me before Edie can turn to check who it is.

Maybe she doesn't care. Maybe she's so into kissing him that she doesn't even notice any ruckus.

Good for her.

My face twists into a scowl and that knot in my stomach gives a sharp yank to remind me there's something about Edie and Mathias that I don't like.

Like I need reminding.

"Did you get rid of the big bad with that bag of garbage?" Chase asks as I brush past him on the way back out to the bar area.

My security number two stands at the sink washing martini glasses and Chef's good knives while Tyler, the regular dishwasher, helps out at the bar during the rush. Chase says doing the dishes relaxes him, and considering he used to work for the Directorate-General of France as one of their top spies, he's due for a little relaxation.

He's the best-paid dishwasher in all of Laandia, but it works for me since it lets Tyler learn more about manning the bar.

"There's no one out there," I lie.

"No? Are you sure? That was an aggressive toss."

"I feel aggressive," I growl.

"That's never a good thing," he calls after me.

It would be easier to deal with this mood if I were still playing sports. Baseball, hockey, even curling—I've done it all. And I wasn't nearly as angry when I had something to focus on.

Not that I have an anger problem but things often irritate me.

Apparently, Edie kissing Mathias is one of those things.

The two families aren't close. There were times in my childhood when Mom made an effort to pull Uncle Dante and his family into our orbit, but it's difficult when it's obvious they didn't want to be a part of our orbit—they *wanted* our orbit.

They still want it all.

My uncle Dante has never forgiven my father for being the first-born son and not abdicating his role in the succession like Odin just did.

Dante has always wanted to be king and if he can't have it, he wants his children to rule Laandia. And Odin stepping down makes it that much closer for him.

Because if I say no—which Dad, unlike other monarchies, has always given as an option for me—without Odin, the crown would go to Bo.

That would be a hard no. Bo would back out of that idea quicker than Edie jumped back into the kitchen that time when she saw that "mouse" by the garbage bins.

Gunnar would be next after Bo, and I... I don't know what he would want. Six months ago, I would have said his response would be a big *hell no*, but now? He asked for a role in Dad's advisory council. He's planning on taking on an ambassadorship role when he and Stella go to Taiwan next month.

I don't know what Gunnar would do if he had the option to become king. But if he says no, that leaves Lyra and...

Still lurking by the back door, I shake my head at the thought of my little sister as queen of Laandia. She'd do a bang-up job, but the drama...

This line of thought, as common as it's become lately, does nothing to take my mind off what's going on in the alley right now.

I brush past Chase and head back into the pub to find Fenella Carrington sitting at the bar, taking a sip of her French 75 cocktail, which means Tyler had to open a new bottle of prosecco.

"Hiya, cowboy." She waves slim fingers tipped with a pearly white polish. "Thought you might be hiding from me."

I met Fenella at Odin's wedding; I had been paired up with Edie—she was one of the bridesmaids, me a groomsman—but both of us knew it wasn't a date. Once we got the pictures and the dancing done, we were there solo.

Edie made that perfectly clear when she started dancing with my cousin Mathias.

Gunnar had invited Fenella Carrington, and enlisted her help to keep the focus off whatever news story was about to break about Camille. I'm not sure anyone thought pictures of *me* and Fenella would show up all over the internet the next day, almost overshadowing the bride and groom.

Fenella is used to getting attention. Being the daughter of a billionaire does that.

We have that in common—not the billionaire father but the getting attention wherever we go. But unlike Fenella, I don't enjoy it.

I'm also not as pretty as she is.

"Taking out the garbage," I grunt. Even the sight of Fenella's violet eyes and smiling face that graces countless magazines and gossip sites doesn't appease me.

I had fun with her the night of the wedding. There were dances. A kiss.

Okay, maybe a few.

There might have been more, but I had been reminded—like a bucket of cold water being thrown over my head—that Fenella was an ex-girlfriend of Gunnar's. My brother has had his share of exes—almost as many as me—and he stayed friends with Fenella. They're almost as close as Edie and me.

There is nothing between her and Gunnar—I made sure of that before any kissing took place.

But still, Fenella's past with my brother doused most of my interest, but I can't help the intrigue.

Or maybe it's the intrigue of knowing that a woman like Fenella Carrington wants to spend time with me.

"Is that code for something or were you actually taking out the trash?" I raise an eyebrow at Fenella's question. "Wow," she muses. "You certainly are a full-service bar owner. I bet you're the only crown prince who does that."

"Should be a mandatory rule."

I knew Fenella was still in town, because she's been staying in one of the guest suites at the castle since the wedding. Despite her past with my brother, I've been toying with the idea of seeing if she wants to hang out but haven't done anything about it yet.

Taking my time. Still toying because Fenella Carrington is a very beautiful woman and I like beautiful women.

Who aren't kissing my cousin.

"What are you up to tonight?" I ask even as I check out the action by the pool table. Fight radar is on full alert now because things seem tense. Coy Schmidt has wandered over and is now leaning on the table as Jubblie Mark takes a shot.

They had a falling-out over some lobster traps last season and I don't think it's been resolved.

"I thought I'd stop in for a fond farewell," Fenella is saying and I pull my attention back to her since she's far more interesting than the grudges of the two grizzled old-timers.

"You're leaving?" My surprise sharpens my tone.

Fenella smiles as she sips her drink, clearly pleased with the reaction. "That usually predicates a farewell. I had planned on a few more days but Gunnar is completely besotted with Stella Laz and practically ignoring me."

I can tell Fenella isn't a woman who likes to be ignored.

"At least Gunny's flying me to New York tomorrow," she continues." Are you going to miss me?"

That question is not getting a response. "Gunny's not flying anywhere tomorrow," I tell her instead. "Bad storm's coming in."

"Does your brother not know this?"

"Is he with Stella tonight?"

Fenella nods. "They're at the shelter with a couple of new dogs."

"Then no, he has no idea what's going on in the rest of the world. You'll be here another day, maybe two."

She hums under her breath and pulls out her phone. "Looks like you're right." She shows me the Weather Network update.

"Did you doubt me?"

"Of course. I'd like to get home."

"Got a hot date?"

"Now why would that be any of your business?" Fenella asks in a flirtatious voice.

"If you're around tomorrow, I'll take you on a hot date," I offer.

Because—why not?

She purses her lips. "I've been here for a week you know."

"I've been busy."

She looks like she's mulling it over but I wouldn't have asked her if I didn't know what the answer would be. "Fine," she concedes. "It's a good a reason as any to stay another day. But I have to tell you, Your Highness, you've got horrible timing."

I glance toward the kitchen and wonder if Edie is still out in the alley. "You're not the first one to tell me that."

5

Edie

MATHIAS KISSED ME.

I knew he would try; I saw it coming as he walked me home after dinner, holding the gigantic umbrella over us both.

It had been a slow, kind of meandering walk home through the drizzle as the clouds threatened overhead and the wind tangled my hair. The storm was coming and it was coming fast, but we took our time.

He didn't mention shoes again but asked about what it was like growing up here.

Halfway back to my place, I decided I would allow it if he tried to kiss me.

He didn't even say anything about the bins in the alley as he paused outside my door, but as his lips touched mine and my eyes closed, I could smell the garbage.

It's the worst thing about living here, the fact that the door that leads up to my apartment opens in the alley. At least it's convenient when I park my car in one of the spots off the laneway, but walking in from the street is an obstacle course of trash that doesn't make it into the dumpster, broken-down cardboard boxes, and most recently, cat dishes because soft-hearted Kalle now feeds every stray in the area.

I've been living here long enough to get used to it, but it's never a pleasant smell in the summer. And it puts a little damper on things; but still, a good first kiss. One that might not go in your diary, but you'd still touch your lips the day after it happened.

Unfortunately, the shouting from the bar puts another damper on it. And then there's the crash.

I pull back, but Mathias's arm still circles my waist. "What's that?"

"Sounds like drunk people fighting. What kind of place does my cousin run?"

Mathias leans in again, but I turn my cheek. "I run." And then I take a step away from him, his hand sliding from my back.

"Are you going inside?" he demands with a sulky twist to the lips I've just been kissing.

"It's my bar," I tell him as I head for the kitchen door.

I don't know if it's a good idea for Mathias to follow me or not. Ducking through the kitchen, I'm reassured at the sight of Chase still at the sink. At the bar, Dillon is in his usual spot—right beside Fenella Carrington—but Kalle is nowhere in sight.

Because he's in the middle of the fray around the pool table.

The King's Hat is a bar frequented by fishermen, so it's normal for there to be the odd skirmish when they need to blow off steam. Actually, bar fights are pretty common, and when they're sober, there's an unspoken rule among the patrons not to touch Kalle.

After a good evening of drinking, that's not always the case. Especially when Prince Kalle of Laandia takes it upon himself to break up a fight. I've seen him take a right hook to the eye and keep standing only to be dropped by a pool cue to the back and then getting his legs taken out from under him.

I've also seen him pick up a man and physically throw him out the door.

Kalle has the Erickson physique, and at six foot four and well over two hundred and twenty pounds, he can hold his own. Plus, there's always Dillon and Chase to back him up. They don't like to interfere unless it's absolutely necessary because it would be too easy for them to seriously hurt someone.

Me, on the other hand...

"That's enough," I shout, heading into the melee, still in my dress and my high heels, lips just a little swollen from Mathias's kisses. "Everyone—drop."

No one listens, or they can't hear me over the shouting and cheering, as well as the Dropkick Murphys blasting over the speakers about going out in style. The music gives the scene a surreal sensation, or maybe it's me wading into a bar fight after enjoying a very nice dinner with a prince.

I pull Teddy Billings away from Danno McElving and give Micky Fish a shove in the chest to send him back against the pool table. Grabbing the still unbroken beer bottle from the table, I give someone a sharp elbow as I make my way over to Kalle, who holds Jubblie Mark in a version of a full nelson wrestler's hold, with Mark's arms over his head. Ken McKibbon still whacks his considerable belly with the pool triangle as Coy Schmidt cheers him on.

Kalle's arms are thick with muscles, his T-shirt hiked up on one side to show an inch of skin.

I tell myself it's not the sight of him like that that has me pausing for a quick moment. I'm just making sure he's not hurt. "Boys!" I raise my voice so everyone in the place can hear. "That's enough."

Kalle turns to me. "Hey, how was your date?" he asks with a grin. His eyes have lost the angry cast from earlier.

He's *enjoying* himself.

"You need to let him go now," I tell him, grabbing the pool rack as Ken tries to bring it down on Kalle's shoulder. "Enough of this, Ken," I bark. "Go home now. Tyler," I call to the bartender hovering wide-eyed behind the bar. "Kill the music."

He does and it's surprising how quickly the ruckus dies down.

Or maybe it's the sight of me standing in the middle of things. Because even as drunk as they get, those who frequent The King's Hat would never lay a hand on a woman.

They're good guys that way.

"Miss Edie," Jubblie Mark gasps as Kalle tightens his grip just before he releases him. "I dinnae do nothin' wrong?"

"Of course not, Mark, but it's time to go home now. Are we finished here?" I ask Kalle.

"I had it under control." And he laughs.

Usually, the sound of Kalle's laughter lightens my heart but not now. "Everyone break it up or I'm sending Chase over," I threaten.

"No, Dillon. I still have dishes to do," Chase calls from the doorway of the kitchen.

The men—and one woman, Shirl Crow, who takes every opportunity she can to get into a fight, and to who the not-hitting-women rules don't apply—back away, returning to their chairs and two-person high tables.

I pick up the broken chair. "Whose tab is this coming out of?" I call. "I told you—leave the furniture and the windows alone."

"Mine." Jubblie Mark hangs his head. "I'm sorry."

"That's twice in the past six months." I shake my finger at him. "One more and I'm banning you and you'll have to go to Sailor's to drink." Without waiting for a response, I turn away from him and head back to the bar with Kalle following me.

"What do you think you're doing?" Mathias is aghast mouth open, eyes furious. "You could have been killed!"

Kalle laughs and slings an arm around my shoulders. "No one's touching her," he assures him, his familiarity for once feeling out of place and uncomfortable.

"Why, because you'll protect her?" Mathias demands. "You were doing nothing of the sort."

"Edie doesn't need protecting," Kalle says, pouring himself a pint.

My gaze flits to a framed picture on the wall. It's too far for me to see the faces but I know where Kalle stands in the middle of the back row, with a huge grin and his arm around the guy beside him. With his skates on, he's almost a head taller than anyone else on the team. It was the first year he played with the Laandia Junior Men's hockey team, and they won it all.

Kalle had been away practicing with the team, but came home for Christmas, a few days before the holiday dance. When he came to see me, I was in tears because I had just broken up with Greg Kaan.

I wasn't crying over Greg, or the fact I didn't have a date to the dance, but because Greg turned out to be the type of guy who had no qualms about laying hands on women.

Women being me.

I had never felt so stupid—for caring about someone who was capable of that, for not seeing the signs, and for letting things get that far. I never told anyone in my family because telling one of my sisters would have been the same as telling my parents and the rest of the town—and I'd rather lick my wounds in private than have everyone know.

But I told Kalle.

"Stop crying," he demanded. "He doesn't deserve you."

"I don't deserve anyone if I'm that stupid to fall for a guy like that."

I wanted Kalle to say something like *you deserve me* but instead, he just pulled me close. I'll never forget the scent of him that day.

"You're not stupid," he said into my hair. "You're brilliant and beautiful and no guy will ever touch you like that again."

The next day, Greg Kaan had a broken nose and Kalle missed the first game of the series because of two broken fingers.

"She's been trained by the best," Dillon chimes in from his seat at the bar, pulling me back from the past.

Kalle notices me staring at the picture and gives me his half-grin. I give my head a shake and turn back to the conversation going on about me because Mathias is like a dog with a bone and isn't letting this go.

"And what kind of security team are you when you sit back and let something like that happen?" Mathias rounds on Dillon, who shrugs.

"I step in when it gets out of hand. They're just blowing off steam."

"Blowing off steam? There was a broken chair."

Dillon frowns. Most of the date/kiss/bar fight adrenaline has vanished and all I feel is annoyance at Kalle.

And Mathias.

"I'm a newbie to the town but even I know that's how things go down around here."

I glance over in surprise. Fenella Carrington stares at Mathias with a mix of disdain and disgust. "Instead of fussing about it, why don't you see that she has a drink, because she looks like she needs one," she adds in her contemptuous drawl.

I never could have imagined I would ever feel gratitude toward Fenella Carrington.

6

Kalle

I SEE HOW MATHIAS looks around the bar.

Like it's beneath him to be there. His eyes flick past my sports memorabilia without interest or the admiration I usually see. I'm the third Laandian who has played professional baseball, part of the only Laandian team that has won the Worlds, and curling wasn't even a serious sport here before I started.

I've created a generation of athletes who know that even though they're from a tiny country on the edge of Canada, they will be able to compete on a professional level on the global stage.

I've done more already than Mathias ever will, but still, the way he looks around brings me right back to twelve-year-old me, overhearing how I won't ever amount to anything.

I finish my beer and try to control my breathing: inhale for four, hold, exhale. Edie made me watch this meditation stuff she found online to help with my "ball of anger that won't go away."

That's what she calls it. I'm not angry. I'm just mad some of the time.

Tyler makes Edie a gin and tonic before pouring me a second beer. "Care for a drink, cousin?" I ask Mathias, trying for polite but it ends up more scornful.

Polite scorn.

"Why would I drink in here?" Mathias asks in a cool voice. "There's nothing but heathens who can't control themselves."

Wow. He's not even trying to hide his superiority complex. I really hope Edie heard that because she's just as proud of this place as I am.

But no. She's settled onto the stool beside Fenella, reaching down to slip off her shoes, and misses that. I resist the urge to ask Mathias to repeat himself. I may not think much of him, but I'm not petty.

Instead, I point at Edie. "Because she's having a drink. Unless you want to cut your evening short, which is fine by me, because then she can get back to work."

I've never had a man look at me with such dislike.

I wouldn't make Edie go back to work. She asked for tonight off, and that means the whole night.

There's a lot of reasons I don't like Mathias. When we were kids, he'd find a way to get me in trouble every time he came to visit. When I was a senior in high school, he came for a visit one weekend and ended up stealing the girl I was head over heels for. And when I was twenty-seven and skipping on the Laandian national curling team, he showed up at my last tournament and made me look like an idiot on television.

Truthfully, me losing my temper was the reason I looked like an idiot, but it was Mathias who got me mad.

That's only a few of the reasons. And I'm not one to air the dirty laundry of my family, so I don't say much about him. For the last few years, it seems we've settled into an uneasy truce brought about because we haven't been around each other.

The truce is starting to crumble and I have a feeling it's because of Edie.

I can't let her know that though, because I don't want her to think she's come between me and my family.

"Scotch. Two fingers. Neat," Mathias barks and Edie looks up with surprise.

"You can really tell they're related, can't you?" Fenella asks and Edie's shoulders shake with sudden laughter.

The sight of the two of them seated together, being friendly, is strange. They aren't friends. They are nothing alike—Fenella, heir to a billion-dollar empire; Edie, daughter of Bob England—save being beautiful women.

But Fenella, with all her bling and pretty eyes, pales in comparison to Edie, and that gives me a jolt because not many men would think that.

"What?" I demand.

"He sounds just like you," Edie says with a tired smile before turning to Mathias. "Mathias, thank you for your concern, but this is all part of my job. I manage a bar; there are often bar fights. I know how to handle myself when they happen."

I try not to let my gaze rove over Edie to make sure she didn't get a bump or bruise from wading into the fray. She hates me checking up on her. "Guys were just blowing off steam," I add.

"There has to be better ways than starting fights in a bar around to do that," Mathias protests.

Dillon rolls his eyes and I agree. They should check paternity tests because Mathias can't be related to me.

"Jubblie Mark and Ken McKibbon are both fishermen. Most of the men here tonight are as well," Edie explains to Mathias.

"With such a bad storm coming in, they won't go out on their boats tomorrow. They'll be stuck on shore, worrying about the storm and what it can do to their boats and their catch, which they need to feed their families. No one meant any harm, and it'll all be forgotten by the morning but they need to blow off some steam. It was bound to happen tonight or tomorrow. Maybe both." She shrugs. "It's just how it is here."

Some days, I'm just so proud of her because she gets it.

Being a member of a royal family means a certain amount of pressure. Constant pressure. And that's for us, one of the lesser monarchies. I can't imagine what it's like for the Windsors over in the UK.

My family has come up with ways to relieve some of the pressure when it gets too much. Odin has his sword fighting; he'll disappear into the fitness centre at the castle for hours at a time, swinging a sword against imaginary opponents. He's so good that if I were a medieval king, I'd want Odin to be the head of my kingsguard. Jaime Lannister has nothing on my brother.

Odin has his swords and Bo has his axes. Bo will walk into the forest, find a dead tree somewhere and chop it up. Give him a stressful day or one of those fancy engagements we sometimes have to go to, and half a day later, he'll have a nicely stacked cord of firewood.

Sometimes he gives them as presents, just a load of firewood dropped off in the middle of winter at a random house.

Gunnar has speed, and now he's finished racing, he'll just leave and travel to some exotic country. Lyra has to work on her outlet because when the stress gets to her, she usually ends up in trouble with the police, a foreign government or with some guy's girlfriend.

It used to be sports for me—the rush of winning, the heat of competition, the cheering and, yes, the admiration of the crowds was the best way for me to get rid of the pressure. A game or a match, something where I could use my skills, would give me a clean slate, ready for the next time things would get tense.

But I don't play anything now, except for darts, and I get wanting to be in the middle of a ruckus to get rid of the pressure bearing down on you.

Edie gets that. I've never had to tell her. She just gets me.

Does she get Mathias too?

She drains her glass and sets it on the bar. "Good drink," she says to Tyler. "Give the lime a squeeze before you drop it in, everyone likes extra lime. I think I'll head up," she adds to me but is looking at Mathias.

Being able to swing a couple of punches got rid of some of the tension, but that knot in my stomach tightened even more with the thought of Edie inviting Mathias upstairs to her apartment.

"Thank you very much for dinner," she tells him. "If you're here for a few more days, maybe we can do it again."

And then I click to what just happened. Edie has just dismissed Mathias in front of everyone and his surprised expression sours, but he's too polite to say anything.

I feel like I've just hit a three-run homer. I wave as Edie leads Mathias out through the kitchen.

"Did you stage that fight to ruin her night?" Fenella asks in a lazy voice. She's still there at the bar, taking in everything with those eyes.

I set down my glass with a bit more force than necessary. "What?" I growl. "Her night wasn't ruined."

Fenella sighs, rolling the delicate stem of her glass between her fingers. "Are you always this observant?"

"I observe."

"She was wearing a dress that cost at least two hundred dollars, wearing shoes that kill your calves because you have to tiptoe in them. Neither of those things are a big deal to me, but I suspect they're not part of her usual wardrobe. Plus, the two of them came in through the kitchen, which means they were probably in the alley and I know for a fact that's how you get to her apartment."

"What are you saying?"

"I'm saying you getting in the middle of that fight ruined her night. You *interrupted* her, Your Highness."

"I don't know what they were doing," I mutter. "I didn't tell her to come in."

"Right."

"Right," I echo. I didn't ruin anything. It's not my fault Jubblie Mark took that moment to curse Ken McKibbon, or that Ken—who has an even worse temper than me or his cousin Jonathan—would throw the first punch.

Fenella smirks and turns those purple eyes on me. "Still want to take me out tomorrow?"

What does that have to do with anything? "Yeah."

"Yeah?"

"Yes, I want to take you out tomorrow," I say, enunciating each word.

"Okay then." Fenella slurps up the rest of her drink. "You asked for it."

7

Edie

I WASN'T SURE HOW the night would end but I did not see that coming.

After Mathias says goodnight—no kissing this time—I head upstairs to my apartment. I hang up the dress, wipe off the makeup and pull on the battered sweatshirt and old gym shorts I sleep in and then crawl into bed.

Ernie climbs in after me, settling at my side.

It's not long before the rain starts driving against my window as hard as hailstones, the wind whistling through the cracks. The storm will empty the bar quicker than ringing the last-call bell can, and Kalle will be able to close early.

I lie awake in my dark bedroom and wait for Kalle's light to come on.

His apartment next door is twice the size of mine and lacks the curry scent that drifts up from the Indian place below, but both of us agree mine is much more comfortable. Our bedrooms are in the same spot, the windows both looking over the alley.

Kalle got into a fight tonight.

Or maybe he was trying to break one up. I wasn't there, I didn't see the cause.

I hope he didn't start it.

The thing with Kalle is that there's always been an undercurrent of bad temper simmering under his surface. Sometimes it boils over into anger but most of the time it's a mild annoyance at the world around him. I've learned long ago not to take it personally, and I've mastered some skills to head off a really bad mood.

Kalle hates having no choice about his future.

He's never come right out and said it, but I can read him pretty well. I know him pretty well. He lives with the uncertainty of *when*, of *how* he will follow in his father's footsteps. Of *why* it has to be him.

And whether it should be. I know that keeps him up at night.

The order of his birth has put him in this position and there's nothing he can do about it.

But learning from Mathias that there might have been a different path for Kalle sets my thoughts spinning.

What would Kalle be if he wasn't a prince of Laandia set to inherit the throne? Would he even stay in Battle Harbour?

He had been happy when he was playing sports—it's amazing that he could be so successful in three different sports. Kalle is a natural athlete and I knew, seeing him in the midst of a drunken brawl last night, he wouldn't be hurt.

Seeing him holding Jubblie Mark, with his T-shirt pulled up to show a few inches of toned, tanned skin...

I'm not blind. I know how attractive Kalle is. Even with his grunts and growls and monosyllabic answers to important questions, Kalle Erickson is *hot*. He's the second tallest with shoulders and biceps that strain the best of cotton T-shirts, darker than Odin and Gunnar with his dark blond hair with streaks of red and brown, and perma-tan. The haughty slash of a nose that somehow remained unbroken despite the fights and hockey pucks during his short career on the ice, and five-day scruff covering a strong jaw. Those eyes that can make you feel—sometimes at once—both like a tiny bug and his favourite person ever, and mirror the ocean on a calm day.

It's amazing how many different shades of blue eyes there are in that family.

If I were a painter, I could commit Kalle to paper by memory alone. But I don't, because there's not a creative bone in my body.

Kalle is attractive despite his temper—

Or, some women might be more attracted to the bad-tempered, brooding type.

Not me. I've always tried to stay away from men who remind of Kalle. It's easier that way. Because Kalle is in my face every day.

And he is a nice face.

He smiles at a lot of women with that face, and every time he does more than smile, I'm forced to talk myself through the sensation that something just isn't right in the world. It never lasts for long, though, because they never last for long. The architect working on Odin's Viking exhibit. The Sports Illustrated model who got a chance to interview anyone for the magazine and picked him. The city councillor who won't give us a permit for a patio after Kalle stopped seeing her.

Fenella seems different.

She's the type of woman he should be with: the strong, smart type who can help lead him through the pitfalls of celebrity life. When Kalle becomes king, he'll be known throughout the world for more than being a three-sport professional athlete with killer abs and a fine backside. People will watch and question and make comments on what he does for Laandia and what he can't. He needs someone beside him to shoulder the scrutiny.

And Fenella, with her background and family could help him.

Plus, she's so incredibly gorgeous, that he's probably not even thinking of the other positives.

It takes a while before I finally manage to fall asleep.

I'm not awake to see Kalle's light turn on.

The next morning, I wake up to a full-fledged summer storm. Rain pours down in curtains, and thunder rumbles in the dark clouds hanging low. The wind is almost as loud, and outside everything that's not held down has taken flight.

Kalle must have opened early; when I go down for twelve, it's clear the fishermen of last night and more have chosen to hunker down and wait it out here. Skywalker, our chef who rules the kitchen with teasing and good temper, mans the grill while Leah, his wife, smiles good morning as she carries plates of eggs and bacon to a table.

My father sits at the bar beside Dillon.

"Hello, sweetheart," he says. Even the tubes up his nose pumping oxygen to clogged lungs can't mask his cheerful smile.

"Mom kick you out because of the rain?"

Bob England kept the grounds at the castle immaculate for almost fifty years, taking over as a young man after his father passed.

Under my father's care, the lawns were always lush and green and free from crabgrass and skunks digging for grubs, the gravel drive and paths raked and clear of weeds. But it was the gardens that were his crowning glory, and where I have so many happy memories learning about the plants. I had lessons in what can handle the shade and what does best in the sun. He taught me how to deal with pests, possums and persistent weeds but would never let me touch the roses for pruning, because he wouldn't trust anyone else with the Queen's favourite flowers.

He instilled a love of plants, and I would like to have my own garden, but I need a house for that. And while Kalle does pay me enough, living right beside the bar is too convenient to make a change.

Dad had to retire two years ago because of the disease that has corroded his lungs. I think telling the king he could no longer do the work he loved did more damage to my father than the scar tissue slowly filling his lungs.

Still, he's kept his cheerful good nature and does his best to keep busy puttering in the gardens at home, but the storm would drive him indoors and under my mother's feet, and so he's here instead.

Dad taps the newspaper folded on the bar. "I figured I'd help Dillon with his crossword."

A fun fact about the king of Laandia—each morning, he has a plane fly into St Johns to pick up the New York, Washington, Toronto, and Ottawa newspapers, as well as a large Double Double coffee from Tim Horton's. Technology has advanced enough so King Magnus can read the news from a tablet instead of actual newspapers, but he's not ready to give up his favourite coffee.

Battle Harbour doesn't do franchises, the one thing in recent times the king has argued for.

"The plane got through the storm this morning?" I ask Dillon, but he shakes his head.

"It's a bad one out there, worst I've seen since I got this gig. This is yesterday's paper."

"You know there's apps and online sites where you can do crosswords and sudoku and your puzzles, right?" I ask him.

"I like being old school."

"There's something to be said about putting pencil to paper," Dad says. "Coronary. Eight down." He taps the page and Dillon prints the answer.

"Wordle in three," Dillon tells me as I pour myself a cup of coffee from the pot behind the bar. I'd rather have a large latte from Coffee for the Sole but I'm not committed enough to brave the rain to get it.

"Did you help him?" I ask Dad. The way he keeps his head down gives me my answer. I laugh as I take the pot around to the tables, greeting the regulars and topping up cups.

It's a far cry from what I walked into last night. The broken chair is gone but that's the only evidence of the fight, save a few guilty expressions and muttered apologies. And Ken McKibbon asks me under his breath not to say anything to his wife.

Managing The King's Hat means I do a bit of everything, from ordering kegs and scheduling shifts to waitressing and keeping the peace. Both Kalle and I share the office jobs, taking turns in the cramped space beside the kitchen because there isn't enough room for both of us in there at once.

We work well together.

Chase is missing, so I suspect Kalle went back upstairs but I don't ask about where he is because...

It feels strange to say his name this morning. I don't know why.

"How was your date last night?" Dad asks when I return to the bar. When I raise my eyebrows in a wordless question, he smiles sheepishly. "Your sister told me."

Thanks, Ella. "I wondered because I don't remember saying anything to you or Mom about it."

If I told my mother Mathias had asked me to dinner, she would have been excited, to say the least. Coronary—that was eight down in the crossword puzzle. My mother might have had a coronary. She might be the biggest royal supporter in all of Battle Harbour.

She named my sisters Ella, Enid and Eloise, and me Edwina, because she thought double E's would look great for a queen's initials. She's been planning our weddings to the princes since we were born, and every time one of my sisters gets married—Enid and Eloise both found their happily ever after with non-royals—she cries with disappointment.

I didn't want to tell her until there was something to talk about and I'm not the type to discuss goodnight kisses with either of my parents.

"How was it?" Dad repeats, and just from those few words, I know he's not as excited about Mathias as my mother probably is.

"It was dinner," I say noncommittally. "I had the pesto penne and some nice wine."

"Prince Mathias."

"Would you like to know what he had?" Dad shakes his head. "You don't like that I went out with him?"

"Sorry, pet, just finding it hard to wrap my head around it," he admits.

"You don't think your girl deserves a prince?" Dillon looks up from the crossword. He's spent many hours with my father at the bar, and I would say they're friends.

"My girl—all my girls—deserve the king of the world. But I worked for that king for years, and while he's a good man, it's difficult to see my girl with one of his sons."

"Sorry, Bob." Dillon gives Dad's shoulder a friendly slap. "That's a *you* problem."

"You've said it yourself," Dad says to me. "With Kalle. You can't see yourself with him."

"That's different," I protest. "We're friends."

And because if I started picturing myself with Kalle, that would be the beginning of the end.

I know there have been times Kalle has been tempted to cross the line. I know him well enough to see that. And some of those times, it would have been easy for me to lean in and let things go where they wanted to go.

But I didn't, because if Kalle and I moved past being just friends, it would put an end to our friendship. It would put an end to everything, because Kalle would never want to end up with me.

He'll be king someday. And the woman he ends up with will be queen.

And that won't be the daughter of the former groundskeeper and manager of his bar.

"About that... How long have you and Maj been friends?" Dillon says, looking up from the paper.

"Sixteen years."

"Huh." Dillon banters and teases and complains, but that *huh* suggests he's got something deeper to say. "Do you know how many lady friends I've had for that long? A big fat zero. Do you know how many lady friends I have? Another, even bigger and fatter zero because when I get friendly with a woman, I want more than just to be friends."

Dad frowns but doesn't argue with Dillon.

I huff with exasperation. I've heard the arguments, the protests that Kalle and I "would be perfect together," "you'd make him a better man," and "it's not natural for a man and woman to be friends like that." "It's not like that with Kalle and me," I say.

Dillon smirks. "I wouldn't bet the boat on that. I saw how he looked at you last night."

Dad raises his hand. "Uh, father sitting right here," he points out. "Who would rather not imagine any man looking at my daughter in any way."

"You got to wonder though," Dillon says.

"Really don't, thanks," Dad argues.

"We're not talking about Kalle."

Why does it always come back to Kalle? Why can't people leave it alone?

Like I willed him, Kalle steps out of the office. He's wearing a brown T-shirt—same shirt as yesterday, only a different colour. He must own at least ten of them.

My eyes stray to the area right along the waistband of his jeans covering the patch of bare skin I saw last night.

Why...? I look away. "You opened early," I say.

"Lineup," Kalle confirms. "Even with the rain. Lots of guys looking for Skywalker's eggs this morning."

"I hope we don't run out." I laugh nervously. "We don't have another delivery for another few days."

A crack of thunder sounds, loud enough to be heard over the din, and I jump. Kalle puts his hand on my back and gives it a soothing rub.

"It's going to be a fun day," he says gruffly.

Customers still, cups and forks held aloft as the rumble continues like bowling balls running the length of Kalle's apartment and it's blessedly quiet for a moment before the chattering begins again. The storm will be discussed *ad nauseam,* comparisons to every other storm in Laandia's history, including hurricanes Igor and Fiona.

Fiona hit Newfoundland hard, but Laandia wasn't as affected. But I have memories of being trapped in my father's greenhouse as hurricane Igor swept across the area, the kind of memories that wake you from your dreams.

I don't like storms.

"I sent Tyler out to FoodMart just in case." Kalle leans over me to reach the coffeepot and I step back, but not before his scent hits me. Soothes me.

Somehow, the combination of Old Spice antiperspirant and Dove exfoliant body wash helps relieve the tightness of my shoulders caused by the crack of thunder. I know what products he uses because he stole mine a few months ago when his shower wasn't working.

I know what soap he uses in the shower but I've never seen him naked.

And why am I thinking of Kalle naked?

"I gotta run up to the castle," Kalle says, pulling me out of my thoughts about things I have no business thinking about. "You okay here? Call Bethie in early if you need more help."

"I'll be fine. Leah is here and Tyler. Worst thing, I can get Dad to start pulling pints."

"Works for me." Kalle gathers my ponytail in his hand and gives it a playful tug. "Later, dude."

"Not a dude," I call after him. Whatever was bothering him last night, Kalle seems to have shaken it off this morning.

Now I just have to shake off how two simple touches have unbalanced me, like I'm navigating the deck of a boat.

We're friends. We touch.

Dillon leaves his paper and follows Kalle into the kitchen. Dad watches them go, waiting until the door swings closed after them before he says anything. "Prince Mathias, huh?"

"He's nice." Why do I sound defensive? Mathias *is* nice. He's—

"You need more than nice, pet," Dad says, interrupting be beginning my list. "You deserve the best."

"As long as he's not part of the royal family," I remind him with a smile.

Dad shakes his head. "Your friend Dillon is right. That's a *me* problem. You deserve the best, and if that's one of Magnus's offspring—"

"Mathias is the king's nephew," I point out. "And I don't even know if anything will come of it. It's not like it would be convenient—Mathias lives across the country and I'm here."

"You know you don't have to stay here."

"Why would I leave? Everything I care about is here."

"We'll still be here, but there's a lot more in the world that you can care about. You got a big heart, Edie, my girl. I still haven't forgiven myself for you turning down that job a few years back."

I had started in hospitality, working at one of the two hotels in Battle Harbour. I had risen up to assistant manager when Kalle convinced me to come work for him. About a year after, a hotel chain in Newfoundland contacted me about a managerial position.

My dad had just been diagnosed with idiopathic pulmonary fibrosis, so there was no question of me leaving. I stayed in Battle Harbour. Only my parents knew about what the company offered me.

I don't let myself wonder how my life might have turned out if I had taken the job because I'm happy. My family is here.

Kalle is here.

"It was my decision, and one I didn't hesitate making," I tell Dad, wiping down the counter. "I'm needed here."

Dad glances over his shoulder, at the busy tables, the laughing customers tucking into eggs and pancakes. "What happens when Kalle sells the place?" he asks quietly. "When he becomes king and doesn't need you anymore?"

I don't know the answer to that.

8

Kalle

Leaving the bar in Edie's capable hands, I throw my coat on and head out through the alley to where my truck is parked. The rain is still pouring down, and another front is predicted to reach us this afternoon so I need to be back by then to help out Edie.

The meow stops me.

"There's your cat," Dillon says, pausing in the rain with me.

"Not my cat." The tabby pokes her head around the garbage bin, looking bedraggled and very wet. A pile of boxes gives her a bit of shelter but wet cardboard can only do so much.

I want to toss the poor thing into the kitchen so it can get out of the rain but it would be my luck to have the health and safety guy stop by.

Every time I see the cat, I tell myself to call Stella Laz. She would be better off if she was adopted or even took up residence in Stella's pet rescue rather than scrounging for scraps in the alley.

She does keep the rodent problem down though.

And it's not that she's alone—I put food out for her every day. She's a well-fed stray cat.

But still, my heart gives a hard tug that I'm walking away from her in the rain, and I tell myself to call Stella as soon as I'm done with Dad.

Dad. King Magnus of Laandia.

I haven't had a chance to talk to him since Odin's wedding and the fallout from his announcement. Dad had been busy entertaining the VIPs who stayed at the castle, and then, three days later, he left for meetings in Paris, Madrid, and London, the city in Ontario, Canada.

But now he's back and it's about time I find out what Odin stepping down means for me.

It means the same as it always did; as the firstborn, I'm next in line to inherit the crown. That won't change.

But I've always wanted it to.

I don't want the responsibility. I'm not interested in power. I can't handle the pomp and circumstance and silly frou-frou that comes with being a king.

Those are only a few of the excuses I tell myself as I make the twenty-minute drive up the hill to the castle. Dillon sits shotgun—Gunnar and Odin may sit back and let their security do the driving but I'm too stubborn to let anyone else take the wheel.

Besides, it always reminds me of when Edie and I were learning to drive and I let her take the heat for something I did.

I've never forgiven myself for that, and I've never let anyone else take the fall for me.

Still, Edie was so insistent; back then she was even more earnest and opinionated and slightly scary. My Edie has mellowed over the years, while I get grumpier than a bear woken up too early in the spring.

"You're smiling," Dillon points out when we're halfway up the hill. The rain comes down in sheets, with wipers doing double time.

"I smile."

"Not really." Dillon leans forward and ups the defrost. "I smile more than you."

"You never smile."

"My point exactly."

I rest my hand on the gearshift. "Did I ever tell you Edie's the reason I learned to drive stick?"

"You did not."

"Duncan set it up with Dad's security to teach me. I sucked at driving—"

"Maybe not the best thing to admit when we're driving up a mountain during a severe thunderstorm."

"Edie was much better than me," I continue as if Dillon hadn't spoken. "Not that I would let you know that. I hit the garage once and ran into the tennis court another time—and this was before I even got my proper license, so my mother told me if I hit anything else, I was going to have to wait another six months. I wasn't about to wait, plus I needed to learn how to drive a stick shift."

"Because you wanted to follow your little brother into racing?"

"Because Edie could drive stick and back then, I didn't want to let a girl do something I couldn't."

"Take about a male ego. So glad you've gotten over that."

I ignore the sarcasm. "The day after I finally master the clutch, Bob gives me the keys and sends me out to practice with Edie. She was so cute back then." For a moment I'm caught in the past, sixteen-year-old me trying so hard to impress Edie, the one girl in town who didn't give a damn about me or my family. She knew who she was and refused to bow to anything or anyone.

"Have you seen her lately?" Dillon demands. "She's still really cute."

"Got a crush, do you, Dillon?"

"You'd be an idiot if you didn't. She's a good woman, one of the best."

"She reminds me of my mother," I say suddenly. "In a good way. Not a... creepy way."

"I figured it was the good way. How does she remind you of your mom?"

Dillon wasn't working security when Mom had the accident, but people talk about her enough, so he could imagine what she was like.

Except for me. I don't talk about her. But something about the rain and the castle looming ahead of us brings it out of me. "She was smart, with all these different interests," I begin. "She was into everything we were, but more. She's the reason Odin got into the heritage stuff, got me coaching to give back. She'd set up daily breakfasts for kids at the schools, actually went in to do some counselling because that's who she was. She worked as a therapist before they got married."

"I didn't know that," Dillon says quietly.

"Yeah. Yeah, she was amazing. She didn't take any crap from anybody, just like Edie. Did you see her wade into that fight last night?" I shake my head. "Fearless. My mother was like that. She stood up to Dad about a couple of things, and she'd bring him back to the real world when he'd start getting too big for himself. Edie does that for me, too. Plus, Mom loved that Edie called Dad

Maggot by accident when she was a little girl, and kept calling him that. It was awesome. King Maggot."

I laugh quietly to myself, the memory still funny, but like a lot of things about Mom, it's taken on a tinge of sadness, like one of those Instagram filters that turns the picture blue.

"Anyway," I pull myself back and continue. "That day, Bob gave me the keys and sent us out. We were driving on one of the roads behind the castle, out toward the farms, in the middle of nowhere; I was driving and there was this huge turtle on the side of the road."

Dillon peers out the window. "I see no turtles. You may proceed."

"I didn't know what it was, but Edie started yelling about turtles, and I don't know, I panicked because I thought I was going to hit one. I swerved, hit the shoulder, hit the other shoulder, and then the ditch. I landed us in the ditch."

"Always a great way to impress a girl."

"Tell me about it. We weren't hurt but I had no clue how to get the truck out of there. Edie was so calm and pushed me out and just drove it out. I was freaking because I knew Mom was going to tell me to stand down and not let me drive at all because of the other stuff, but we got home and Edie stepped up and in this voice—I swear she sounded just like my mother—told Bruce and my mother that *she* was driving. She wouldn't let me say it was me. Shot down all my arguments, and that was that."

Dillon grins. "Sounds like an Edie thing to do."

"It was such an Edie thing to do. But because of her, I focused and paid attention and practiced at the arcade, in one of those driving games with the steering wheel, and I got better. Once I knew I wasn't going to embarrass myself, Edie was the first one I took for a drive. No turtles this time."

It always gets me that for as long as I've known Edie, we don't share a lot of firsts.

"The two of you have been friends for a long time," Dillon says as we pull up to the castle.

"Yeah."

"I don't know, you ever think—" Dillon continues.

I cut him off. "What are you, trying to be some kind of matchmaker? Edie and I are just friends."

"I hear that a lot. But have you really looked at her lately? Like, last night when she got all fixed up for her date with the prince?"

I did look. I couldn't help myself.

Because she looked amazing.

I've seen her fixed up to go out with other guys before and it never hit me like a kick to the crotch like it did last night. She was almost... glowing.

Because of Mathias.

So it's got me thinking. "Yeah," I concede. "She looked good."

Dillon looks sideways at me. "Shame it was because of a guy like the prince."

I park in my usual spot between the west side of the castle and the garden. "Yeah," I say heavily.

And then I wait for Dillon to tell me it was time to do something about it, but he doesn't.

"You good today?" he asks instead.

I frown. "Why?"

"Never heard you talk so much."

I give a bark of laughter and race Dillon into the castle.

I can't deny that Edie is on my mind as I head through the halls of the castle to my father's office, especially how she looked in that dress last night.

And the pink of her lip gloss.

Whatever my uncertainty about the possibility of becoming the next king of Laandia, I can't deny that I loved growing up in the castle. Built back in the sixteen hundreds, the place has secret passages, dungeons, and a ton of character. Plus, it really impressed the girls when I was into impressing them.

Except Edie. She was never impressed I lived in a castle.

If she was, she never showed it.

She never treats me like a prince, never refers to me as Your Highness like so many others do.

These days, it's hard to find a woman to date who doesn't make a big deal about my family. Fenella doesn't.

Edie never did.

Dillon takes off for the kitchen as soon as he sees me safely inside, leaving me to the capable hands of Mrs. Theissen and Duncan Laz, Dad's right-hand man.

I say hello to the staff I pass on the way to Dad's office. The castle is both an office and a home for the royal family, as well as a part-time hotel.

I wonder if Fenella is wandering around here somewhere. And since I'm taking her out tonight, should I find her to say hello?

I should get back to the bar instead of looking for someone who might not even be here.

I find Dad in his small office, the one he does the work in, not where he meets with foreign dignitaries and local government and business heads.

King Magnus of Laandia leans back in his oversized chair, feet up on the desk. His sock has a hole in his toe, his jeans have that distressed look because Dad wears his clothes until they fall apart. Case in point is the rough-looking Aerosmith T-shirt he has on; it has holes within its holes and has turned a strange shade that is no longer gray, and not quite brown. It came from an actual concert and it wasn't from this decade.

Or even last decade.

Dad is no one's idea of a king but that makes him kind of great.

He's reading something on his tablet, squinting so he doesn't have to use the glasses he's recently been forced to get. I knock at the open door. "You busy?"

"Ah," Dad says, looking up with his usual cheerful grin. "My favourite kind of distraction."

"I thought that was a cold pint of mead." I take the seat across the desk, sinking down until the worn leather threatens to swallow me whole.

"That's good too, but it's early yet."

"Not at my place. It's packed already."

"Storms are good for business when they don't destroy everything." Dad looks at me and there's a barely perceptible shift from father to king. "How's the town? Any problems this morning? Spencer and Gunnar went in yesterday to make sure the boats were okay, and no flooding."

Spencer is Duncan's son and like a brother to me. If we lived in medieval times, he and Duncan would be courtiers, dukes or other high-ranking aristocrats whose sole purpose is to help the king run the kingdom.

In fact, Dad has tried to give Duncan a title more than once, but he always says no.

Both are more than simple 'yes-men.' It's tantamount to the respect he garners, but the idea of having people around who will agree to his every whim and decision doesn't sit well with King Magnus. He and Duncan have gotten into a couple of fierce shouting matches over the years. Spencer is a lawyer by trade, but the country as a whole is more of his client than Dad is.

It doesn't surprise me that Spencer would venture into town during the worst of the storm. It does surprise me that Gunnar would.

Then again, my little brother did ask to take on more responsibilities. Make more of an effort in being a prince, and looks like he meant what he said.

I don't make much of an effort being a prince.

Today, the realization leaves me feeling hollow, like I haven't eaten.

"Things look good," I report. "No flooding in the square. There was a bit of a ruckus last night in the bar, just some of the guys blowing off steam."

"That's to be expected. You handle it?"

I smirk. "Actually, Edie did."

Dad smiles widely. "That girl. Woman, I guess now. She's been a godsend to you. I've always wondered why—?"

"Things good up here?" I interrupt. I don't want another talk about why Edie and I anything because then I have to ask myself why I haven't, and I don't like looking like an idiot.

Dad mirrors my smirk. "Fair enough. Fenella is still here, you know."

"Yeah. I... yeah."

"You haven't come for a social call, have you. It's a very wet day for you to come all the way up here to say hi, so there must be something on your mind." He sets the tablet on the desk but leaves his legs stretched out. "What's up?"

King Magnus of Laandia isn't your usual monarch. He's a former Olympian (gold medal in shot put), best-selling author (vegan cookbook before vegan was big), and one of the founding members of the heavy metal band Kräftig.

It's not my style of music but I still love to watch the videos of Dad onstage with Duncan, both of them rocking their hearts out.

He gave up a music career to come home to Laandia and prepare to take the throne.

He's also the most laid-back man I know. It pisses me off when I compare his relaxed vibe with my almost-constant irritation, but most of the time, spending time with my father teaches me something, whether it's about the country, his style of ruling, or even just how to take a moment and enjoy it to the fullest.

I've seen my father seriously upset four times in my life: after the attempted kidnapping of Lyra when she was thirteen, when the Canadians refused to concede to our requests in the fishing dispute, once at Bo, and recently, when he found out exactly what Signe Luute, Duncan's ex-wife, had been saying about the castle and those living here.

Not only was the anger directed at Signe, but her stepdaughter Daphne. She, together with Daulton Drake, former secretary to the king, tried to sabotage Odin and Camille's wedding. Daphne had been one of Camille's bridesmaids and found out a few things that Camille had been trying to keep secret. She went to Daulton to spill what she knew. Daulton went to the press.

Thanks to Gunnar and Stella, the media explosion Daulton had aimed for was more a limp *pft*.

But still, I suspect Peter Luute won't be mayor of Battle Harbour for a second term, thanks to the machinations of his wife.

At least he wouldn't be if I were king. I would have forced him to resign the day after the wedding. Dad's a lot more benevolent than I would be.

"How was the trip?" I ask instead of just getting to the point.

Dad lifts an eyebrow. "You really want to know?"

"Shouldn't I be asking these things?"

"Ah." He steeples his fingers. "This isn't really a random son-ly visit. You want to talk about O jumping ship."

I fix him with my gaze. "Did you know?"

Dad nods. "You're asking if Odin came to me first? Of course he did. We had several long conversations about it, with and without Camille."

"Camille? You didn't think I had a right to know what Odin was planning?" My voice rises as frustration surges. "I should have been told this was in motion."

Dad keeps his calm, same as always. "Are you planning on abdicating?" he asks, like he wants to know how bad the drive up the castle was in this weather.

Despite the calm demeanour, the words float between us like some sort of explosive balloon ready to destroy.

There have been hours of discussion about whether I will accept the throne. Sometimes I'm part of these talks, but most times I'm not. I know the security council has regular meetings about it and it's a common topic among the people of Battle Harbour. There's even a group called the Odinites who likes to protest that Odin should be next in line, but they're out of luck now.

As far as I can remember, no one has ever outright asked me if I plan to step aside.

Again, this isn't usual. I know most of the heirs to the thrones in the different monarchies of the world—a few of us are in a group chat and Catharina-Amalia has been trying to get me to join her Facebook group, but I've never been a fan of social media—and the fact that I may have an option to not follow in Dad's footsteps is unheard of. They think I'm crazy to even consider it.

Laandia isn't your run-of-the-mill monarchy either; my great-grandfather Leif didn't conquer Canada to get his part of Newfoundland and Labrador. He helped them. Leif Erickson and a group of men, all with Viking ancestors, defended the country against a secret German invasion during World War Two and the Canadian government, encouraged by the United States, offered to reward Leif.

He asked for a country, and they gave it to him, as unbelievable as that seems.

I don't like history, and I don't know the exact details of what went down, but I think I would have liked my great-grandfather Leif. He seemed like a take-charge type of man. A doer, ready to get into the thick of things.

Like Edie stopping that fight at the bar last night.

Leif started it all; Laandia was his vision and he made it happen. But then it was my grandfather Euan and my father who have really established Laandia's place in the world.

I would rather been like Leif—take what I want and make it happen—than like Euan and Dad who had to fight to put everything in motion.

It's not being a king that I don't like the thought of, it's all the mundane, tedious things I'd have to do.

That's why I have Edie for the bar. She could organize the hairs on my head to stand at attention with a clap of her hands.

"This isn't about me," I say, easily sidestepping the question.

"You're right; it's about your brother." Dad's tone is firm. "Unless you have plans to step away, and then it's your business as well as Bo's. Do I need to call your brother home to talk about this?"

My brother is a good man, but no one really thinks of him as king material. Not that he wouldn't be amazing—Bo is kind and smart and generous—but he's a loner. An introvert, who tries to avoid people as much as possible. I'm sure—and history lover Bo could confirm—that there have been kings and queens both who like the quiet life, but I can't imagine putting Bo in the position of having to step into Dad's shoes.

I'll have a hard enough time with that myself.

I glance down at my hands in my lap. "No. Bo doesn't need to be here for this."

"Does that mean you'll remain in your position in the line of succession?"

I don't know how to answer, because there's so much more to the question than me being king someday in the future. And Dad seems to realize this because he gets up from behind his desk and comes around to lean against the edge.

"When I was your age, I didn't have a clue if I wanted to be king," Dad admits in a casual voice. "Do you remember me telling you this?"

I do, even though it's not something we talk about. Mainly because no one can imagine Laandia without Magnus Erickson as king.

"The band was doing great," he continues like he's telling a story and not retelling the history of the country he reigns over. "I was touring and loving the travel. I might have been prince of Laandia but I couldn't see any reason to come home. I couldn't see a good reason to be king. I liked my life and I didn't want anything to change."

I can understand that.

"My father came to one of our concerts—"

"He came to a concert?" I interrupt. I never met my grandfather, but the portraits suggest he wasn't a man who enjoyed much, let alone live music. Loud live music.

"He came, but he wasn't a fan. But he needed to know what I was going to do."

"What were you going to do?"

The moment stretches on long enough for me to wonder if this is the most important conversation I've ever had with my father.

The pause is so long I have time to study him, notice the dash of silver in his dark blond hair has increased to a liberal sprinkling, that there are new lines around his eyes.

His eyes are still as bright and alive as they've ever been, full of compassion and love without having to say a word.

"Well, I had a pretty good career happening. The band was doing fantastic and—" He paused to lift his gaze to the ceiling with a shake of his head. "The women," he breathed with a sheepish grin. "We would get mobbed at every stop and the girls—"

"I don't need to know that," I cut in.

"This was before I met your mother and became the one-woman man I am today," he's quick to add. "You and your brothers might think you've got game but back then I—"

This time I hold up my hands like it's my only way to stop a bus heading straight for me. "Please. Way too much information."

"Really? You don't want to hear about how your old man once met—"

"Dad. *Mom.*"

"Was the love of my life," he finishes. "Before that... well, I won't say any more. But just know that at one time, I was living my best life and the thought of giving it all up to come back to pokey little Laandia wasn't on my list of things to do." He heaves a sigh, and I get it—I know exactly what he felt back then because it's how I feel every single day. "But my father came to visit," Dad continues. "We went out for a beer and he told me something. He said a great man doesn't seek to lead. He's called to it. And he answers."

I frown. "You were called to lead?"

"Not for a year or so. I won't get into the details about what was going on, but it was before my father got sick, and my brother was ready to step up and into the mess. Dante was ready and willing and... *really* wanted to be king. He thought I had hesitated too long, I was too distracted, and he would do a better job at it. He said he was obligated to step up."

"Dante was going to be king?"

"He thought he was," Dad says heavily. "In my opinion, he felt a sense of entitlement to the position. He was the second son, but your grandfather wasn't as liberal as I am. He was insistent that I declare myself. To give up the band and come home. Dante did a lot of whispering in his ear, in everyone's ear. I had a full life, a few successes—"

I don't bother to hide my snort.

"—Dante thought he had a right to take over. I don't know if it was because of that... I know his attitude had something to do with it because the two of us were even more competitive than you lot. Finally, I came to realize that I... I needed to do it. I was born to be king, and I'd do a damn fine job at it. That was me getting the call and me answering. Someday, you'll figure it out too. And if that day comes, and unlike me, your answer is no, you'll still be the only thing I ever wanted you to be."

My frown deepens because his words sound too familiar. "Did you just quote Dune?"

"What?" Dad asks, his face a mask of innocence.

"Dune, the movie. And the book. You just quoted L. Frank Herbert. Or at least the movie."

"It's a good quote," he says sheepishly. "And I changed a few words, so it's not like I lifted the whole thing."

I have to laugh. "Oscar Isaac said it better."

"I beg to differ. Oscar does a lot of things well, but I think I've got him beat when it comes to heart-to-hearts with my kids."

"I guess so," I concur.

"But Kalle—you'll know. There will be a time in your life when you'll know if you're going to step up and be the leader the country will eventually need—not for a long time, cuz I'm not going anywhere any time soon. And you'll know if it's time to step down and let someone else take over."

"And what if I do?" I ask. "Step down and let someone else. Let Bo. Or Gunnar?"

Dad shrugs. He shrugs like it's not the very thing that kept me awake at night for the last week. The last year. My entire life. "They'll deal. Either one of them is very capable of leading. Even your sister, as unbelievable as one would think, after seeing her latest picture on the cover of *US Magazine*."

"Oh, god, what did she do?"

"I think it's more about what she was wearing. But whatever you decide, Kalle, you'll always be the only thing I've ever needed you to be." He gives me a toothy grin. "My son."

I groan. "Oscar said it better."

Dad laughs like that was the funniest thing he's ever heard, slapping his thigh and roaring. "But seriously, my boy, there *is* something you might want to pull forth from the back of your mind."

I give another groan. "That doesn't sound good."

"It could be," he says mildly. "If you do decide this king stuff is going to be up your alley, you're going to want to find a queen before that happens. It'll be a lot easier for you."

"What does that mean?"

"It means that as a prince of Laandia, your options for dating are pretty good," Dad explains. "Girlfriends are great, girlfriends don't have a lot of pressure. Wives, on the other hand—especially when your wife will eventually be Queen of Laandia—wives are under a lot of pressure. And there may not be many options if you wait too long. I want you kids to all marry for love—we lucked out with Odin, and it's still early, but Gunny seems to be headed in the right direction." He studies me intently, like he's trying to read what I'm not saying. "It's hard enough to meet a good woman you think you can fall for, but I'm telling you, it's exponentially more difficult when you're already the king." He grins ruefully. "Trust me on this. It worked out for me, but I don't want you to have to go through what I did."

I know the story of my parents—at least I thought I did. "What did you go through? You met Mom, fell in love, and got married."

Dad grimaces. "Yeah, but it wasn't really in that order. I did meet her soon after my father passed away, and I became king, but it wasn't exactly love at first sight like everyone assumes. In fact, I don't think she liked me that much."

"I definitely didn't hear this side of the story."

He waves his hand. "It's too long to go into it now, but ask me again next time you catch me with a couple of pints of mead in my belly. Long story short, I knew I needed someone to do this with me. My father was gone, my brother wasn't speaking to me, and I had Dunc, but I thought a wife would be good. I set to find her, sort of like Odin did."

"But…" It feels like the chair tips as my seismic plates shift and react to this new information. My parents' love story was known to all, and the type of relationship every one of us wants to emulate.

They met. Fell in love. Married, in very short order. Five children and twenty-five years later, we lost her in a tragic accident.

There were no difficulties or challenges Dad is now suggesting they went through.

"I know," he admits. "We kept that part of things quiet because we weren't proud of it. I met your mother six months after I was crowned king. She was working in Ottawa and I knew she'd be the perfect person to help me figure out how to be a king. I proposed that night."

"Just like that?"

"She said no. Three times, actually. I was very persistent. I was also very frightened and your mother—Selene—she made me feel like it was all going to be all right."

"She did that with everything," I say, the ever-present sadness when I think of my mother building the usual lump in my throat.

"She did." We share a smile. It says a lot about my father that he's always acknowledged his grief and worked through it. The family had a therapist for almost a year after we lost her, with group and individual sessions.

I hated the idea of sharing my feelings but it was Edie who convinced me to talk.

"Selene eventually agreed to marry me. Either I wore her down, or she took pity on me... or it might have been the conversation I had with her father. He worked for the governor-general; it was easy for me to convince him I needed his daughter. I'm not proud of that," he admits cheerfully. "But I'm glad it worked because I can't imagine my life without her."

I shake my head. "I had no idea."

"Yeah, it's not the love story you want to broadcast. And it will be broadcast," Dad warns. "Your life will be under a microscope, which, I promise you, you'll get used to, but it's the relationship stuff that is the worst to handle. Keep that in mind."

"What am I supposed to do?" I had come to talk to my father to settle my nerves and get some assurance that I could do the job of running this country, if that's what I wanted.

This conversation has done *none of that.*

Dad's advice comes with a cheerful grin. "If you've got your mind on someone, go for it sooner rather than later. Stop playing and make it real."

I don't like that advice.

9

Edie

I'M SURPRISED TO SEE Kalle back so soon. Usually when he's up at the castle, he's gone for at least half a day, hanging with his brothers and taking advantage of the castle's facilities.

There's a lot one can do at a castle because—castle.

But he's back sooner than expected, rain shining on his hair from the run through the alley. Kalle's last haircut was a mohawk fade with the sides shaved brutally close, enough to see the white of his scalp. I'm glad to see the sides finally growing in because every time I stood beside him, I was tempted to stroke the soft hairs behind his ear.

My father stayed long enough for a second cup of coffee and to finish Dillon's crossword. He didn't say anything more about Mathias but I'm sure he'll be pressed into giving up any information he's gleaned to my mother when he gets home. I urged him to stay until the storm breaks but he headed out not long after Kalle left.

The breakfast/early lunch rush has ended but the pub is still packed, so much that newcomers have crowded around tables full of friends and relations, and the bar is standing room only. The screens mounted on the wall are showing the 1992 World Series with the Braves versus the Blue Jays and causing as many cheers and complaints as if it were a real-time game.

I sense The King's Hat will sell a lot of beer today.

I get a text from my mother.

> Mom: You need to tell me everything about Mathias!

She adds an emoji of wide eyes and big smile.

I tuck my phone in my pocket instead of answering. I don't feel like thinking about Mathias right now. Last night was... nice...

Mathias is nice.

Am I old enough to settle with *nice*?

There's no sense dwelling on this, or giving my mother any information because it was a date. Dinner.

A good-night kiss that was also nice.

I need a new descriptive.

Kalle is quiet when he comes back. No one would ever call him loquacious, but now he offers more grunts and growls than his usual monosyllabic answers.

"How's Maggot?" I ask in a low voice as I follow him into the kitchen. The first time my dad took me to the castle gardens, the king came out to say hello. I was flustered and scared, because as wonderful and gracious a person as King Magnus is, he's still a king and I was a five-year-old girl. So when my father introduced me and the king bent over to shake my hand, I stumbled on his name and out came King Maggot.

The king loved it and still insists on referring to himself as Maggot when I'm around.

Chase chats with Tyler by the sink and Skywalker has taken a quick break from the grill, and this is what will constitute alone time for me today.

"Good." Kalle doesn't look up from where he's slapped a burger on the grill.

"Did you have a meeting with him?"

Kalle makes a garbled noise that sounds like one of his grunts got caught up with a word. I peer around him to look at his face. His expression is strange, one I've never seen before.

"What's going on?" I demand. "You look weird."

"You look weird," Kalle counters dully.

I sigh. "A bad comeback will not distract me. What happened? Is there word of Daulton?"

How Kalle never knew his father's secretary was such a slimeball is beyond me.

"What about him?" The strange expression is replaced by that look in his eyes that makes any drunk back down. I don't much like angry Kalle, but any woman would agree he's very attractive when he's in a temper.

I don't step back. I also do my best not to breathe deeply because lately, Kalle's scent has been doing strange things to my insides. I've trained my insides not to react to anything Kalle, so I can't understand *why now*? "Stella told me Daphne is back," I tell him. "Alone."

He *humphs*. "That didn't last long."

"Which is probably a good thing. Apparently, Silas is trying to come up with a reason not to give Daphne her job back, but he really needs another person in the coffee shop for the summer."

Kalle grunts.

When he gets like this, I know there's something wrong, and my first instinct is to try and chatter it out of him. Sometimes it works.

Sometimes he tells me in no uncertain terms to go away.

"Your father didn't say anything about it?" I ask.

He flips the burger. "I didn't ask." His heavy sigh is audible even over the sizzle of the cooking meat. "And it'd be Dunc who'd know more. Or Spencer, if the castle is planning on pressing charges."

"I'm not sure what you could press charges for." I hand him a slice of cheese and a bun for his burger.

Kalle has a great smile—when it comes out—all white teeth and full lips, but when he's mad and smiles, he ends up looking like a shark. "Spence could figure something out."

"Is that what's bothering you?" I press. "Daphne and Daulton stuff?"

"I haven't given it a thought until you brought it up."

"That's a good thing." Everything about Kalle tells me to let it go but I've never been one to take the easy way out. "What did your father say?"

Kalle glances up at me for a moment before he adds the cheese to the burger. "He knew Odin was stepping down."

Abdicating. That's the proper word. Prince Odin abdicated his place in succession. Kalle has never talked about it with me, but I know his brother was Kalle's safety net if he abdicated. Odin would make a great king.

So would Kalle, but he's never been able to see that.

"That's not surprising," I venture.

"It was to me. And now I can't... I can't do that to Bo."

"Bo would be okay."

Bo, third son of King Magnus, lacks the gregarious nature of his father and younger siblings, and while he shares the sense of responsibility all of the siblings have, Bo thinks he's best serving the country by living alone in the middle of the country and setting up nature reserves and animal preservation sites. I've always liked Bo with his quietness and soft sense of humour, but I don't know him well. I wonder if anyone really does.

The royal children of King Magnus are many things, but none of them really have close friends. Spencer is more family than friend, and Gunnar has Fenella, but she lives in the US. Kalle has Jonathon, and me; Lyra has Kate. The Laz sisters, Stella and Sophie used to be close to Lyra and the boys, but things happened there.

They have many acquaintances, but few can be considered close to them. It's as if there's an invisible line separating the princes and Lyra from the rest of the town and very few are allowed to get past it. Or maybe that very few try.

My heart warms at the thought that I'm one of them to get past the line into their inner circle.

Kalle rubs the back of his neck. "No one ever told you about Bo, did they?" he asks with a grimace. "About him and Hettie Crow?"

I haven't heard that name in a while. Hettie is the younger sister of Mabel Crow, and Mabel was the inspiration for many stories and scandals in Battle Harbour, including the allegation that it was her who broke up Gunnar and Kate McKibbon years ago. While unlikely, it wouldn't be unheard of with both Gunnar's and Mabel's reputations. She's a year younger than I am, and often comes into the pub. I don't think life has been easy for her. Or too kind.

I don't think I've ever seen Kalle have a conversation with her.

Mabel's sister, however, was a different story. Before she left town years ago, Hettie was the complete opposite of Mabel, save the long dark hair and pretty face. Hettie was sweet, soft, and beautiful.

She was like Bo.

I scrunch my nose as I try to remember past gossip. "I knew they were together for a year or so and then they weren't," I say. "And Hettie moved away. Just disappeared and no one talked about it."

They might have talked about it but not when Mabel was within earshot. Because the Erickson family might be loyal and watch each other's backs but Mabel is a lioness when it comes to her little sister.

Kalle nods. "Yeah."

"Just yeah? There's got to be more to it if you brought it up."

"Well... yeah. But..." He shakes his head and mutters something that sounds like "You're family."

I face him, hands on hips. "You're going to have to tell me now," I demand. I'm not much for hurtful gossip, but working here, it's impossible not to hear the talk. And there was lots of talk when Hettie up and left one night. "What happened between them?"

Kalle leans around me to make sure no one is within earshot. "Hettie left."

"Yeah..." I impatiently motion for him to continue.

"She left because Bo didn't want her to have to deal with the media scrum that comes when one of us dates. Because he hates dealing with being in the public eye—hates it so much that he went off to live in the woods. You can't live in the woods and rule a country."

I watch Kalle flip the burger onto the bun and scrape the grease into the trap.

He's right. Laandia doesn't have a president or a prime minister—King Magnus is head of the government, and you can't run a country from a little house in the forest, as cute and quaint as it might be.

"If I don't become king, it falls on Bo. And that would be a hard no for him, so then Gunnar. And if anything happened to him, then Lyra." Kalle actually shivers at the thought as he adds ketchup and mustard to his burger.

I know there's more to the story of Bo and Hettie, but I make a hard right back to Kalle being king because he never talks about it.

He's content to let others talk, but his true opinion on the subject is unknown.

"Have you actually seriously considered abdicating?" I ask in a quiet voice. "Do you hate the idea that much?"

Skywalker pushes open the swinging door to the kitchen with his barrel belly, Leah chattering behind him. But when she notices our serious expressions, she grabs Skywalker's arm and pulls him back into the bar area. "Fries can wait for a minute."

"No, we'll take this into the office," I call to her as I motion for Kalle to follow me. The office itself is neat and tidy with bookshelves and a filing cabinet in the corner, but invoices and receipts are strewn around the PC because Kalle was in here last.

I make a point to take a minute to deal with them when we're done talking.

"I should have made you something," he says apologetically.

"I already ate, and don't change the subject."

Kalle takes a bite of his burger, forehead furrowing as he chews. "I don't hate the idea," he finally says. "I just... Dad gave me the line from Dune, about being called to lead and answering it, like it's a bloody phone call."

"It's a good line." Kalle huffs at my response so I continue, folding my arms across my chest. "Did you want more from him? Like for him to tell you to stop being wishy-washy and accept that you'll be the king Laandia needs when the time comes?" We've been friends long enough to not have to pull our punches, but I've never gotten into this with him. And I'm not about to coddle him because Kalle would be an amazing king.

I know that. Everyone should realize that.

But the main problem is that I'm afraid Kalle doesn't see it.

Another huff and I give a hiss of frustration. "I've never understood why you don't see yourself like the rest of us do."

His mouth twists into a frown. "Because I know myself better than the rest of you."

"Really?" I cock my head and stare him down. "You think so? I know you miss playing baseball more than any other sport because you'll grab anything round like a lime or one of those squishy stress balls I buy for you and hang onto it like you're getting ready to throw it across the room. I know you pretend to hate being dragged up to the castle for family dinners, but you secretly love spending time with your family because they mean everything to you. And I know you'll be king someday because you won't put the pressure of it onto Bo, but you're so scared of not being enough that you can't just come out and say it."

Kalle narrows his eyes, the blue darkening like the night sky. "You think you're so smart."

"I *am* so smart, that's why you poached me from the hotel to work for you."

He gives me a lopsided smile. "Yeah, but you've stuck around so that proves you're not as smart as you think you are."

"I stick around because you pay me to."

"Yeah yeah," he grumbles. "Remind me not to give you a raise when you ask."

"And I'm asking for a big one. Soon." I grin at Kalle until his smile falls and I know he's ready to dish more. "What else did he say?"

"I'm not scared," he says instead.

"It would be perfectly natural if you are," I tell him in a gentle voice. "I'd be terrified."

"You... you'd walk in there and have everything organized and get the perfect people to do the perfect things for them and have the country fall in love with you within the day," Kalle says in a rueful voice. "You'd be amazing."

"Yeah, maybe," I concede with a sly smile and Kalle scoffs. "But so would you."

"I don't know..."

"What else did your father say?"

Kalle presses his lips together as if he's trying to stem the flow of words. It has been a lot for him. But then he opens his mouth and: "He said I should get married before I become king."

I take a step back into the door because the thought of Kalle getting married is as jarring as sticking a finger in a light socket. He... Married? To a woman who would be his wife.

"Oh," I manage. Kalle with a wife. Kalle with a woman longer than four dates. Kalle in love and with his happily ever after. I want that for him but—

But...

"Yeah," he says heavily. He finishes the burger in about three bites, and all I can do is watch him, and try not to picture my life without Kalle.

Because if he marries, I won't be part of the package. I won't be...

I stare at my crossed arms and blink furiously. "Married," I manage. "Huh."

"Yeah.""Like... now? And who would you marry?"

Kalle shrugs helplessly. "I don't do relationships. They never work so getting married would be... Yeah. No."

"You've never tried to make one work," I point out, trying to get back my sense of equilibrium at the thought of Kalle with a wife. "Your father obviously wants to be around to see you get married, so it makes sense."

He scrubs at the back of his neck and I worry about the skin back there. "I dunno. The thought of dating—"

"You've been dating for years."

"None of them mattered. I wasn't looking for a wife."

Things start to get blurry and I know it's because of this conversation. At the thought of Kalle... I rest my back against the door to steady myself. "And you think you should look for one now."

It's not a question. It's a statement, and all I can think of is that Kalle is about to tell me that he's going to marry Fenella Carrington.

She's practically royalty; her father is one on the one percent list in the United States, so it makes sense.

But Kalle and Fenella... it doesn't make sense to me.

There's never been a woman with Kalle who has made sense for me.

"Maybe?" That is definitely a question. Kalle falls back to asking questions when he doesn't want to answer them, and so I know...

My heart gives a thump of disbelief. Of disappointment.

"Well, then. Who?"

"I don't know," he says, with frustration.

"You have to have an idea."

"I really don't."

"You have to. If you think you can just up and get married... If you could have any woman in the world marry you, who would it be?"

He shrugs. "I don't know. I just—You."

My heart jumpstarts as if Kalle had given it a shot of adrenaline. "I'm sorry—what?"

Kalle stares at me like he's seeing me for the first time, and then he gives me such a smile of relief that I'm reminded of how my baby nephew looks when he's done a load in his diaper. "You should marry me."

"No." Even as the word escapes like a puff of cold air from a freezer, I know that's not what I'm supposed to say. But this isn't what Kalle should be saying either. Because friends like us don't get married.

And friends don't ask friends to marry them like that.

I can't have heard him correctly. There's no way Prince Kalle of Laandia... there's no way my best friend Kalle Erickson...

There's no way either of *them* wants to marry *me*.

No way. But still—

"You should marry me," Kalle insists. The relief has vanished and now he looks like he did when he had the brilliant yet drunken idea to dare Gunnar to strip naked and run through the town square. "Yeah. You'd make a good queen. A great one. You said it yourself."

I laugh. I can't help it. The thought of a sentence including the words *me* and *queen* sends a burst of laughter—a guffaw, really—bubbling up and out. Some of the guffaw heads out through my nose and I snort. "No way."

"Seriously, Edie, think about it."

"*You* can't be thinking about it. Me and you, and me queen?" I stammer, searching for the right words, when there can't be any words because this can't be happening. "You're kidding," I insist. "You have to be. Plus, that's the worst proposal I've ever heard."

"It's not a proposal, it's a—it's you." Kalle stares down at me from his height and all I can think is that he's so tall and so broad. And so Kalle—and he can't be serious.

But he looks serious. He looks like he means it.

"It's a good idea," he says quietly, holding my gaze like it's my hands in his.

My hands are actually in his. I hadn't realized Kalle had grabbed my hands and *ohmygod*, if he goes down on one knee—

"I think you'd be perfect," he says, still upright on two legs.

Not, *I think you're perfect* but *you'd be perfect* like I'm auditioning for a role. Interviewing for a job. Kalle thinks I'd be perfect for a position, but not for him.

If I keep that train of thought, I can overlook the position he has me in mind for would be queen. Because that just can't happen.

That is fairytale land, and my life has never, nor will it ever exist in fairytale land.

"Are you serious?" Any humorous aspect of this conversation vanishes. "You think it's a good idea to marry me, but you don't want to propose?"

"I don't need to... Okay, it was a proposal." Kalle backtracks when he notices my expression.

I know exactly what expression I'm wearing because I've seen it on my mother's face many times.

"No," I say.

"No...?"

"No, I'm not going to marry you."

"Edie..." I think Kalle knows he did something wrong, but I don't let him finish.

"I can't believe you did that. Unlike you, I value the idea of marriage. I want a love like my parents. Like your parents. I want a husband to love and respect me enough to get down on one knee and tell me all the ways he plans to make me happy for the rest of his life. Not some pity—hey, we should get hitched because I need a queen."

"I just thought…" Kalle says miserably. "We're friends."

"And so you should know that is not the way to ask me anything. You may be my best friend, Kalle Erickson, and I want to marry my best friend, but not you. And not like this."

And I yank open the office door and storm out, leaving him there, scrubbing at the back of his neck.

10

Kalle

ALL THE AIR IN the office seems to be sucked out as Edie slams the door behind her.

That didn't go how I thought it would.

It makes sense that it didn't go well since I didn't even think about it. That could be the problem right there.

It hit me when Edie was talking—how incredible she would be as a queen. Edie has the ability that I'll never have to make everyone love her, even when she's rearranging their lives in one of her organizational kicks.

And in the same breath, I realized how easy it would be to have her as my wife.

Edie has always been important to me. I don't think she knows just how much. All the big things in my life—she's been a part of. When I was playing ball, I called her after every game. She came to the Briar to watch me win it. She sat in the pew behind me at my mother's funeral, tears sliding down her face, her hand on my shoulder, my back, making sure I knew she was there for me.

The thought popped into my head fully formed and ready to be spoken aloud—that I could be king with Edie at my side. So I said it. Sort of.

And she said no.

I slump into the chair behind the desk. *Crap.*

That's why I've never made a move on her. You don't mess around with your best friend because what happens when things go wrong—you lose your best friend. And that's the last thing I want.

Because there have been times that I've wanted Edie.

Lots of times.

The night of our high school graduation when Dad let me host the party at the castle. Edie, wearing those cut-off shorts that showed off long legs and the Katy Perry T-shirt I bought her when she took me to the concert, was beside me all night. I had thought *maybe...* the beer I drank made me think, *why not...*

And then Stef Davies pulled me into the gardens.

The day I came back from Baltimore, cut from the team, my shoulder messed up, and I stopped at the hotel where she was working. She looked up from behind the desk, her dark hair cut short to her chin, and smiled.

I didn't do anything then because I knew I was as messed up as my shoulder, but I lived with the regret for quite a while.

There have been so many of those *I want Edie* moments over the years that most have blended into a heaviness in my heart. If I could guarantee the safety of our friendship, I would make so many moves on Edie, in a heartbeat.

But she's not interested. And I would mess it up.

Like I just did.

11

Edie

WHAT JUST HAPPENED?

I lean against the office door for a moment to catch my breath.

He... Kalle *proposed?*

I can't believe him.

Kalle asked me to *marry* him.

Marry, as in husband and wife. As in, more than friends. As in, sharing a bed.

At least, that's what I assume he meant because I know Kalle and he wouldn't want to be married and not enjoy marital relations with his wife, friend or more than friend.

The thought of me and Kalle in bed together—

When he asked me—which technically he didn't, now that my brain is working properly. It was more of a *yeah, we should do this,* like asking a buddy to get a beer.

I'm the buddy he wants to marry.

It's not a good feeling. It was a great feeling for a split second; all I could think about was *Yes!* Yes, I'll marry you and *ohmygod-momisgoingtofreak.*

And then reality crashed down. The fear. The disappointment in the certainty that he doesn't *really* want me. I'm like a security blanket for Kalle, nothing more.

And then—did he just do that because I'm dating his cousin?

Because Kalle has never, ever given any indication that he thinks of me as anything other than a friend. Sure, there might have been times where I got the sense that he might have been tempted to make a move, but he's never, ever said anything to me.

And now he wants me to go from best friend to potential wife? To being the *queen*?

What is he thinking?

He's not thinking. That's the problem.

And as for me, I'm thinking too much.

I love fairytales. I've read all of them, keep a collection of fairytale retellings. To say I have never considered the possibility that Kalle and I... that sitting beside the future king of Laandia was something I might enjoy—it's laughable.

Of course I've thought about it.

Every woman in Laandia has thought about marrying one of the princes. To become queen or a princess—it's like a hive mind. Everyone has had that thought.

Only I make it a point to stop myself whenever the chaotic thought invades the calm of my mind.

Because it would have to be a real-life fairytale to have the daughter of the castle groundskeeper end up with the future king. It's just not possible.

Or at least I never thought so until Kalle opened his mouth.

I push off from the door because I don't want to be standing here when Kalle comes out. I'll have to say something to him, and I have no idea what that might be.

He thinks he wants to marry me. *Me.*

No.

I head to the kitchen and straight to the door that leads to the alley because that's where I go when I need a breather from the bar. But it's still raining, water pouring down in sheets like a biblical flood is about to wreak havoc in Battle Harbour.

Screw it. I grab the short and stubby umbrella we keep by the door, the one with the bent spindle, and step outside before anyone says a word to me.

It's very wet, but at least I can breathe.

I stand in a puddle in the alley, the umbrella not doing much to protect me as rain spatters my shirt and my arms, and I take a deep breath.

And another. And, "Oh, my god," I cry. "He said *what*?"

For one moment, and one moment only, I let the excitement wash over me. I let the unbelievable become believable. For one moment, I let myself think about marrying Kalle Erickson, prince of Laandia.

And then I shut it down.

I get angry because *how dare he* think he can make that leap from friends to so much more without giving me an ounce of warning? No warning. None at all.

No warning, plus *what kind of proposal was that?*

Another deep breath.

I'm in the middle of a long drawn-out one when I hear the squeak of *meow* from behind the bins.

It's Kalle's cat, and it's a sorry sight that breaks through my anger.

I try to coax it to come out from behind the bins, but no luck. She's a cute cat, so tiny with tortoiseshell fur plastered to her little body. I finally give up and head back into the kitchen, where I call Stella and arrange a rescue.

She promises Ajax and Gunnar will be there as soon as possible and I do my best to explain where she's hiding because I don't want to stick around and talk to one of Kalle's brothers.

Of course, when all this is finished, and I head back into the bar, who is sitting there but Prince Bo and Spencer Laz.

Bo looks like a lumberjack, with his flannel and thick beard, and shoulders that can heft a full tree over his head. Spencer, lifelong friend of the family, is as close as a brother to the princes, but doesn't look like it with his slim built and dark hair. He's a lawyer by trade, and usually up to his elbows on some case or other, but his intelligent green eyes still know how to smile.

I do not smile when I see them, and Spencer raises his eyebrow, right away noticing my mood isn't as cheerful as usual.

"Afternoon, Edie," Bo says.

"I suppose you're here to see your *brother*." I don't mean for it to come out that way, but that's how it comes out.

Bo looks abashed. "If he's around?"

"Or not," Spencer adds. "We can just drink our beer in peace."

I don't even serve them a pint before I go find Kalle.

12

Kalle

EDIE BANGS ON THE office door and tells me Bo and Spencer are here. She's gone before I open the door, and that's when I know I really messed up.

The bar is quieter as some of the after-lunch crowd has gone home for afternoon naps before they return for the evening shift.

Bo sits with Spencer at the bar, with empty seats around them. Both men are a common sight in here, but there's still a space around Bo that most people won't enter unless they're personally invited. Spencer is fine, as he's technically not family, but really is, but the rest of us have the same space.

Lyra explained it to me once—that we could pretend to be regular people, but we'd never really get there because of that space. We intimidate or scare; I'm not sure why it's there. And I usually can ignore it because I've got Edie, and she never makes me feel like that.

I really messed up.

I give Bo and Spencer a grunt as a hello, and busy myself with pouring us pints, the head thick and foamy.

In unison, we pick up the glasses.

I make it two-thirds before I run out of air.

Bo finishes the entire twenty ounces, then pushes it back to me for a refill.

"That good?" I ask him, giving him another one.

"He had a lunch with the Minister of Wildlife," Spencer says, setting down his glass at the halfway mark. "It turned into a meet-and-greet with a tour company going whale watching."

"It was a lot of people," Bo mutters. "Not used to that."

"Time to go back to your house in the woods, little brother?" I ask sympathetically. That's why taking Odin out of the succession has been so rough. I know my brother; Bo is a good man. A smart man, smarter than the rest of us. But he's also a man who likes his own company. His privacy. He'd have a tough time with people constantly demanding his time and energy like they were trying to peel off pieces of him.

I know Bo would hate to be king, even more than I would, and that's saying a lot.

"I like my house in the woods. I want to talk to you." Bo leans over the bar to where I keep the bag of potato chips and pulls one up. I take it from him and pour some into a bowl because if I leave him the bag, the whole thing'll be gone in a second.

"I figured, since you didn't call in the cavalry." We have brothers' text chat, along with Spencer, that is used to call a gathering when one of us needs something.

Because he grew up at the castle, and his father has been such a constant in life at the castle, we all treat Spencer like another brother. Each of us has a different relationship with him, though. He hangs out with Odin socially, because they are the same age, but also worked with him on castle stuff. He plays with Gunnar, doing Gunnar stuff. I go to him for business issues. But it's Bo who uses him as a confidant, more than we do. If there's something on Bo's mind, he talks to Spencer first.

Sometimes I wonder if we could somehow convince Spencer to take over. That would solve everything.

"No, Gunny doesn't need to hear this." Bo taps the counter, clearly uneasy because if I'm not one to discuss my feelings, Bo is even worse. He glances at Spencer, who gives him a nod.

I frown. "What's going on?"

"I know you went to see Dad earlier."

No clue how he knows that, but the Battle Harbour grapevine is frightening at times.

"I get you're trying to figure things out," Bo continues. "Odin stepping down didn't make it easy on you. I think we all thought he'd eventually take over after Dad." He gives me a rueful smile. "I know if it's a no for you, nobody wants me to take over."

"You'd be okay," I tell him automatically because, what am I supposed to say? Tell Bo that I worry about his mental health if he has to be king?

Bo shakes his head. "You don't think so, and that's okay. I don't have the big game temperament that the rest of you do. If I was firstborn, I would have already given up. But you..." He meets my gaze, and it's like looking in the mirror. Bo and I look the most alike, with our darker blond hair and beards, but it's our eyes that show us as brothers. "This is what you were born for. Not just because you were the first," he stammers. "But because you'll be good at being king."

"I'm not dad," I tell him quietly.

"Nobody is. But you could be great."

"You have to believe it, though," Spencer adds quietly.

I shrug. They make it sound so simple. *Believe in Yourself*, which should be a title for one of those old Chicken Soup for the Soul books Mom used to read.

"I believe in you," Bo continues. "And so do most of Laandia, more people than you can imagine. I doubt this will make it easier, but I'm saying it out loud—if you don't do this, I'm not going to either."

I wipe away a non-existent smudge on the bar top. As soon as I saw them here, I knew this was where Bo would eventually end up at. I don't blame him. I can't, because I think about the same thing. "Then, Gunnar..." I trail off, not needing to finish.

"*I* think he'd be great. I really do." Spencer meets my gaze, looking earnest and serious. "He's grown up. He's not the little bugger racing all over the world anymore. And this happened before Stella, so who knows what magic she's going to work on him? She really steadies him."

I've noticed that too.

But Bo isn't finished. "I guess what I want to say is that it'll be cool, no matter what you want," he says slowly. "I trust you."

"Sometimes I wish Dad never gave us the choice. The option." I rub the back of my neck, staring idly at the pockets of customers. I've spent so much time here, making it into a place I could be proud of. If I grew up without having an option, I wouldn't have started the bar. I wouldn't have played hockey or ball, or anything but stayed home and learned everything I needed to know. I might have been better off.

"That's not Dad's way. He made this his choice and you get to as well. And just so you know, I think you needed to do all those things because they made you the man you are."

I chuckle to break the seriousness of the discussion. "Now you're going deep."

Bo nods with a bemused smile. "Done, now."

I finish my beer, attention caught by the T.V showing the old Jays game. Bottom of the sixth. I've watched repeats of it enough that I know exactly how it ends. It's still fun to see.

Edie was right about me missing baseball most of all.

I pull my mind off of her for another moment. "When I was talking to Dad, he told me some stuff about Dante," I start carefully. "Do you ever wonder what it would be like if Dad had let Dante take the throne back then?"

"Laandia would be a very different place," Spencer says.

"Yeah. Dante... can't really see him as a king." And that's probably the nicest thing I can say about my uncle.

"Don't think it matters because we wouldn't be here," Bo says, always the pragmatic one.

"Yeah. Yeah, I guess."

We finish our beers. There hasn't been much time in the last few years where I can hang out with my brothers and Spencer without big conversations. Questions to be asked. Decisions that need to be made.

Sometimes I wish we could go back and be kids running wild around the castle. It was a good childhood. There might not have been a lot of outside friends that I was close to, but we had each other, and Spencer. And I had Edie.

I really hope I didn't mess it up with her. Because that would—

I don't even want to think about what that would be like.

I watch as she comes from the kitchen with a tray of nachos, the smell of cheese making my stomach rumble. For a moment, I think she's bringing them to us, but she veers off to the back corner where a group of kids are parked.

"What's up?" Bo asks, watching me watch Edie.

I scrub a hand along the back of my neck, thinking of this morning when I woke up alone. "I don't know," I admit. "But I'll let you know when I do."

After Bo and Spencer take off, I hide out in the office for a bit, tidying the papers on the desk because I know Edie will disappear back in here to do it, as soon as I come out.

When I finally emerge, I keep my head down as Edie stews, storming her way around the bar prep, snapping at Dillon when he asks about Wordle.

I give her time and space because fixing things with women has never been my strong suit. But when she keeps answering me with one-word answers, I can't take it anymore.

I come up beside her when she's cutting up limes at the bar and brush her shoulder with mine. "Don't be mad at me," I say in a quiet voice.

She turns, still with fire in her eyes. "And who should I be mad at, then?"

"Don't be mad at all. Dad said stuff and I didn't know what to think and you're *here*, you've always been here—"

"You want to marry me because I'm *here*? You know you're only making it worse."

Dillon lifts his head from his tablet where he's playing online Scrabble. "What's this now?"

I shake my head at him. *Later*, I mouth but he keeps his attention on us. "I know. I know I'm making it bad, but the kids can't handle it when Mom and Dad fight." I smile winningly at Edie, putting every ounce of charm that Lyra says I have into it, and nod to the other side of the bar where Tyler and Bethie are staring at us with trepidation.

"I'm allowed to be mad at you," Edie insists. I don't know if it's the concern of Bethie and Tyler, the undivided attention of Dillon, or maybe even my smile that takes away most of the fire in her eyes.

"You are allowed, but you won't be." Another grin. "I'm irresistible."

"You're really not."

Taking that as an opportunity, I step behind her and wrap my arms around her slim waist. Edie is tall but I have the Erickson height, so my chin rests on the top of her head. "That was…" I stumble for a moment over what word to use before giving up. I've never been a wordsmith. "I don't know what that was, but I know I made you unhappy and for that I'm very sorry."

Edie rests a hand on my arm. "I don't know what it was either."

"You're my best friend," I say into the top of her head.

"Oh, I know."

"You might be my only friend."

"Oh, I know that, too." She squeezes my forearm, her thumb rubbing circles on the inside of my arm, and I wonder if I should be alarmed at how much her touch soothes me. At how comfortable it feels to have my arms around her, pressing into her back.

She fits. Edie fits with me.

"I know I shouldn't be mad," Edie begins hesitantly, "but that felt callous. Kind of selfish. Like... like I don't matter to you."

"You matter," I insist. "A lot. A whole lot of a lot."

I keep my arms around her because it feels good. Being this close to Edie always feels good, but this seems different. I like the way she leans back against me, her head against my chest. How her thumb keeps stroking my arm.

How she smells like strawberries and coconut because I know what kind of shampoo she uses.

I really like how her breathing matches mine, deep and easy. Content.

Being around Edie is easy—

It's more than that. I'm aware of the softness of her stomach where my hand rests against it. It would be simple to brush my lips against the top of her head, to tuck her hair behind her ear, the tiny diamond studs I gave her for her thirtieth birthday gleaming in the overhead light of the bar. To trail my mouth down to her cheek, sliding across to her—

"Maj, what time do you want me back for tonight?" Dillon asks me.

Edie stiffens and pushes my hands away. I step back, feeling unsteady, like I've had too much to drink.

What just happened there?

"Sorry, did I interrupt a little moment there?' Dillon asks with a strange look in his eyes.

"No," Edie says at the same time I open my mouth as if to say, "Yeah, I think you did."

But I don't say it.

"What's going on?" she asks Dillon. "I thought you have tonight off?"

"Duty calls when his Highness goes out." Dillon, who has handled everything from a tourist who fainted at the sight of me, and another that I needed a restraining for, looks irritated. Annoyed.

Mad at me.

Edie turns to me and my stomach sinks because— "Oh, sh..." I begin.

"What are you doing tonight?" she demands.

"I gotta go out for a bit..." I swallow, wishing I could rewind my conversation of last night. "I told Fenella..."

Edie stiffens again and the fire in her eyes returns, only this time it's worse because she looks like I've slapped her. "You just asked me to marry you and now you're going on a date with Fenella Carrington?" Edie throws out each word like a dart.

"I didn't think."

"You haven't been doing that much lately, have you?" And she stalks away; lucky for me because she looks like she's about to throw me across the bar. Or something across the bar *at* me.

"What did I miss?" Dillon asks.

I sigh. "Too much to get into."

"But you're still going out with the Carrington girl tonight?"

I check my watch. I told Fenella I'd meet her at seven, in only a couple of hours. "It's too late to cancel now," I tell Dillon. "Edie's already ticked at me so there's no point making two women mad at me."

"What did you do to make the woman mad?"

"What makes you think I did something?"

"Did I, or did I not hear something about getting married? You and her?" Dillon points to where Edie takes an order from a table on the other side of the bar, smile miraculously back on her face.

She's so pretty when she smiles. She's pretty all the time, but when she smiles, it's like she's opened a window to see what she's really like.

"No." I shake my head. "It was an idea and I shouldn't have opened my mouth."

Both of us watch Edie walk to the kitchen, black jeans hugging her curves, the strings of her apron crossed and twisted at her back.

"It's not a bad idea," Dillon offers.

I turn away from the sight of Edie as she heads into the kitchen. "I know, right?"

"It's a big step, considering both of you insist you're just friends." He waves his hands as he says it, which cracks into the miserable feeling in my stomach. "But what are you going to do about *him*?" And he points to the phone sitting on the bar.

Edie's phone.

And I glance at the screen to see a notification of a text from Mathias pop up. *Are you working tonight?*

And that's when I realize I'm going to lose her. And I don't have the faintest idea what to do about it.

13

Edie

K ALLE ERICKSON IS AN intelligent man. I've seen proof of this—or at least I think I did, because, now, there's no evidence of *anything* inside that pretty head of his.

Or maybe he's still intelligent but the beer he shared with his brothers has wiped out any other feelings.

He proposed to me. Then he said all this nice stuff, how I'm his best friend, and *then* he goes out with Fenella Carrington.

Hell, yeah, I'm mad.

I got Mathias's text after that, and told him I have to be here all night but to come over if he has time. It's possible I was a little more flirtatious in my response than usual because why wouldn't I when the man who just proposed marriage was leaving to go on a date?

Who does that?

Technically, it wasn't a proposal, but still.

I can't even look at Kalle when he leaves. We were having a *moment*... But maybe we weren't, because—only friends.

Just friends because that's how it's always been. That's how we've always wanted it.

So why did my stomach twist into a knot when Kalle showed up wearing his favourite jeans, the ones I helped him track down online because he needed athletic fit because his thighs are so muscular, and his dark purple shirt with the white squiggles that make his eyes even bluer.

It's his date shirt. His favourite date shirt and he's never once worn it with me.

I had to look at him then because I can't not. It's like he's a magnet and I'm a piece of metal.

He probably wore the shirt because it matches *Fenella's* eyes.

Seeing him leave to meet her does *things* to me. The ego takes a beating; the whole episode has done a number on my self-esteem. I've never had an issue with self-confidence. I know who I am, and my worth, but a half-hearted proposal because we're friends? It doesn't feel nice. It's as if Kalle smashed a mallet into a gong and the vibrations are still being heard.

And then there's how it felt to have his arms around me. It felt like it shouldn't feel. Even though Kalle isn't the most affectionate, we've hugged lots of times but that felt... different.

It did a thing to me too.

"Edie? Earth to Edie?"

I come back from my angry internal monologue to find Leah before me. "Sorry, what's wrong?"

Leah has been at The King's Hat longer than I have. In fact, Kalle would have given the older woman the job of manager, but she wanted nothing to do with it. "I'm retired," she had said in her slightly nasally voice. "I'm fine with slinging drinks and helping Luke in the kitchen but no more than that."

Luke, her husband, used to be a cook at the castle. Both he and Leah worked there for years, retired at fifty-five with benefits and a nice pension, and then were persuaded to come work for Kalle.

Everyone calls Luke by his nickname, Skywalker, except Leah.

"I wanted to make sure you'll be okay if Luke and I take off," Leah says with a concerned frown. "We got the last of the supper crowd plated and served and this lot left—" she waves a hand around the tables— "—are here to drink."

"It's all good," I assure her. "Bethie and Suze are here, and Kalle won't be late."

"Oh no? I thought he was out with the American." Usually I ignore the disdain in Leah's voice when she talks about Kalle and the women he dates, but right now I want to give Leah a fist bump for being on my side.

"He's with Fenella but..." Kalle looked good in those jeans and had even replaced his well-worn boots with a nice pair of shoes. I've seen Kalle leave for countless dates and I can tell when he's trying to impress. "I don't know when he'll be back," I admit. "But we'll be fine. It's a quiet crowd even with the storm."

"If you're sure." Skywalker will stay for as long as we ask him to, but Leah, despite her words of concern, comes to work, does her shift, and clocks out.

I don't blame her; my feet hurt after being on them all day, and Leah is a lot older than I am. "Get home and see you tomorrow. Stay dry."

"Tyler is still in the back if you need an extra set of hands. Or if there's trouble."

As soon as Leah says that, the door opens and Princess Lyra blows into the bar with a gust of rain-soaked cool air. Kate McKibbon, her best friend and personal secretary to Prince Odin, is right behind her, shaking the droplets off her hair with a grin.

"I can't see there being trouble," I say wryly as Lyra and Kate wave and head for a couple of empty stools.

"I wouldn't hold my breath," Leah mutters as she ducks out the back door and I make my way over to play bartender.

"Hey," I greet them, unable to summon up my usual cheeriness. And it's not like I'm not pleased to see Princess Lyra; Kalle's younger sister is like a breath of non-beer-scented air whenever she drops in. The King's Hat welcomes everyone, but the clientele is primarily men content to sit and drink beer and watch whatever is on the screen. Lyra always gives the place a more fun vibe.

I could do with a vibe of fun tonight.

"What bit you on the bottom?" Lyra demands. "Let me guess: my brother. From the absence of Big and Brawny, I'm guessing he's not around."

I roll my eyes. "What can I get you?"

"Information, for a start. We have family dinner tomorrow night, so what mess am I going to walk into? I heard he braved the storm to come talk to Dad today."

"On Kalle? None to give," I lie. "Drinks?"

Kate asks for a beer, but Lyra likes them fancy and instructs me step-by-step on how to make something called a Jet Pilot.

"Because I'm stuck here, and can't fly away," she says as I set the cocktail in front of her.

"I thought you were going back to Chicago tomorrow?" Kate asks her. All it takes is one look at her for me to deduce that Lyra dragged her here because of Kate's mood

A glance around the bar tells me Bethie and Suze have everything under control and I settle in to do my part to cheer up Kate.

Like me, Kate is born and bred in Battle Harbour, with family sprinkled on every street. I know her brother Jonathan, who is a good friend of Kalle's.

"I'm not going anywhere with this storm." Lyra waves her arms like she's pretending to be a tornado. "Rain, rain, go away. I thought I'd hang out for a few more days and see what you decide." She nudges Kate with her shoulder.

"Still haven't made up your mind about going to Saint Pierre with Odin?" I ask Kate. Odin abdicating his spot in the succession means there is nothing official holding him in Laandia. Lady Camille—*Princess* Camille now—will be taking over as prefect of the island country of Saint Pierre at the end of the year when her father retires, so the two will be moving there when they return from their honeymoon.

Kate, as Odin's secretary, was invited to relocate, as was Camille's secretary, Jackson, who came with her from Saint Pierre.

Kate shakes her head with frustration. "It's a good offer and seems like a nice place, but I don't know. Laandia is my home."

"And then there's Jackson," Lyra says slyly. Jackson, from what I heard, declined Camille's offer and will be staying in Laandia.

"He shouldn't have anything to do with it," Kate snaps, uncharacteristically for her.

"Trouble in paradise?" I ask sympathetically.

"There is no paradise because Jackson refuses to acknowledge... anything."

I mirror Kate's frown. "I saw the two of you at the wedding. The whole town saw the two of you ga-ga over each other. The boy is crazy about you, so what's the big deal?"

"Apparently he's not." I hear the hurt in Kate's voice. "I thought we had something but the day after the wedding, once Camille and Odin left, it was all business with him. He…kissed me at the wedding," she admits. "I thought it meant something."

I feel bad for Kate but her trouble is a welcome distraction from my *whatever it is* going on with Kalle. "I'm not sure I can be much help, but have you talked to him?" I ask.

Kate rolls her eyes. "Jackson isn't much of a talker."

"But can he kiss?" Lyra wants to know.

"I'm not answering that," Kate says in a prim voice studying the bottles lined up behind the bar. "If I say he's an amazing kisser, you'll pity me more if it doesn't work out between us. If I say he's not great, you'll look at him funny if we do get together."

"I've never really looked at it that way," Lyra muses.

"Don't look at him in any way," Kate tells her.

"I'm looking at him with the death glare unless he makes you happy."

"Walk up and kiss him," I suggest. "Men aren't good at talking about stuff. At least not the men around here."

"That's a great idea," Lyra cheers. "Only, I told her the same thing and she poo-pooed it."

"I'm not doing that," Kate protests. "If he wants to kiss me, *he* can kiss me."

"Well, aren't we an independent woman from the 1950s," I drawl, heavy on the sarcasm.

Kate's offended expression makes me laugh and makes Lyra switch her attention to me. "So what did my brother say—or not say— that got you hot and bothered? Not in the good way," Lyra adds. "Cranky-pants bothered."

I pause for a moment, wondering if it would be a good idea to tell them what he said. If I wasn't so annoyed, I wouldn't have said a word, but Lyra is his sister, and Kate is practically family. "Kalle came up with the idiotic idea that he should marry me."

Lyra spits a mouthful of her cocktail across the bar.

"He what?" Kate gasps.

"He went to talk to the king about Odin and ended up thinking it was a good idea for me to marry him. FYI, it was a pretty pathetic proposal. Not that it was a real proposal. Definitely not."

"Did he—was it—did he actually say *will you marry me*?" Lyra's eyes are practically popping from her head.

"We didn't get that far. It was more of a sketching out the parameters."

"I'm amazed he got as far as he did." Lyra gives me a searching look. "After Mom died, Kalle vowed never to marry."

Hearing any of the family mention Queen Selene always gives me a jolt of sadness. Today it's a little different since I'm reminded that Kalle will be looking for a woman to replace his mother. "He never told me that," I murmur.

Lyra shrugs. "It might have been just something for a guy to say after he loses his mother, but you have to admit, Brother Dearest has sort of been on the no-marriage path for a while."

"Maybe," I concede. Kalle has never been open to commitment. He likes to play the field and he likes to have fun. When a woman starts thinking long-term and begins to check out the window of the Jade's Jewels in town, it's his signal to bail.

I've seen it happen so many times I've lost count.

"Why haven't the two of you...?" Kate begins but trails off. Maybe it's the way I quickly shift my gaze to her, knowing exactly what is about to come out of her mouth. "I'm only asking because of the half a beer." She gestures to the half-empty pint glass before her. "You and Kalle. What's the real story?"

"I'm not going to serve you if you ask things like that."

"You make him smile." Kate turns to Lyra. "He smiles so much more when Edie is around, don't you think? And Kalle is..." Kate widens her eyes and gives me a knowing nod.

"Don't talk like that about my brother," Lyra snaps. "Watching you and Gunnar—" She makes a variety of kissing noises, plus a motion with her tongue— "—was bad enough. Take your heart-emoji eyes away from the rest of them."

"I don't have heart-emoji eyes for Kalle," Kate protests. "The man is—" She falters under Lyra's glare. "He's a little, maybe kind of... he's totally hot," she finishes in a rush, dropping her head and grabbing her beer. "He was Sexiest Man of the Year for the magazine."

"They all were," Lyra grumbles with another slurp of the straw. "It made them all positively insufferable."

"I love that Bo was first of them to get it." I laugh, remembering how Kalle had discredited *People* magazine, telling all who listened about how they objectified men. It had been totally sour grapes because Kalle said nothing when *he* was featured on the cover two years later. "Besides, I've always thought Bo has the best bottom of the bunch."

"Oh, totally," Kate agrees.

"Stop!" Lyra cries, cupping her hands over her ears. "La lala la la... I can't hear you."

"You have to admit, you're kind of perfect for Kalle." Not to be distracted, Kate heads back to her earlier question. "Perfect for each other."

"People perfect for each other are boring," Lyra complains.

"Like you and Spencer?" Kate asks, mirroring her friend's sly tone from earlier.

I've long had the suspicion that Spencer had more than familial feelings for Princess Lyra. I guess I'm not the only one.

Lyra looks aghast. "Did you start drinking before we came out? You're a spicy one tonight."

Kate heaves a huge sigh. "I just. Don't care," she manages. "And I'm sad. I either lose my job or my boyfriend. Only I don't know if he's my boyfriend because he won't kiss me again and that's all I've been thinking about."

Things are worse than I thought. Before I change my mind, I line up three shot glasses on the bar. "I'm sure this won't make it better," I say, pulling bottles.

"But it will certainly help." Lyra grabs the shot as soon as I finish pouring the spirits and downs it in a mouthful. "More please."

Kate puts her elbow on the bar and slowly sips. "Tell me about your reasoning for staying just friends with Kalle," she invites. "So I can get behind you and Mathias."

Lyra makes a face. "It'll have to be a pretty good reason for me."

I down my shot, the half-ounce of cranberry juice lessening the heat of the vodka, melon liqueur and amaretto, but not much. "We don't like Mathias?" I ask Lyra, checking the door to make sure he's not walking in.

"*We* don't have a say in it," Kate answers before her friend. "*We* are your friend and want you to be happy. Are we friends?" she asks with a shy smile. "I mean, we got along really well at the wedding. At least, I thought we did."

Lyra looks at me expectantly, replacing her usual blasé with a wistful gaze.

Princess Lyra wants to be my friend. And *aww...*

"I don't make Killer Kool-aid for just anyone," I tell them, pouring another round. I also don't normally drink while on duty, but it's been a strange day. Besides, with another wave of the storm rolling in later tonight, a few drinks under my belt might help me sleep with the thunder.

"Mathias is perfect," Lyra says. "And boring. So what happened with you and Kalle?"

"Nothing," I admit.

"Is that the problem? Haven't you ever?"

"There *may* have been a few times over the years that I... I thought about it," I confess, stacking the shot glasses.

"Why didn't you?" Kate wants to know. "More than think about it?"

"Yeah, you could have just walked up and kissed him," Lyra echoes and Kate makes a face at her friend.

"It's not that easy," I say. "My father worked for his father. Your father. The king."

"He doesn't work for him anymore," Lyra points out. "Besides, half the town works for my father."

"It felt... weird," I admit, wondering if the alcohol is making me open up like a video of a flower blooming in time release. "Like it was crossing a line that shouldn't be crossed."

"This isn't the time of Jane Austen," Kate points out.

"So get over that," Lyra adds.

"Says the princess in the castle."

"It would be the same thing for you and Spencer." Kate nudges Lyra. "Haven't you thought of that?"

"I do my best not to think of Spencer Laz and *that* in the same thought. And no one brought him into the conversation."

"I brought him in," Kate says proudly.

"Take him out. You want to know about Edie and Kalle, so focus on that." Lyra's tone has the authority of her father when she wants to, which is just one more reason why she has followers all over the world. Not just social media followers but actual people who would follow her into a pool at midnight or onto a plane across the world to watch a football game. Lyra has everything going for her—beauty, charm, social status. Loving family.

She reminds me of Fenella Carrington.

"I'm going to add my two cents before you ask," Lyra continues.

"I don't think she's going to ask," Kate whispers.

"I think you'd make an amazing queen."

I down another shot quickly, closing my eyes against the flame licking my stomach. "That's what he said," I mutter.

"Well, what's the problem?" Kate demands.

"We're not together," I say. "And won't ever be."

14

Kalle

I'VE HAD A LOT to drink tonight.

The beer with my brother, and another one when I was getting ready.

There was a little shot of whiskey before I left. Okay, maybe two. And now, most of the bottle of wine is gone, and I don't think Fenella had more than a glass.

I'm fine though—I am an Erickson and Vikings can handle their alcohol. It just helps get Edie's expression of disappointment out of my head.

And hurt. That one still sticks.

I can honestly say it's not the best night to take Fenella to dinner, but it's the least I can do. I look at it as if I'm doing her a favour because while the intrigue is there, the interest in Fenella has definitely dwindled.

And that's a me thing—nothing to do with her.

So while I sit across from her, trying to pull out the charm and make conversation, there's a whole *what am I doing* here vibe going on for me. I'm a little stunned that I'm there, but I wager being with Fenella would stun most men.

She's like my sister—Lyra is a force of nature as well, but unlike her, Fenella has the billions to fix the destruction she leaves in her wake. At least her father does.

Halfway through Nonna's finest lasagna, I have a flurry of thoughts, wondering if I should be thinking of Fenella as a potential queen.

Edie said no. She doesn't want to marry me.

And now—it's not like I'm fixated on the idea of getting married, but it's something to think about so I don't have to think about other things.

Like me being king. And how crappy I'll probably be at it. If I think about who I would want to become my queen, I don't have to think about me being king.

Do I need to give every woman I date the queen test? Or should I go with the arranged marriage route, like Odin? It worked out pretty well for him.

No. That's not for me.

I never thought marriage was for me until my father shoved the idea into my head and now that's the only thing I can think about. So maybe I am fixated on the idea.

It's hard to imagine Fenella with Mom's emerald and diamond crown on her head when I look at her across the table. She'd look pretty good in it though.

I brought her to Nonna's Ristorante because I had a hankering for the lasagna, and the light from the tiny candles in the glass jars gives her face a softness it lacks in the daylight.

It also makes her prettier, a more approachable prettier.

I chew on a piece of bread and try to pay attention to Fenella's story about the last Met Gala; something about a dress that resembled someone else's and what was said in the ladies' room.

I don't do a very good job paying attention. At least I seem to nod in the right places as I continue to mull over the fact that Edie turned me down.

She said no to marrying me.

Edie said no.

Not that I would expect her to ever want to marry me, but hearing the no come out of her mouth was a shock. I thought she'd give a reason, argue a bit but a flat-out, no? And like I offended her with the question?

I wasn't expecting that.

I don't hear no very often.

"Earth to Kalle."

I glance up at a pair of bemused eyes. Purple eyes, because of course Fenella Carrington would be the only woman I know with purple eyes.

I haven't asked if that's her real colour, but I want to.

"Yeah," I grunt.

"You're in your own little world over there."

I take another piece of focaccia and dip it in the saucer of garlic oil. "I'm right here," I assure her.

I've never brought a date to Nonna's. I've been told I'm a bit of a romantic when it comes to dates. My go-to spots are the castle garden—asking the kitchen staff nicely to set up a table with champagne and dinner so we can eat in the moonlight—or in the fields behind the tennis courts where you can lie on the grass and see the stars. I took one woman to Stella's pet rescue when she said she loved cats and borrowed a friend's fishing boat for an evening sail for another.

Or I just take them back to my place.

But I take Fenella Carrington to Nonna's, so that should say something.

But I'm not sure what I want it to say.

"Kalle." The snap in her voice pulls me back to reality. "One more time and I'm out of here."

Those full lips twisted into almost a frown, violet eyes narrowing. She looks *almost* annoyed.

I wonder if Fenella has trained herself not to show emotion when she's in public or if that's something her family taught her. "Have you ever walked out on a date?" I ask.

"Do you really have to ask that?" she counters.

That gets a smile out of me. I can picture her sweeping out of the best restaurants in Paris and New York, leaving a half-eaten dinner and a date who happened to say the wrong thing.

Fenella is fun and feisty, her good heart countering the spoiled and indulged side. She makes me laugh, she makes me think—not always a good thing.

I've enjoyed the time I've spent with her. But something is missing.

"I'm leaving as soon as this horrible storm lifts," she announces.

"Not enough to interest you here?" I offer her a lazy grin. "I can see about offering more amusement." I dip into flirtatious charm—at least that's what I'm aiming for. I *can* pull it out as easily as I can growl out a monosyllabic sentence. It just depends on who I'm with, and who's watching.

Everyone is watching us at Nonna's, so it's all smiling eyes and flirting banter. The restaurant is surprisingly busy with the storm still raging. Some people just don't want to stay at home during a storm.

I'd rather be at the bar. Make sure everything is quiet, with no outbursts of fighting. Edie can control things, but I want to make sure she has enough help.

I want to make sure she's not mad at me.

I know the night will not end how the diners think it will. I can put up a good face, but my heart isn't into this tonight. My heart isn't into Fenella, period.

It's too bad, really.

"It's not happening with us, Your Highness," Fenella says echoing my very thoughts.

Which gets my full attention. I might know something is missing but that still doesn't mean I can't show her a good time. "What?"

Fenella smiles kindly, like the babysitter letting down her ten-year-old charge with a crush as gently as she can. "You know it, too, Kalle. You've been playing for a long time, same as me. But you're ready for something real now. Same as me. And—" Fenella waves between us. "This isn't real. Might end up being fun, but it wouldn't last."

This is a new one for me. "I don't understand."

"Have you never had a girl break it off with you?"

"Uh... no?"

Fenella gives a peal of laughter. "Oh, to be a prince with no kingdom."

"I have a kingdom."

"Do you?" She leans back in her chair, half of her mushroom ravioli uneaten. "I didn't think you wanted it."

"I never said that," I say, my gaze straying to the door like I'm looking for the quickest way to make an exit.

"You never *not* said that either," Fenella points out. "Maybe that's the problem—you haven't found your person because you haven't found yourself yet."

How did we get to be talking about this? I change my mind about Fenella being fun. "I know who I am."

"Of course you do," she soothes.

"I'm the crown prince of Laandia, and someday, I might take the throne."

"Is your father planning on acquiring immortality?"

"What?"

Fenella leans across the table, gaze holding mine. There's something in the way she looks at me that calms the surge of temper. "There's that word. *Might.*"

I shake my head. How else am I supposed to say I'm going to be king some day? I hate even thinking about it, let alone saying it.

"*Might* implies that there is a possibility that either you might not take the throne or your father will be there indefinitely," Fenella says, dropping her voice so the table next door can't eavesdrop, which they've been doing all night. "Or that there might not be a throne to take." She blinks those purple eyes at me like she's waiting for me to unleash all my emotions and concerns and thoughts on the matter.

I'm not doing that.

Why would I?

Just because the possibility of me not taking over as king has dodged me for my entire life despite doing what I can to avoid it. Instead of being like Odin, and learning what I needed, I played sports, excelling at everything I tried.

Unlike being king. I won't be very good at that. In fact, I'm going to suck at it. I'm an athlete, a dumb jock, and a bar owner. Who would ever want me as their king?

I'm not telling Fenella that. I'm not telling anyone.

"So what's the real thing you're leaving for?" I ask, trying to move away from the part of me who wants to tell her all of this. The thought of telling someone is very tempting.

Must be something in this bread.

"There's someone back home," Fenella admits with a smile. "In LA, which is sort of my home base these days. At least I hope he's a someone."

"Who?"

"Ever heard of Opium?"

"The drug or the band?"

"The band. The lead singer, Tiger Hennan and I... well, there's something."

"Enough to give up your chance with a prince?"

Fenella smiles prettily. "We both know there's no chance here, as tempting as it may be to think so. You agree."

"I don't really have a choice," I tell her ruefully.

"But you agree. I'd love to have another Laandian prince pining after me, but it's not going to happen. Now, are we ordering another bottle of that pinot noir? You'll need something to drown your tears in."

"There's no tears."

"Exactly why it would never work with us, handsome. Besides, I saw you at the wedding before I moved in. You've got something with Edie, and that—" She nods knowingly. "Is going to end up being more real than this."

I don't have it in me to argue.

15

Edie

L YRA INSISTS I DO more shots with them.

Shots, as in plural.

Princess Lyra has always struck me as a person who doesn't like to drink alone and persuasive enough to convince anyone to be her new best friend.

Apparently, I am now one of them.

Lyra and Kate are both younger than I am—I had graduated high school before they even got there—and except for Kalle, I've never been particularly close to the rest of the royal family. But I got to know them being part of Odin and Camille's wedding.

And now, it looks like I am close enough for Lyra to want to drink with me.

Or it could be because I make good cocktails.

The rain still pours down, and rolls of thunder shake the windows and make me jump. The bar is Thursday-night busy, but the chaos of the lunch rush has thinned out as pitchers of beer and sitting at a table all day have sent many back home to more comfortable furniture.

There's still enough to keep me serving between making shots. Battle Harbour is a beer and mead type of town, with the odd customer drinking too much whiskey or Screech, but more than a few regulars are curious enough about the bottles being used to order what Lyra and Kate are having.

I took a mixology course a few years ago and it's fun to revisit some of the recipes. I pull down the blue curaçao, coconut rum, and every fruit-flavoured vodka we've got, and even unearth the dusty bottle of absinthe. Add them together and I can create cock-tails and shots that have Kate cheering over the colours and taste.

I'm clearing up a row of sixteen shot glasses when Mabel Crow joins the crowd grouped around Lyra and Kate.

"What can I get you?" I ask her.

Mabel nods at Lyra. "Whatever she's having."

Mabel is a common sight in the drinking establishments of Battle Harbour, but after the rumours about her and Prince Gun-nar that broke up him and Kate, I've never seen a conversation between Mabel and any of the family.

And I've definitely never seen her speak to Kate.

"Make us something fancy," Lyra instructs, leaning with her elbow on the bar to face Mabel so that Kate is blocked. "How's your sister?" she asks.

Mabel smirks. "Which one?"

"The one my brother was madly in love with until she skipped town and broke his heart. Hettie."

There's a flicker in Mabel's expression before it smooths into a masklike blandness. "She's good, last time I spoke to her."

"Where'd she end up?"

"Don't you leave town to make sure nobody knows where you end up?"

Lyra sniffs and stiffens when Kate tries to push her aside. "I talked to Gunnar about what happened between the two of you," Kate announces.

I hold the bottle of vanilla vodka aloft and hold my breath.

"Did you now?" Mabel narrows her eyes. "And what did the Playboy Princeling say about that?"

"Nothing. He said nothing happened."

Another flicker; I only notice because I'm watching Mabel. It almost looks like relief. But her voice is cool. "If that's what he says," she says with a shrug.

"It's what he says. And I believe him."

"Goody for you."

"And I'm sorry," Kate continues doggedly, "that everyone thought of you like a scarlet woman."

Mabel glances down at her plaid shirt, which is tight around the chest and has one extra button undone. "I do like red."

"It wasn't fair," Kate says. "And I'm sorry I didn't believe him."

"You're apologizing to me?"

"Yes," she says with a proud lift of her chin. "And I'd like to pay for your drink."

Another shrug. "Suit yourself. I'm not one to say no to that."

"I should have believed him," Kate repeats.

Lyra nudges her. "It's okay."

"It is okay," Mabel agrees. "You were young, and he is the Playboy Prince."

"But he wasn't then," Kate says.

"No." Mabel gives her a tiny smile. "He wasn't."

I let out the breath that I've been holding and Mabel glances at me. "What? Did you think I came over to cause trouble?"

"I think there's a lot of history between you and them," I tell her. "I came back last night to find a bar fight, so I don't want Kalle coming back to the same thing."

Mabel has a pretty, musical laugh that doesn't go with the rest of her. "Shame I missed that. Don't worry, Edie, I'll be good."

"Even though being good is boring," Lyra cuts on.

"Have you grown up to be the royal rebel, then?" Mabel asks her. "I always thought it would be Kalle."

I set three shots on the bar before anyone can make another comment. "No more for you?" Kate asks.

"I'm still working."

"I want to go dancing," Lyra complains as she clicks the tiny glasses with Mabel and Kate. "There really isn't a good place to go around her for a girls' night. Of course I like drinking for free at my brother's pub—"

"Who says you're drinking for free?" I demand.

Lyra waves a hand at me, nails bitten but still painted a vibrant turquoise. "Don't worry, I tip exceedingly well. When Kalle started this place, I was still pretty depressed by our mother dying, and he promised that I would never have to pay for a drink here. You can ask him." She blinks innocently at me.

I laugh. "I think I will since I've never heard that one before."

"I will pay, because these are really good drinks." Kate holds up her glass.

"I'd like somewhere to dance," Lyra continues. "I haven't been dancing since I've been back."

"We danced at the wedding," Kate said. "I danced with Jackson. It was nice." Her smile droops.

Lyra nudges her shoulder. "We're not talking about Jackson. We're talking about dancing."

"You can dance here." I jerk my chin at the tiny piece of hardwood behind the pool table at the back of the room. "We push the tables back."

"What do you do for music?" Lyra cocks her ear to listen for the background music all but drowned out by the raucous laughter at the pool table and the curling tournament playing on the three televisions mounted on the walls.

"I turn it up." I set Kalle's old iPhone on the bar before Lyra. "What do you want to listen to?"

Ten minutes later, Lyra has stopped the pool game, got the tables pushed back, and along with Kate, is bouncing on the makeshift dance floor to Olivia Rodrigo.

It just goes to show how beloved Lyra is, because there is only a murmur of complaint when the music starts, and quickly the girls are surrounded by a group of fishermen, Mabel and her friends, and Jubblie Mark, as drunk as he was last night, but much happier. All of them are in varying degrees of intoxication but having fun. And no one is fighting.

The only fight there's going to be in here tonight is between Kalle and me when I tear a strip off of him for going out with Fenella.

Or maybe I won't. Because after I get Tyler to man the bar, I go and join them dancing and soon, I'm having too much fun to stay mad at Kalle.

That's usually what happens.

16

Kalle

AND SO ENDS THE story of Kalle and Fenella.

I knew it wasn't going to work out with Fenella. She was a fun girl, a gorgeous girl, but ultimately, Fenella was Gunnar's girl. And it would have eventually been awkward.

It sounds like I'm making excuses because she decided *I* wasn't right for *her,* but it's more than that. Fenella would have only been a distraction, another in a line of women I wouldn't let myself be serious about.

She's a nice woman and I wish her the best, but it won't be with me.

"What now?" Dillon asks as we linger under the awning of the restaurant, watching Fenella drive off with Minka, Gunnar's security detail. "Damn, you should have let me drive. We're going to get soaked."

Rain pounds the pavement in front of us, and fast-moving rivers flow toward the town square. There's a real concern about flooding in town but the mayor has sent people to check the drainage system, and thankfully, the waves haven't crested over the pier yet.

Over twenty-four hours and it's still raining.

"I got an umbrella." I show him the compact black one that Leah thrust in my hand before I left to meet Fenella. It hadn't been raining this hard then.

"That's not going to do a damn thing in this storm," Dillon grouses. "You just want to go back to the pub and shake like a dog, and make it look sexy."

"Dogs shaking are not sexy."

"Yeah, but you with the hair—" Dillon demonstrates, shaking his head as if he still had hair and it was long and luxurious.

"You're jealous because you have no hair?"

"I'm not jealous and if you give it another year or so, you won't have much hair left either."

"I cut it like this." I thrust the umbrella into his hand. "Quit your complaining." I flip the hood of my jacket over my head. "It's not far. Race you." And then I take off toward the pub, with Dillon's curses lost in the rain.

I like storms. I like rain. And the quick run through the empty Battle Harbour streets back to the bar lets loose some of the tension that's been building today. There are only a few places open and it seems later, as if the town has already shut down for the night. Even Coffee for the Sole has closed early and the bartender for Sailor's Salon stands at the open door and watches us run past with a forlorn wave.

The people are bracing for the worst of the storm, and here I am, running through the rain.

But when we yank open the door to the pub, bringing in a rush of cold air and wet, I find no one here is bracing for bad weather. There's a fair crowd lined up along the bar, the pool table has its usual game going, but the tables have been pushed back and there's a scrum in the middle of the floor.

Unlike last night, no one is fighting.

They're dancing.

And I find my sister, arms up and red hair thrown back, in the middle of it.

Of course.

The music drowns out the rain and the thunder, and I give my head a shake—but not like a sexy Dillon dog shake—as I peel off my wet coat.

"Seems like things have picked up since you left," Dillon comments with a snort.

I nod wryly to Lennie Tak as I make my way to the bar. It's not the first time Lyra went looking for fun in here and it won't be the last.

At least I hope it's not. We all complain about Lyra, but I know my brothers share my worries about her. She was hit the hardest over our mother's death and even seven years later, I notice shadows cross her face when she's home.

She's not home a lot.

The storm has kept her in town for longer than she wanted to and I'm glad she's found something to amuse herself with.

I just hope my place doesn't pay the price.

Along with Lyra is her usual accomplice, Kate, and hey—

Bethie and Suze look like they decided to take a break from their serving duties to join the dance party. Bethie catches me watching her and gives a guilty wave, but Suze ignores me as she backs out of the group and heads to the bar to pick up a pitcher, delivering it to Jem and Leodie from Coffee for the Sole, sitting with Silas and singing along to the music.

Guess they closed early to trade coffee for beer.

And there, right beside my sister, is Mabel Crow. Why is she—?

And then I forget about Mabel and my staff and everyone else because there's Edie, her ponytail waving as she bumps hips with Kate.

Edie's wearing her oldest jeans that she can't bring herself to throw out. They look exactly like the denim you can buy with rips and tears but every rip in Edie's jeans has a story to tell. She's had them since high school, and they look really good on her.

Plus they're low rise and when she bends over, sometimes you can see the edge of her underwear.

Less than a week ago, I watched her glide down the aisle, gorgeous in a fancy blue-green dress and heels, hair and makeup done, and even with one of my mother's necklaces. She looked amazing.

Tonight she wears the jeans with a plain black T-shirt and her apron. I just left Fenella Carrington, who wore an outfit worth more than Edie makes in a year, and she can't hold a candle to Edie.

Seeing Edie in those jeans and T-shirt, arms up and *smiling* as she moves to the music, looking as happy as I've ever seen her, is like a kick in the gut.

I actually hunch my shoulders, clapping a hand to my stomach.

She's...Edie... and I'm—

"I wondered if you would make an appearance."

Wide-eyed at the rush of... *whatever* that was, I look over and see Mathias leaning against the bar.

And then my feeling-like-it-just-got-kicked stomach takes a nosedive because Mathias is here for Edie.

The King's Hat is not the sort of place my cousin normally frequents. In fact, before this visit, I don't remember him ever stepping foot inside.

I don't blame him. He clearly doesn't fit in, looking like a fairytale prince in his tailored pants and white polo shirt without a drop of rain marring it.

"What makes you think you have what it takes to become king? You're nothing but a jock—a dumb one at that—and you'll only bring this country to its knees if you become king."

The memory hits me like a slap. *Memories,* because it wasn't the first time someone—family—questioned my ability to take over after my father.

First when I was seven, then not again until I was seventeen. But after that, every time Mathias and his family were at the castle, for family events or political obligations, I would overhear things. Dante questioning my studies, the role I take in my father's counsel. Mathias's younger brother Jonas, outright criticizing my choices of relationships, activities, and even my clothes.

And Mathias—he would comment on a few things but mainly stepped back with his smug smile, looking the epitome of a prince.

I told myself it didn't matter, *they* didn't matter because I would be king someday but over the years, I hated to admit the little bug they put in my ear only grew and spread until that was all I thought about when I considered the steps I need to take.

Before the wedding, I hadn't seen my cousin in well over a year.

But now, thanks to Edie, he's going to be here all the time.

"Cousin." I nod to him as I duck behind the bar, hoping he didn't notice me staring at Edie.

"Your Highness," he says smoothly and with a hint of bitterness.

"Quite the crowd you've got here tonight."

"Yeah."

"Is that all you have to say? Half your staff is out there dancing with those they are supposed to be serving, and all you can say is yeah?"

I look Mathias up and down. "Yeah. Want a beer? Is that the problem?"

"There's no problem."

"Then why aren't you out there dancing with Edie?"

Mathias has the gall to sniff at the thought, like something here is beneath him. I don't know if it's my place or those enjoying themselves... or Edie...

I don't like it.

Granted, the sight of Edie dancing does that thing to my stomach, but honestly... she's not the best dancer. Top marks for enthusiasm but she's always lacked some rhythm. She loves to dance, but when the place becomes an impromptu dance club, Edie might take one turn around the floor and come back to her customary spot behind the bar.

She's about a half beat behind Kate but still going strong. It's a while since I've seen her let loose like this.

It wipes all the bad thoughts away.

Except that Mathias is right here and if I wait long enough, he's going to say something to get me annoyed again.

I watch him watching Edie, and there's no smile of appreciation on his face. There's no admiration. He looks *bland*, handsome but bland like he's wearing a Mathias Halloween mask.

There's no way he should be watching Edie without even any expression on his face.

I won't allow it.

I wait for a response, but all he gives me is the sniff.

"Seems to me that when a man is interested in a woman, he shows her he's interested," I say, moving behind the taps.

And I pour him a pint of honey mead to keep him at the bar. It's obvious if he even thinks about wading into that mass of dancers, he'd lose his beer sooner than he could smile hello at Edie.

"It's not my style of music," he says, accepting the glass and staying right where he is.

Style of music? I might not enjoy females wailing about *getting him back* and *not hooking up,* but when I see a woman alone on the dance floor clearly in want of a partner...

"Good thing it's mine," I tell him with a wolfish grin. "Yell if you need me," I say to Tyler, happily mixing drinks for a couple of just-nineteen-year-olds, their hair damp from the rain.

Then I slide into the group on the makeshift dancefloor.

It's Edie's playlist, heavy on the female artists and 1990s pop-rock. Kelly Clarkson switches to a cover of Total Eclipse of the Heart and I move beside my sister.

Kate sees me first. "Kalle?"

"Big brother is in the house," Lyra cheers, arms over her head and shimmying like my sister should not be shimmying. But still, I step up and show her my moves.

I have moves, but mainly they're used for picking up females, which is to say I should not use them on my sister. But it makes her laugh, and a happy Lyra is good for all.

And it gets me closer to Edie.

Her face breaks into a smile that loosens the knot in my stomach. "You're back," she says loudly, glancing toward the bar like she's looking for someone, her gaze passing right across Mathias standing there looking as out of place as a three-piece suit on a baseball field. "I didn't think you'd be back," she admits, raising her voice so I can hear her over the music.

I put my hand on her lower back. "Shouldn't have left."

Edie tries to frown but her eyes are dancing. "That good?"

I lean down so I don't have to shout above the music. "Does that make you happy?" Edie only shrugs, so I try again. "Are you still mad at me?"

Instead of answering, Edie moves even closer. I don't realize she's smelling me until she scrunches up her nose. "Are you drunk?"

"I don't get drunk." My hand is still splayed on her back and she's still very close... and that's okay with me.

"You do get drunk if you drink with your brothers, which you did this afternoon," she points out. "Plus, if you have a bottle of wine—" She sniffs again. "—possibly several bottles of wine..."

"What wine?" I grin down at her, and the way she smiles back at me tells me peace has been restored.

That makes me very happy.

"You're going to ruin my floor again, you know," I tell her.

"Just so you know, it was the pitcher of beer that spilled and someone forgot to mop up that ruined your floor, not the dancing," she says in a pert voice that makes my grin widen.

"Is this your idea or my sister's?"

"You left, so you'll never know," she shoots back.

"I'm back now," I tell her, holding those big brown eyes, until someone smacks my butt.

Mabel Crow. Mabel Crow just smacked my butt with her hand. There's no way Mabel should be around Lyra and Kate, given their history, because that would lead to—

Lyra laughs out loud, and Kate covers her mouth with her hand. They're dancing together. Lyra and Kate are right there with Mabel Crow, and Edie is here too...

I shake my head. What did I miss?

But I'm not missing this chance.

The song changes abruptly to Home for a Rest and I look at Edie.

One night, before The King's Hat opened, a group of us hung out in the gutted downstairs of Bruce's attempt at a gentleman's club and sampled Dad's latest mead offering. Bo had been here, and Jonathan McKibbon, Kate's brother, and a couple of guys I played high school ball with, and one of my curling buddies, and Edie.

Edie was always there.

Someone had put on Spirit of the West, and I got up because Home for a Rest is the best song to dance to. I grabbed Edie, and we *danced*, whipping around the room doing a quickstep in fast forward.

I convinced her to come work for me that night. If she had said no, I would have made a move on her.

And now, I look at Edie, and she looks at me and I know she's remembering the same night. The connection that's always been there. The pull between us and the disappointment I felt when I picked friendship over more.

Maybe Edie had been disappointed too.

I slide a hand around her waist. "There's no room," she warns, taking the hand I offer.

"There's always room." And with Edie's laughter trailing after us, we're off.

People are jumping and stomping and clapping as I lead Edie through the dancers and into the maze of tables. I resist the urge to flip Mathias the finger as we flash by the bar, my hand wrapped around her waist, holding Edie as tightly as I can so that her laughter rumbles through me.

We're flying, Edie and I, and this time, I wonder if it's really time to take off.

17

Edie

I'M BREATHLESS FROM RACING around the bar, the cheers and clapping echoing in my head, laughing every time Kalle's deep voice sings out, "I've been drunk for a month."

I've never been much of a dancer. I know for a fact that everyone at the castle, including Kalle, had to endure dance lessons when they were younger, but for once, Kalle makes me feel like I'm floating with the stars. I should be wearing one of the flowy, sequins-and-feather-type dresses on Dancing with the Stars, his big hand engulfing mine, his other warm on my back.

To be honest, it might be being held by Kalle that makes me a little out of breath as well. I've danced with Kalle plenty of times, even to that song, but that—

He holds me differently. Tight, but somehow wrapping himself around me as he leads me through the tables so I'm not getting bumped or bruised. People move out of the way as we fly around the room, but I don't worry about running into anyone because of Kalle.

It's like he's got me in a little bubble, and no one is part of it but him and me.

He's never smiled down at me like I'm the only person in the room.

So much so that when the song ends, I blink with surprise. "That was... I can't believe we did that," I gasp as the laughter rolls through the room. Another song comes on, something by Great Big Sea and the dancing starts again.

Except for Kalle and me, now standing off to the side.

"Yeah." It's Kalle's customary reply but the way he's looking at me isn't. His blue-eyed gaze roves around like he's checking for something, and his smile—

I step back, breaking his hold. "What?" I demand.

"What?" he echoes, still gripping my hand in his.

"Do I have something on my face?" I slap my free hand to my cheek. "The way you're looking at me..."

Like I'm a woman.

"Can't I look at you?" Kalle asks in a low voice, tangling his fingers with mine.

The way he says it—

"That was quite the performance."

I turn, and there's Mathias, his smile not quite meeting his pale blue eyes. "Looks like the dancing lessons certainly paid off," he says to Kalle without much of a glance at me.

My fingers slip out of Kalle's grip and it's as if I've stepped out into the rain.

Mathias is here. He texted and said he'd stop by, but seeing him here in the bar, with me breathless and slightly sweaty, makes the shots I had with Lyra and Kate begin to swim in my stomach. I can't help but feel like Mathias is intruding, like he's someplace he shouldn't be and reprimanding us about it at the same time.

Kalle's smile changes into something like a grimace. "I've never heard any complaints."

"You wouldn't, since conversation's never been one of your strong suits."

"With me, it's *what* I say that matters, not how much. Worthless conversation has never been my thing."

"Am I missing something?" I glance between them. Kalle, who had been laughing and pressed tightly against me only a moment ago, is now ramrod straight, jaw clenched with tension. "You're like two dogs trying to pee on the same stump."

Mathias stiffens, before he forces a laugh and finally looks down at me. His smile still hasn't reached his eyes. "Not at all. The two of you looked like you were having fun."

"I was." I tell myself to relax, that I haven't done anything wrong. It was just dancing.

"I almost got pushed out of the bar area by the crowd."

I glance over to see that some of those who had been dancing have followed Lyra off the floor to swarm around the bar. Bethie is with Tyler serving drinks with Chase flitting around and trying to help.

I back away. "I should get back there." A roll of thunder, the loudest one yet, crashes overhead and I flinch.

"It's fine." Kalle reaches out like he wants to grab my hand, stopping just before he touches me. "They've got it covered."

Mathias reaches for me as well. He doesn't stop and his fingers tangle with mine, long and slender and cool to the touch. "How late are you working?" he asks, his smile finally reaching his eyes. "I thought if Kalle is back from his date... We should talk."

Kalle's face instantly shutters and now he steps back from me like I've insulted him. "Leave whenever you want," he growls.

I watch him stalk back to the bar with a pang that feels a lot like regret. He's quickly swallowed into the group waiting to be served, leaving me by the pool table with Mathias.

"Always so cheerful," Mathias scoffs. "He should work on his manners rather than his dancing."

I turn to Mathias. "What was that all about?" I demand. "With you and Kalle?"

He smoothly shrugs a shoulder. "It's always been like this with Kalle. We like to needle each other. Cousinly teasing."

Mathias is *always* smooth. "I don't like it," I say flatly.

"Don't like what?"

I shake out of his grasp as a laughing Coy Schmidt passes between us, followed by Ken McKibbon, and I step back with a frown. "Your needling. Kalle is my friend," I tell Mathias after they pass.

Mathias's eyes flash before he returns to his smooth expression. "You work for him. How does that make you his friend?"

"He's been my friend longer than I've worked for him."

"Is that all it is? Because I get the sense..."

I roll my eyes. If Mathias had said anything two days ago, I would have laughed it off. *We're only friends.* But now I don't know what to say. Especially being faced with Mathias's jealous possessiveness, or whatever this is.

Because that's exactly what it seems to me. "I'm here until at least midnight and I should be getting back to work," I tell him in a cool voice. "Thanks for stopping by, and I'm sorry we didn't get a chance to talk."

"Edie..." Mathias's expression shifts, changing into something not so smooth. Something that might be real, and makes him even better looking. "I wanted to ask you..." He chews his lip. Is he actually nervous? "Will you come and visit?"

"Visit?" I parrot.

"Come see my home. My part of the country. Get to know me, away from here."

To me, *away from here* means away from Kalle. And the thought of that...

I'm not sure what that does.

It makes me glance over at the bar where Kalle is now laughing with the group crowded around Lyra, lifting a shot that looks suspiciously like Screech, the high-octane rum that has left many a non-Laandian weak and woozy in the morning.

"That sounds great, but can we talk about this later?" I say automatically, forcing a smile. It's exhausting, jumping from growling Kalle to dancing Kalle and smiling Mathias to not-sure-what Mathias—and now he wants me to visit him? "Maybe tomorrow? I really should get back to work."

"Tomorrow." He frowns. "I hoped to leave tomorrow. With you."

"What?" Is he serious? "I can't leave just like that." I match his frown with one of my own. "I have a job. There are things I need to figure out, schedule—"

"Of course not," he says, back to smooth like the moment of vulnerability never happened. "Let's talk timing tomorrow. But I would like you to visit me. There are things to discuss."

My heart skips a beat—and not in a good way. "What things?"

He chuckles and leans closer. "Don't look so scared."

For me, discussions are a prelude to bad things, but I'm not about to tell him that.

Mathias leans down to kiss my cheek. "I've called for a car, so I'll let you get back to work. Hope it stays uneventful."

I watch as he winds his way toward the door, keeping as much distance from the group around the bar as he can. As the door shuts behind him, I glance back to the bar to find Kalle watching me.

There's something in his eyes that I've never seen before. I can't read it.

I stand motionless, caught in his gaze like a deer in the headlights.

I don't like not being able to read Kalle.

Thunder booms, and I'm not the only one who jumps. Lightning flashes outside, for a moment making it as bright as day, and I see Mathias out the window getting into one of the castle cars.

It pulls away from the curb and I still stand there.

Mathias wants me to visit because there are "things to discuss."

There can't be much to say, since we've only had one dinner. To invite me for a family visit seems quick, and out of place.

And then I remember Odin and Camille had planned for a six-week engagement.

Kalle just asked me to marry him out of nowhere.

Things move fast in the royal family, but that doesn't mean Mathias...

No. There's no way.

I glance back at Kalle and he's still staring at me. He gives me a lopsided smile, and I smile back because that's what you do when a man like Kalle looks at you like that.

And then the lights in the bar go out.

18

Kalle

THE GENERATOR I BOUGHT last year, the one Edie insisted I get, kicks in twenty seconds after the lights go out. The darkness is just long enough for a few shouts, a scream, and a few glasses to fall and break, and then the power is back.

The first person I find is Edie, eyes wide. I know she doesn't like storms, but just as I start across the bar to her, she gives herself a shake.

"Everything is okay," she calls out. "Generator works. But let's ring up your tabs so you can get home."

"Buddy system out there," I add in a loud voice. "We'll call some cabs, and I don't want to take your keys, so leave your cars if it's not a good idea to drive."

It's chaos for the next half hour as we close the tabs and get people into cabs. Battle Harbour has a surprisingly large taxi fleet, but it's still not enough as some who walked here now refuse to go out in the storm. I call Jonathan McKibbon and promise free lunches if a couple of police cruisers can ferry people home.

Still, it's quick to clear the place out as everyone rushes to go home to check on pets and parents and children.

Except for a few—Lyra and Kate among them. "Who've you got for security tonight?" I ask Lyra, looking around the bar for her security detail. Now that I think about it…

"Ah, well… no one," she admits with her best beguiling smile.

That smile might work on some, but not me. "What are you talking about?" Each of the royal siblings has a security team in place that accompanies them everywhere.

Lyra shifts with a flash of her guilty expression. It's only there for a moment, but as her big brother, I can always tell when she's done something wrong. "I left without telling them," she admits.

I cross my arms and glare down at her. "Which you've been told not to do."

"I felt bad dragging them out in the rain."

"That's what they're paid for." This growl is from Dillon, who stands at my back, mirroring my stance and expression.

"Mathias left in one of the castle cars," Edie says, stepping forward to play mediator as usual. "It's too bad you couldn't have gone with him."

"And now you're going to have to call and drag somebody else out in the rain," I glower.

"Can we deal with this tomorrow?" Edie suggests. "There's enough to deal with the power being out. Can you put her under your protection for the night?" she asks Dillon before turning to me. "And maybe let them crash at your place?"

Dillon doesn't like it, but he sends Chase to my apartment with the girls.

"How do you do that?" I ask Edie as she makes quick work of the floors. I was ready to leave the clean-up until tomorrow but Edie has already said if the power stays out, we should open early.

"Mop the floor?" she asks with confusion. "I've seen you do it a few times."

"Fix things," I clarify. "Defuse tempers. Settle people down."

"I have three sisters." She smiles as she wrings out the mop. "Someone has to be the level-headed one."

"Yeah." I reach for the bucket of dirty water at the same time as Edie does, which means our fingers touch—and that happens at the same moment as another thunder boom hits, which makes Edie jump. A splash of water tips out of the bucket.

"You really don't like thunder." I take the bucket as Edie mops up the spill. "Are you going to be okay tonight?"

"I'll be fine. I have candles."

I forgot that the power would still be off in her apartment and make a mental note to get the generator hooked up to the house. "I'll come up and make sure you're settled. I can stay with you." It's not unusual for us to hang out for an hour or so after closing, when we're both wired and sleep will be slow to come.

"I'll be fine," Edie repeats.

"I won't be." She looks up, brown eyes wide and questioning. "Not unless I know you're okay."

Is she thinking of how I held her while we danced? I can still feel the curve of her hip under my hand.

Is she thinking of Mathias? Has she realized how much of a dick he is?

Has she changed her mind about marrying me?

That one is probably a long shot.

"You don't like storms," I point out when she doesn't say anything. Edie always has something to say, and when she doesn't, I'm forced to fill the silence and usually end up feeling like an idiot.

"The girls'll be giggling for a while and I don't want to listen to them."

"Good idea," Dillon says, and I start. As impossible as it seems, I've forgotten my security detail is still here. "Let Chase deal with them. I'll crash outside your door tonight."

"You can't do that," Edie protests as we move into the kitchen. Dillon takes a last look around before hitting the light switch. "I have a couch."

"Which I assume Maj will be sleeping on tonight, but if that's not the case—" His expression is pure innocence, but Dillon's eyes are dancing.

"I'll pull a chair out into the hall," she says quickly, and Dillon chuckles.

After a last check of the kitchen, we get ready to make the dash to the door of Edie's apartment. Dillon starts out first, his head bald and bare, like he's daring the rain to land on him. I push an umbrella into Edie's hand before she makes a run though the alley as I lock the kitchen door behind us.

I'm halfway there when I remember the cat.

"Cat!" I shout, stopping to rummage around the garbage bins. The collection of cardboard from yesterday is floating in a puddle. "Kitty? Kitty, kitty—Cat! You out here? Goddam cat," I mutter, hair dripping down my back.

Edie pauses, one hand on the door. "What are you doing?" she calls back.

"I need to get the cat," I tell her but a crack of thunder masks my words. I motion for her to go inside.

Of course she doesn't.

"What's wrong?" Even with the umbrella, Edie's hair is plastered to her head, ponytail drooping like it's run out of energy. Her eyelashes are like starfish.

"Get inside," I tell her.

"No. Why are—?"

"The cat," I insist. "She should be inside."

"She is," Edie surprises me by saying. "I called Stella today and they came and got her. She's safe. She'll get her checked out by the vet and hopefully adopted. No more eating garbage for her."

I stand in the rain and stare at Edie because she does it all. Everything. There is nothing this woman can't do.

Then I grab her hand and run with her to the door, her burst of laughter following us.

"When did you call Stella?" I demand as we leave a path of wet footprints up the stairs, trailed by Dillon.

"After you—when Bo was there. Gunnar and Ajax came and grabbed her, so she's safe and warm at the shelter," Edie says, pulling her keys out. "I didn't realize you were worried, or I would have told you." There's a puddle on the floor outside the apartment by the time she gets the door unlocked and a little of the tightness in my chest dissolves.

"I didn't worry about it. It's a cat."

"You were. You liked her."

"I never—she's a cat. I think it's a her. She eats my garbage. Course I don't like her."

"A cat you've been feeding for months. You did. I think you should call Stella and adopt her. I'll get you a towel," she promises Dillon as she opens the door.

"Maybe more than one." Dillon turns to me. "I didn't know you liked cats."

"I didn't either," I say, bewildered.

As Edie gets him a towel, we manhandle one of her armchairs out the door and into the hallway. I've always hated the thought of inconveniencing the men who are paid to protect me, but I've talked to them both enough about it to realize they accept it as part of the job. Still, I'm glad to see Edie return with a few towels, a warm blanket and pillow as well as a bottle of water and a muffin for him.

"I like watching her place," Dillon says, stuffing half the muffin in his mouth and drying his head with a towel.

"Careful you don't wake up Miss Bessie." Edie points to the other apartment door where Edie's seventy-year-old neighbour lives. "Actually, she might like it and come keep you company."

"I know Miss Bessie," Dillon says tightly. "I'll keep it down."

"I hate the thought of you out here," Edie frets.

"Just doing my job m'lady." He pulls out his phone so we can see the puzzle app he's pulled up. "You get some sleep, and don't let Maj keep you up."

I nod good night as I shut the door, leaving him in the hall.

Leaving Edie and me alone in her apartment.

Lightning flashes outside the big living room windows, illuminating the room to a hazy gray rather than pitch black.

It's about half the size of my apartment but cozy and clean with woman things like candles and books and plants, with a vase full of pretty flowers on the table.

It's more of a home than my place, and it smells like Edie.

She stands a few feet away from me, shoulders tight and uncertain. I'm over here enough to know where she keeps the corkscrew and her stash of cookies, but it feels different tonight. Maybe it's the storm and the lack of power that means we can't sit and watch Netflix like we usually do.

Maybe it's just because it's been a strange day.

I—kind of—asked her to marry me today. The echo of that, plus the ghosts of Fenella and Mathias drift between us.

"I don't like him out there," she says quietly, like there really are ghosts listening.

"I don't either, but that's what he does." When I'm at my apartment, there are two bodyguards with me at all times—one outside the door, the other staying in the spare room. When I stay in other places, one of them is always with me, the other outside in the car.

There's not a lot of privacy being a prince, but it's the only way I know. At least with Dillon and Chase, I get to live my life.

"He appreciates the muffin," I tell her. "And the blanket."

"I didn't want him to get cold. You," she bursts out, like she's only now realizing Dillon might not be the only one who is cold and wet. "I'll get you towels."

"That would be great since I'm kind of dripping all over your floor."

By the time Edie is back with a stack of towels, I've kicked off my shoes, soggy and ruined from the floating garbage in the alley. And I've shucked off my jeans so that I'm standing by the door in my boxer briefs and a soaking-wet shirt.

"Oh." Edie stops a few feet away, eyes even bigger than usual.

"I didn't want to drip through your apartment again," I tell her, unbuttoning my shirt. "We made enough mess getting the chair out."

I don't see her watching until I lift my head and the expression on her face looks like...

It kind of looks like she hasn't eaten in a couple of days.

"Is this okay?" I ask her quickly.

"You standing here naked? Um... sure?" She looks everywhere but at me, which is funny since we're standing in the dark.

I can't help the smirk. "It's not like you haven't seen me naked before."

"No, no, I'm fairly certain I've never seen you naked before," she corrects.

"It's not a big deal." I finish unbuttoning with suddenly unsteady fingers and let my shirt hang open for a moment before I shrug it off.

She looks at me with an expression I've never seen in her eyes, but I can read her pretty well. "Uh-huh," she says.

I stay like that for a moment. I know Edie is looking and I want—

I'm not sure what I want.

Finally, Edie draws a shaky breath and thrusts the towels at me. "I'll find you something to wear," she mutters, and heads to her room.

"You should get out of your wet clothes too," I call after her, just to be a jerk. In the dim light, I see Edie's cat watching me.

He doesn't seem impressed.

19

Edie

K ALLE IS...

Incredibly hot.

It's not like I saw much of him—my apartment is dark but a little shade of gray shines through the window, right to where Kalle was standing. I could see enough.

There were muscles on muscles, his abs divided into eight little sections, all cumulating into the sharp V-ridges above his hips.

And I had no idea how strong the urge to reach out and *touch* one of them would be.

Reach out and touch *Kalle*.

I lean against my bedroom door. I shut it so I can change, not that there's enough moonlight coming in the window for anyone—Kalle—to see me. It's still the principle of being without clothes with a man in my apartment, even if it's a man I've known most of my life.

Kalle is my friend, not some random guy to be ogled. And he doesn't need to see me undress, since with my luck the power will come on at just the wrong moment.

If I close my eyes, I can still see him.

I've seen him without his shirt on before. We've gone swimming, hung out at the beach. I even interrupted him once after he got out of the shower, wrapped only in a towel.

That was a nice image to remember, but it didn't throw me like this.

I draw in another shaky breath. A crack of thunder sounds and I let out a little yelp.

"You okay in there?" Kalle calls, breaking me out of my trance caused by a fine set of abdomen muscles.

"Good. Fine." The lightning that follows lights up my room. "Great."

I hear Kalle chuckle. "I never thought you'd be scared of anything."

"I'm not scared, I just don't like storms."

"Don't like seeing me naked either."

"I did not see you naked," I cry. "I can't see. It's dark."

"Didn't stop you from trying."

"I'm glad you're enjoying this," I mutter, peeling my wet T-shirt over my head.

"What's that you said?"

"Be quiet or I'll make you stand like that all night," I snap. He laughs.

When at last I manage to get out of my wet jeans—I have no idea how Kalle undressed so quickly—and into a pair of flannel pants and a thick sweatshirt, I figure Kalle should be shivering by now.

"I don't have much that would fit you but—" I stop short when I come out to find Kalle in the middle of the room, holding Ernie to his chest. "Oh. He never lets anyone pick him up."

"He's warm so I didn't give him much of a choice." He sets down the cat to take the clothes I hand to him, my baggiest pair of pink tie-dyed jogging pants that I wear as a second layer in the winter, and an old University of Laandia sweatshirt that I stole from Kalle years ago. "That looks familiar."

"Maybe," I say primly.

"I'm going to have to go commando," he tells me. "Unless you've got a pair of my boxers stashed away someplace."

"I'm not going to dignify that with an answer, and please commando yourself in the bathroom. And take your wet clothes and hang them up in the shower while you're at it."

I'm not thinking I'm not thinking I'm not thinking...

With another chuckle, Kalle takes his nakedness into the bathroom while I start the hunt for candles.

By the time he comes out, I've lit a handful of tea lights left over from the pumpkin-carving episode of two years ago, a pair of beeswax tapers, and a fat three-wick vanilla candle and there's enough light for me to really look at Kalle when he comes out.

And laugh, because the pants are snug, to say the least, and only come to mid-calf. And the sweatshirt may have fit him when I took it, but it certainly doesn't now. The shoulders cling to him like a Harry Styles fan given a chance to hug him.

"You comfy?" I ask with a grin.

Kalle rotates his hips and gives a little shimmy. "You have no idea."

The man is in an awfully good mood in the middle of the storm of the year that's knocked out the power.

And then I remember he's been drinking most of the evening.

"I'm hungry," he says, grabbing a light and moving into the kitchen. "What food?"

"Not much," I admit, following him. "Plus, no microwave." I know he's got a childish preference for pizza pockets.

"You've got peanut butter."

I hover nearby, holding a candle as Kalle moves with familiarity around my kitchen, collecting bread and my mother's homemade strawberry jam, and makes two peanut and jam sandwiches. "I thought you had dinner," I say, and get a one-shoulder shrug in return. "How *was* dinner?"

"Fine."

"And things with Fenella?"

"How are things with you and my cousin?" The abrupt change of topic makes my stomach flip over. Or maybe it's just talking about Mathias.

I've had boyfriends, and I've talked to Kalle about them He's given me advice, told me who wasn't good enough for me, or who would never take the next step.

He has a good read on other men.

But talking about Mathias with him seems wrong. Disloyal somehow. I'm not sure if it's because of the "needling" as Mathias called it, but there's something not right between the cousins.

And I have the strange feeling it might be me.

"He's leaving," I say, watching him spread jam.

There's a pause, and then— "Do you like him?" Kalle asks in a gruffer voice than usual.

Do I like Mathias? If Kalle had asked two days ago, my answer would have been an unequivocal yes. But now... "He's a prince," I hedge.

"That doesn't mean you have to like him."

"Why don't *you* like him?" I ask in response.

"Family reasons." The aggressive way he cuts off the crusts suggests there's more to his answer.

"Which you're not about to tell me," Kalle grunts his response. "How are things with you and the Lady Carrington then?" If he can ask, so can I. Unlike me, Kalle never says much about his other dates or girlfriends, so if I get anything from him, this will be a first.

"She's not a lady."

"With her family, it's just as well she should be."

"*She's* leaving," Kalle offers, reaching around for plates, and my stomach gives a leap of relief. "Just like Mathias."

"Do you like her?" Why am I holding my breath? Why does Kalle having an interest in Fenella Carrington suddenly seem like the worst idea ever?

Kalle grunts. "She's nice."

I answer his grunt with a snort. "That's not how you describe Fenella Carrington."

"Works for me."

"Are you going to visit her?" I hadn't given Mathias's invitation another thought, but if Kalle is going to see Fenella—

"No."

"No?"

"She'll be back sooner or later. But... no. There's no need to visit. There's nothing there."

"Nothing where?"

"Between me and Fenella." Kalle hands me a plate and I give him a questioning glance. "Your sandwich. I'm not making one for myself and not for you."

"You made a burger without making me one," I remind him.

"I was so in my head that I didn't even know *I* was making a burger."

Kalle's gaze holds mine as his white teeth tear into the sandwich. Is this how we're going to start talking about it? Standing in the dark?

"Anything happen tonight?" he asks.

So, no. Does he mean anything that happened at the bar when he was gone, or anything that's happened today? And what does he mean about there being nothing between him and Fenella?

He means did anything happen at the pub while he was away, I decide. Kalle isn't one to recap conversations. I expect my refusal to be the last I hear of his marriage suggestion.

"We had drinks with Mabel Crow."

He looks at me closely. "Yeah. I saw that."

"We had shots. Kate says she believes Gunnar that nothing happened. She apologized to Mabel."

"We," Kalle repeats, already finished half his sandwich. "*You* were drinking. You don't usually do that."

This is how we're going to talk about this—standing in the weak candlelight so that looking at Kalle is like watching a night scene on TV in the bright sunlight—you can't see much at all. "You can say it's been a weird day."

"Storm bothering you?"

I give a choked laugh. Maybe he's really concerned or maybe he's being deliberately obtuse. I've never been one to beat around the bush and I'm not about to start now. "I'm talking about how you asked me to marry you earlier today."

The only sound is the hiss of the candle flame and Kalle setting his plate on the counter. "Ah."

It doesn't matter if Kalle won't bring it up. There's two people in this conversation and I've never held back from saying what I feel. "Yeah. Ah. Is that all you're going to say?"

Kalle looks like he's mulling it over. "Yeah?"

"Seriously? That's all? We're not going to talk about it?"

"'Bout what? You said you didn't want to marry me. No means no. What else can I say?"

His face is expressionless and I think for a moment that he did make a mistake. That it was a total fluke and he didn't mean it at all.

And then he rubs at the back of his neck. Kalle has got so many tells and I can see through each and every one of them.

He really thinks he wants to marry me, and that does strange things to me.

And the worst is the leap my heart gives, like it's ready to jump off a big cliff.

"Tell me where that came from," I say in a quiet voice, trying to steady Kalle as well as my now leaping heart. "Tell me why, out of nowhere, you think you should be looking for a wife."

But more important is what I don't say. *Why do you think it should be me?*

Because I am not queen material. I'm the girl you want to manage your bar, that you hang out watching television with, that you joke and laugh and maybe have a dance with.

Not the woman that you hold close and look at like she means everything to you.

Kalle looks at me and I can see there's more behind his eyes. But all he says is, "You should go to sleep."

There's more going on but he doesn't know how to tell me.

That realization calms me a little, but I don't stop wanting more.

I know he'll tell me. He always does.

But it's not going to be now. "I'm going to crash on the couch."

"That's silly because you don't fit on the couch. Take my bed."

"I'm not kicking you out of your bed."

"You can sleep—stay—with me." The words come out wrong, too high-pitched. We've shared a bed before, so there shouldn't be a problem.

The problem is that Kalle has just opened a door that had been locked and double-bolted.

I don't want to be queen.

But I want Kalle. I've always wanted him and I don't know what to do about it if he only thinks I'm good for the country.

20

Kalle

SHE FINISHES HER SANDWICH and now there's nothing to do but to go to bed.

I know I should talk to Edie about what my father said. She's the person I go to when I need to get something off my chest, but it doesn't seem right when she's part of what I need to get off my chest.

I can talk to her about Fenella because there's nothing there. Maybe there was never anything there but a mild attraction. Two good-looking people finding their way together.

I hope she'll be happy with her rock star.

As for me, I check on Dillon while Edie uses the washroom.

The power is still off and she insists we blow out the candles. She lends me a toothbrush, but I can still taste the peanut butter, and I forgot Edie likes the all-natural kind that doesn't have enough salt or flavour.

Plus, these pants are *tight*. I pull off the sweatshirt before I crawl under the covers, but that's not an option for the pants. Being naked in bed with Edie would be a first, and if that were to happen, her clothes would have to be gone too, and there wouldn't be much sleeping going on.

There needs to be sleep tonight because Edie, her head on the pillow, is looking at me with eyes that are heavy and purple-shadowed. We leave the curtains open to get whatever light there is and it's just enough for me to make out the planes of her face.

"Tired." It's not a question and I stroke her hair away from her face with a hand that doesn't feel like mine.

She nods. I know she has questions and I might have to give her answers, but not now. And she's patient enough to wait.

She's always been patient with me.

"Night, Edie." Even though I'm tempted to lean forward and kiss her forehead, I rest my hand there for a moment instead.

"Night, Kalle."

She falls asleep almost instantly. It takes me a little longer.

A lot longer.

When I wake up in the morning, Edie is still asleep on her side facing me, curled up around the cat who is spread long between us like a harbour chain, blocking any entry. I watch her, but not in a creepy, Twilight way.

Edie made me watch the series years ago so I know that Edward was super creepy.

She sleeps with her hair pulled up into a bun that started at the top of her head but slipped off-centre. The sight of it makes me smile. I'm tempted to curl a loose tendril around my finger.

Now, that might be creepy.

Over her shoulder, I notice her clock radio blinking. The power is back on, but I have no idea what time it is. I can hear the rain against the window, but the wind has died down.

I have no desire to get out of this bed. It's soft and comfortable, and while my feet may be hanging over the end, it smells of Edie, and I like how Edie smells.

I like a lot of things about Edie.

Like, really like about her and more keep popping up, like those seeds she started last year. One day there was only a thick expanse of dirt, and then the next, there were all these little green sprouts.

I never saw it happen, but one day they were just there.

I never saw the change from Edie-my-friend, to Edie-maybe-more.

"Maybe more" might not be enough.

She's dating my cousin, my arch-enemy. My nemesis. Is that what prompted this shift into the maybe more?

I roll onto my back and stare at the ceiling. There's a little water damage in the corner. If Mathias hadn't asked Edie to dance—if he had asked Kate, or even Fenella—would there still be this strange vibe between me and Edie?

I think so, yeah. If I'm being completely honest, I'd say Mathias gave it a kick in the pants, but he didn't cause it.

Edie causes it, because she's Edie. And I'm going to lose her if I don't do something.

I watch her sleep, listening to the steady intake of breath that borders on snoring, but not obnoxious snores. Sweet snores. I'm fascinated by the way she flexes her fingers. How her hair curls at her temples.

And then I notice the cat watching me watch Edie. "What?" I hiss.

Ernie closes his eyes.

As if she realizes I'm watching her, Edie's eyes flicker open. "You're here," she whispers in a sleep-thickened voice.

"Yeah. Power is back on."

She rolls over to check the clock radio beside her bed but comes back to face me. "Is it still storming?"

"Maybe. But not for long."

I wake up in her bed and we're talking about the weather.

"Mathias asked me to come visit him," she whispers.

I'd rather keep talking about the weather.

"He wants me to go with him when he leaves," she continues.

I close my eyes and fight the urge to roll away, to roll far away from this conversation. "Yeah?"

She strokes the cat and his purring is loud in the room. "Why don't you like him?"

This is getting heavy way too fast. "Doesn't matter."

"It does to me."

"It shouldn't."

"It does." Her brown eyes, suddenly wide awake, stare at me. A gust of wind rattles her windows.

"It's not him," I hedge. Talking about the past is like trying to dig a hole with my bare hands—time-consuming and it's going to leave my fingers scratched and bleeding.

I should have gotten right out of bed when I woke up.

But I stay beside her.

"It's your uncle," Edie guesses. She's always been able to see inside me, to know what I'm thinking, sometimes even before I know it myself. "What did he do?"

"It's what he said," I say, my voice tight. "What they said."

"About you?" It takes a moment to swallow, so I nod instead. "Tell me," she urges.

"That I shouldn't be king," I say in a dull monotone. "That I would never amount to anything. That someone like me had no right thinking I could rule because I would only end up ruining what Leif wanted." There's more. I remember everything that was said to me, word for word, but I remember what I overheard even more, because Dante and his sons wouldn't have to hold back about what they really thought of me.

Stupid. Incompetent. Selfish. Unable to rule.

I close my eyes so I don't have to look at Edie pitying me.

"Kalle…"

"It doesn't matter," I say gruffly, dropping an arm over my eyes.

She slips her fingers under my arm, stroking my cheek, and at the simple touch, everything inside me squeezes painfully. "It does. Of course it does." I shrug and her hand slips to my shoulder to give it a squeeze.

Her hands are so small, but strong.

"Do you want to be king?" she asks in a quiet voice. "Honestly."

"No. But I could do it with you."

She gives a quick intake of breath. I've caught her off guard. "That's not fair."

I lift my arm and peek at her. "Maybe not, but you wanted me to be honest. It's the truth. You've been with me through everything, Edie, and I can't imagine—I can't honestly picture me being king without you being there beside me. When Dad told me to grab whoever I have my eye on, I thought of you. Because... you. You need to be there when I do this."

"I'm not your security blanket." But Edie sounds wistful, and her eyes are a little glassy.

I pull up her sheet so it's covering her shoulder. "You kind of are." And then I mean to tweak her nose but end up resting the back of my hand against her cheek. "I like it."

"Kalle..."

"I meant it when I said you should marry me. I know I messed up the delivery." I wait for her to agree but she only waits for me to continue. "I think we'd be a good team."

"But we haven't ever—"

"Gone on a date?"

"Kissed."

The air goes heavy in the room and the cat stretches, his paws kneading the blanket. "Why haven't we kissed yet?" I ask.

Edie's eyes flick to my mouth, exactly like I did to her a moment ago. For once, she seems to be at a loss for words.

"Ever wanted to find out what it's like?"

21

Edie

I CAN'T LOOK AWAY from Kalle.

My heart breaks for him, to have to endure all the insults and condescending remarks. I wonder if the king knows and then decide no. Dante wouldn't be welcome if Magnus knew how he treated his son. The lack of respect is appalling, all because of jealousy.

But that's not why I can't stop staring at him.

Last night, seeing the undressed and very wet Kalle was one thing. Those abs will live on forever in my mind. But not only did he spend the night in my bed, this morning he's also shirtless and his muscled chest with the sprinkling of hair looks like the best kind of pillow right now.

I should get up.

We can talk about this upright, and fully dressed. That would be best.

We should get up, get dressed, and figure out what's going on in town. Was the power off all night? Are there any problems after the storm? What about the bar? Plus, Ernie needs to be fed.

But I stay right where I am because I can't believe Kalle just asked if I've ever wanted to kiss him.

Kissing Kalle…

I nod helplessly. It may ruin everything, it might be the worst thing I could do, but I'm past lying about how I feel.

Yes, I've wanted to kiss Kalle, every day for the last sixteen years. I want to kiss him when I see him in the morning, I want to be the last one to press my lips against his at night. I want to find out if his lips are as soft as they seem and if his beard will leave a burn on my cheeks.

I want to know if his kisses are soft and gentle, or if he's demanding.

I think Kalle would be demanding.

I want to know how he tastes.

"Yeah?"

That's all? That's all he has to say?

But no— "Me too," he admits. "Last night."

I swallow, thrown by his honesty. I only managed a nod, but here he is with his truth-telling. "You wanted to kiss me last night?"

"Most nights," he says with a rueful grin. "Pretty much since I've known you."

I sit up because I can't comprehend what he's telling me while I'm lying down. "You can't say that."

He sits up as well, the blanket pooling around his hips and leaving his chest gloriously, beautifully bare. "It's the truth." His voice is gruff but his gaze, when I meet it, is soft.

How can women not melt under that gaze?

"It sounds like you've always wanted to kiss me." My voice is shaky, unsteady but Kalle only shrugs. It might be the most infuriating thing I have ever seen, this morning or ever. "Why didn't you, then?" I cry.

Ernie is off the bed like a shot and even Kalle seems surprised at the ferocity of my words.

"I'd mess it up," he says.

"The kiss?"

"I don't mess those up, sweetheart."

The air around us heightens, stretches. The way Kalle looks at me is how I've always wanted him to look at me but I still *don't know.* I don't know what he wants, what he means, what he's trying to say.

He's saying that he's always wanted to kiss me—but how is that possible when that's all *I've* ever wanted?

And why didn't he? That's... that's what I really don't understand, because this is Kalle Erickson, Prince of Laandia, and he's kissed *a lot* of girls. Women.

Women other than me.

"Have you ever wanted to try?" I've never heard Kalle's voice like that—soft, shy. Hesitant. Kalle jumps in with both feet and figures things out when he lands.

I don't understand why he's never done that with me... if he wanted to. "Try...?" I think I know what he means, from the expression on his face, but I don't know for sure.

I don't know anything right now.

I know I'm not a fairytale princess. I'm just regular Edie England, daughter of the man who cuts the castle lawns.

The royal family is held in high esteem in Laandia; they are the monarchy that rules the country. King Magnus has held the throne for over thirty years and does a great job of it.

Someday Kalle will be king.

Whoever his wife is will be queen.

I've never once, in all our years of friendship, regardless of my mother's irrational daydreams, considered myself to be in the running for that. To be queen of Laandia.

It's laughable.

But yes, I'll admit, I have thought about Kalle like that over the years; that our friendship is so important, but what if there were more between us? What would that be like?

But I never thought of us having a happily ever after together.

Kalle has dated countless women, and every time he came through the door with another one, I wondered if she would end up being The One.

Never me.

I'm not queen material, and that's fine.

But I'm thirty-two years old—we both are. When a relationship fails when you're twenty-two, you think you've got years left to find your person. But when you're thirty-two and thinking of starting a relationship that can't end well...

Kalle and I would never end well because he would never want me for his queen.

Except, didn't he say something like that?

I think maybe I should stop him right there, before he can say something he'll regret.

That might break my heart.

But then Kalle smiles like I've always wanted him to smile at me. Things shift, soften. Begin to melt like chocolate left out in the sun and I can't help but wonder... maybe?

Maybe...?

"This." Kalle says, motioning between us. Because there is very much an *us* at this moment. We've always been a team, but this feels different.

It feels like I should get out of bed and stop this before it's too late.

But I don't get up. "Together," he continues, "but... more."

No, I want to say. Because it's not possible. And I'll get hurt. "I don't know," I tell him honestly. "We're friends."

"We could be more? More than just friends." He sounds almost... hopeful.

How can that be? "I thought you..."

"I think it was you."

Does it matter now? If it was Kalle who put on the brakes or me who wouldn't take a chance. It doesn't seem important, not with the way Kalle is looking at me.

But it was me. I know there were times when Kalle looked at me just like he's looking right now, and I stopped it. I'd move or say something or just leave.

Like I want to jump out of the bed and leave.

Because when you've been in love with a man as long as I've been in love with Kalle Erickson, it hurts too much to even consider anything more than the status quo.

I've been happy with him as my friend but if he's asking me to try...

"I don't know," I admit because I have no clue what else to say. One minute I was asleep and the next Kalle is still here and asking why we aren't together, and right now, I can't seem to think of a single good reason why we're not.

Edie and Kalle. It makes sense. The best kind of sense.

Kalle lies down again and my goodness, that's a nice chest. "There is a problem though."

"What?"

"Who, you should ask."

"Fenella?"

He chuckles. "Fenella is not a problem. Fenella was a distraction from the real problem."

"Which is…"

"You're dating my cousin."

I honestly draw a blank for a moment. Maybe it's seeing Kalle's taut stomach or just my sleep-addled brain… or maybe it's because Mathias means nothing to me.

Huh. Mathias means…

I think it's all three.

Mathias invited me to visit, insinuated that he has something important to discuss with me, and I went to bed last night without giving it a single thought. Yes, Kalle was a distraction, but some part of my mind should have wondered. Questioned.

Gotten excited?

But nope. Nothing. Am I okay with that?

"You need to end things with Mathias before anything happens with us," Kalle informs me as casually as if he's back to talking about the storm.

"I don't know," I say.

His face shutters closed like it's a store at the end of the work day. "You don't know if you want to end things with him?"

"No, it's just…" I was answering myself rather than Kalle. "Mathias is nice enough—"

Another chuckle but this one doesn't have a lot of humour. "You should tell him that."

"I'm not telling him anything. I mean... I'll tell him I won't see him anymore but... This is confusing," I admit, flopping back on the pillow so I can face him, pulling up the covers. While I have no problem ogling Kalle, there's not a lot of appeal in what I wear to bed.

But still, Kalle is smiling. At me. And maybe it's because of what I just said, or maybe it's because of the faded Snoopy I have on my shirt.

"It's a lot," I admit. "I'm—I don't move that fast. Last night you were out for dinner with Fenella, and this morning, you're ready to de-friend zone me."

He smirks. "Is that a thing?"

"I don't know what is a thing. Are we a thing? Is this because things didn't work out with Fenella?"

Kalle's mouth tightens. "I'm going to forget you said that."

"But Kalle, I can't forget that we've gone sixteen years without anything more than friendship and now, out of the blue—"

"It's not out of the blue," Kalle says, pointing to the window. "The sky is still pretty gray."

I look at him, exasperation rising like the storm and then, inexplicably, Kalle gives me a mischievous, very Gunnar-like grin, and I can't help but laugh

And then I open that door, the one I've kept closed and locked for sixteen years. The door I've kept my Kalle feelings behind, the one that I've never thought I'd get to open.

It's surprisingly easy to open. It's not stuck at all.

"You are very vexing," I tell him.

"Are we doing Bridgerton-speak? Is this because we didn't get to watch your episode last night?"

"I'd say you're pissing me off, but vexing is a much better word."

"If I kissed you, would that vex you too? Or would it convince you that we could be more than friends?"

That takes the breath out of me, sucks it clear out of my lungs, and I can only stare at Kalle. Kalle, my best friend.

Kalle, the future king of Laandia.

I can't forget that. But somehow, it's not the most important thing right now. "Maybe?"

Oh, that smile. Sly, flirtatious, cocky... My stomach does a 180 flip. "You don't sound too sure."

I laugh nervously, because yes, I'm nervous. I've had sixteen years of wondering about it, but when the moment is finally here, I have no idea if reality is going to measure up. "Kalle, you can't expect... Where is this all coming from?"

There's a moment as Kalle is staring at me and I think... wow. Maybe. Maybe this can happen, and I lean in just a bit.

"I'm not kissing you now." And Kalle sits up, stands up, moving away from me. Across the bed away from me.

"Ah... You're not?"

"No. Not now, with morning breath and you looking like you're ready to fall over with shock. No, I'm going to take you out and kiss you when the moment is right."

And then he smirks and walks out of my bedroom.

"The moment was right, Kalle," I call after him.

22

Kalle

SO I DID THAT.

I don't know what's worse: I'm freaking out because I finally said something to Edie, but at the same time I'm kicking myself that I didn't kiss her.

I should have kissed her.

She was right—it was the perfect time, only we were already in her bed and if I kissed her, we might have stayed there a lot longer

We probably would have. Definitely.

I would have wanted to, and that would have rushed it.

Edie shouldn't be rushed. I've waited sixteen years for this and it needs to be perfect.

If this is what she wants.

What if she doesn't?

I'm not going there.

When I escape to the washroom, I find my pants are still damp but I pull them on anyway. I don't bother with the shirt because it's no problem running across the alley bare-chested.

Edie catches me when I'm at the door, holding the sweatshirt I left in the washroom. "You can't leave."

"Sweetheart, I don't think it's a good idea if I stay."

I see the moment Edie realizes what I mean. "Oh. Ah. I just meant you can't leave like that." She reaches out like she wants to touch my chest, just like the Steve Rogers/Peggy Carter moment in the Captain America movie.

Maybe it's childish, but I can't help puffing a little with pride. "What's wrong with this?"

Edie rolls her eyes. "If you walk out of here without a shirt, *someone* will see and take a picture and I don't especially think it's *the right moment* to deal with that, do you?"

I laugh, and she goes ahead and rests her hand against my chest before pushing the sweatshirt back at me. "There's nothing wrong about this, by the way," she says with a twinkle in her eyes.

"Good to know." I pause with my hand on the door handle, and look down on her. So sweet and sleep-rumpled, brown eyes shining and those full lips—

I need to leave. But still, I hesitate. "Will this be okay?"

"Us?" I nod. "I think we can make it work." It guts me that she sounds so uncertain. How can she convince me if she's unsure? Maybe we should—

"I can't lose you," I mutter.

Edie cups my cheek with her hand. "You won't."

I really hope not.

Edie doesn't start work until four today, so I'm stuck with my own company for the day, since Dillon and Chase have the day off. I've never gotten close to their replacements, mainly because they usually stay in the car and don't say much when they follow me around.

The rain continues, sheets of it pouring down but the thunder and lightning seem to have stopped. The bar isn't as busy as it's like the town can feel we're near the end of it.

Or else they're sick of my place.

I change the kegs for Bethie, spend a nice half hour talking to Lennie Tak, and even throw some darts with Ken McKibbon. I get the paperwork finished before Edie tells me to do it.

I text her sixteen times.

I spend the rest of the time thinking about her.

Edie has been a constant for half of my life. She's the only person other than my family that I completely trust to have my back. Thinking about changing the dynamic between us should be terrifying, but instead, I find myself impatient.

Regretful. Why didn't we figure this out earlier? We wasted so much time. Or did we? Would it have worked between us?

Will it work now?

What if the first time I kiss her, Edie decides I'm not enough. I'm not what she wants.

I doubt that will happen, but there is the uncertainty of the future. Edie knows what I want—I want her. I want her... forever.

Do I really? And is it only because I think she can steady me if I become king?

What if I wasn't going to be king? Would I still want Edie England?

23

Edie

I GLANCE AT MY phone, at the text that has been waiting, albeit impatiently. What happened with Mathias? Coffee, dinner, kiss. Things going well—until Kalle decided to be a wrecking ball and take a swipe at my burgeoning relationship.

Would it really have been a relationship? Would it have gone anywhere? I had butterflies for Mathias, but they were the tiny, just-hatched type that can't really fly on their own. And how Mathias spoke to Kalle, finding out how he treated his cousin, kind of squashed them flat.

Despite the kiss. It was a good kiss. A solid eight.

Kalle's going to be a ten, I can just tell. If he ever gets around to putting his money where his mouth is.

Or where I want it to be.

The whole morning has been full of thoughts of Kalle distracting me from dishes, laundry, and other chores I was happy to be distracted from.

I can't even have a text conversation with my sister without my thoughts jumping to him. I'm sure Ella is going crazy with the triple dots vibrating on screen.

> *Ella: Why haven't you spilled the tea yet?*

Ah, Ella. She's a grade seven teacher and once she picks up on some slang the kids use, that's all we hear for the next year.

> *Me: Too busy… sorry!*

> *Eloise: I thought you had this morning off?*

I love my sisters and how we're so close, but sometimes… I stop halfway through making my bed to sit down and get the recap out of the way.

I'm not changing the sheets—these ones will be on for a while because now they smell like Kalle. The pillow where he laid his head, the sheet that covered some of his body.

His body…

Hugging my phone, I close my eyes and picture his bare chest. Those abs. His arms.

How he didn't kiss me, despite having the perfect opportunity.

I growl under my breath.

> *Me: there will be no second date with Mathias*

> *Ella: what???*

> *Enid: Why?*

> *Eloise: what happened? R U ok?*

What am I supposed to say to that? Enid is the worst of them, always trying to get me to push through the *just friends* barrier to see what might happen with Kalle.

It's like she knew something I don't.

Didn't. Something I didn't know, because now I know more. Not everything, but enough to... get excited?

Be scared? Hopeful? Resigned that it's not going to work out and it's going to hurt really bad, not to mention destroy our friendship? Over the moon with happiness.

I feel like a ping pong ball.

My sister has carried on the family tradition of the "E" names.

I've always thought the England family was a bit like the Bennets in Pride and Prejudice. I, of course, would be Lizzy, Eloise the sweet sister, Jane. Enid would be Mary, and Ella, the scatterbrained Kitty.

Thankfully, we don't have a Lydia.

But it was our mother with her over-the-top dreams of her daughters marrying into the royal family that reminded me of Mrs. Bennet. And now, like never before, I can relate to the part in the book where Mrs. Bennet says if Elizabeth refuses Mr. Collins, she'll never talk to her again, and Mr. Bennet says if she does marry him, he would never talk to her again. I feel like that.

My mother would be beyond excited to know that there may be *something* between me and Kalle, and my father would hate it.

Would my father hate it? If he knew I was happy with the son of his former boss, would he accept it?

I really hope so.

But there's no way I'm giving up that little tidbit to my sisters. I will report back on Kalle when there is something concrete, not just *maybe we should give it a try* and then *nothing happened!*

I'd never hear the end of it from Enid. From Ella: "Why didn't you kiss *him*?

Why didn't I?

I've made more of a fuss out of a non-kiss than of Mathias kissing me goodnight. I guess that shows where he stands.

Now I've got to tell him.

24

Kalle

I SPEND A LOT of time in the office thinking whether I'd still want Edie if I were just a regular guy.

There's no question about her: me being a prince is actually a detriment to Edie. If I were just a regular guy who owned a bar, would we be a couple by now?

I have no idea because I've never been a guy who just owned a bar, as much as I try to pretend I am.

I've never been one to consider my feelings. Emotions are unknown to me. I like action. I can do gestures. I can't talk about my feelings. It took three whole therapy sessions after my mother died for me to give something real.

This is what's terrifying for me. Summoning the courage to tell Edie exactly how I feel. It has taken a bit for me to figure it out, but now I think I've got it.

I love Edie. Even *thinking* it has my breath clutching my chest with fear, so I don't know how I will ever manage to tell her. But the thought also makes me smile—it's a comfortable thought; proud, like I've managed to fit in the last few pieces of the puzzle.

The thought of Edie makes my future less foggy.

I love Edie. I love her as my best friend, but I'm also *in love* with her.

I might have been in love with her for a long time.

"I'm an idiot," I groan.

"Is there a reason you're talking smack to yourself?" I look up to see Edie standing in the doorway of the office with a concerned look on her face. She's wearing her usual outfit of jeans and a T-shirt, her white apron already tied around her waist.

She's wearing a pink T-shirt today and her hair is down, swinging to her shoulders. She's traded in her usual diamond studs for simple gold hoops and put on lip gloss, so all I can stare at is her lips.

The whole package is the best thing I've ever seen.

It's not—Edie in that black dress the other night was pretty spectacular, but I know she got dressed this morning knowing she would be seeing me. So I can think she looks this good for me.

If there was any doubt in how I felt, seeing her there made it vanish. Disappear like the morning fog over the harbour. Seeing here there makes my insides feel like that dish of butter when Skywalker left it too close to the grill one time. There are rainbows and fireworks. Puppies and spring flowers after the rain.

There is a need to hug her that I can't ignore. I push back the chair and go to her, scooping her up in my arms, lifting her right off the floor.

Edie laughs and it's the best sound ever. I've always loved to hear her laugh, but everything sounds so much better today.

"What are you doing in here?" I ask into her hair. It smells good. Edie smell.

She kicks her legs. "I've got nothing else to do and it's too wet to go outside."

"Or maybe you missed me?"

Her arms tighten around my neck. "Or maybe I missed you."

"Good."

"Is that how it's going to be? I say something nice and you give me a grunt?" She gives my shoulder a playful slap.

I set her gently on her feet but keep my arms around her for a moment longer. "Probably."

I hold her longer enough for Edie to slide her hands from my shoulders all the way down my back to rest on my butt. And then she gives it a squeeze. "Did you just grab my butt?" I accuse.

Edie shrugs and gives me a mischievous grin. "You say something nice back or I squeeze something," she warns.

"I'll tell you right now, that's not much of a deterrent."

She laughs and winds her arms around my waist. And then she rests her head against my chest and sighs. "Is this happening too fast? It feels like it's happening too fast."

"It feels pretty good to me." *She* feels pretty good to me, here in my arms where she's always belonged. "Now I just say the things I've been thinking for years."

"Years, huh?"

"That's what I said."

"I've been thinking this is all so fast since last night, but if you're talking years..." she says into my chest and I can *feel* her smile. Edie is always smiling and cheerful, but this is a different kind of smile. This is the smile she gets because of *me*.

It feels pretty darn good knowing I can make her smile like that.

"You've been thinking of me, have you?" I interrupt.

She tilts her head and looks up at me. "I'm not admitting anything now."

"I've been thinking of you," I tell her, and watch as her smile lights up her face.

"What were you thinking about?"

There's no way I'm admitting any of my uneasiness. "About where I'm going to take you for our date tomorrow."

"Not tonight?" The disappointment rings in her voice. "I thought—"

"I'm gone tonight, so you think you can handle things here?"

"I can handle anything." I still hear the disappointment, and for once I want to cancel my plans. "Where are you off to? A goodbye dinner with Fenella?"

"Why would I be going out with Fenella if I told you I wanted to take you out?" The words come out harsher than I plan, but still—does Edie not think I meant what I said this morning?

"Oh." She looks startled. "I just thought..."

This might take some work.

"Think about what I said and realize that I meant it." I glance at Edie, annoyance fading with the urge to kiss her again. It was strong this morning, it's died down a bit, like the rain, but still—I want to kiss her.

I repress the urge and run a finger down her cheek. "If that's okay with you."

"It's..." She nods. "I'll talk to Mathias."

"Good girl."

Her eyebrows almost disappear into her hair. "Good girl?"

This time I swipe my thumb across Edie's lips, pausing at the centre of the bow and giving the bottom lip a tug. "I like good girls."

My chest puffs when she swallows, and I step back. "I'm at the castle tonight. Bo's still in town, so Dad called a dinner."

"Fun." The word comes out a little strangled and I smirk because I have that effect on her.

Me. Edie likes me.

"It will be. I might crash there, so don't worry if I don't make it back to town."

She looks confused. "I never worry if you don't come home or make it back into town because I can never be sure what you're doing."

"I thought maybe after last night..." It's an adjustment, I tell myself. We can't go from friends only to more without a few stumbles.

Not only do I have a past, but I've got a reputation, whether it's justified or not.

"You mean, last night when you woke me with your snoring?" she asks.

I chuckle. "Yeah, I think that was the other way around. You don't worry about me?"

"Of course I worry," she says, exasperated, "but I never know what you're doing... who you're with..."

"You'll know now," I promise.

Something softens in her eyes. "Okay. Text me when you're back and you can tell me about this date you're planning."

"Maybe I will."

"You will text me," she orders with a note of authority that does... things.

"Yes ma'am." I tip an imaginary hat to her. "I'll head out in about an hour or so. And I'll let you know when I get back."

It's been a long time since I've checked in with anyone when I came home. I thought it would be annoying but it's kind of nice.

It's very nice.

25

Edie

I WATCH KALLE LEAVE for dinner at the castle with a smile on my face. And the smile stays there like a permanent tattoo as the bar fills up for Friday night.

Kalle is going to text me.

Kalle is going to take me on a date.

Kalle better kiss me soon.

I know Kalle isn't one for the witty banter or meaningful conversations but he's one for grand gestures. In the rom-com movie, he would frustrate the main character by his lack of discussion of his emotions, but he'd come through at the end and be the one sprinting through the airport to stop her from getting on the plane.

But in Kalle's life, he could call and shut down the whole airport.

So while I'm a little frustrated with the lack of kissing—okay, a lot; I mean, look at the man!—I know Kalle is planning to knock my socks off.

That's a lot of pressure, for him and for me. I wish I had taken the opportunity when it came—which there have been several of them. Private office, anyone?

But that doesn't stop me from smiling.

The rain hasn't let off but it's a straight downpour, not the thunder and lightning and wind of the last few days. The bar is as busy as it has been, maybe busier because it's a Friday night. I work the taps with Tyler when Fenella Carrington blows in with perfect hair, wearing an outfit that must be worth more than what I make in a year, despite the rain.

The sight of her twists my stomach and I watch the crowd part with some sort of reverence as she approaches the bar. She's with Sophie Laz; an odd pairing, but not unheard of considering Sophie is Stella's younger sister, Stella is with Gunnar now, and Gunnar is friends with Fenella.

Still... odd.

"Hi Edie," Sophie calls as they take the last two stools at the bar. I like Sophie, who, unlike her sister with her crusty exterior, is always cheerful.

"Hey, Sophie. Fenella." I can't help but give her a wary glance. I know more *about* Fenella than I know her—the billionaire father, hot-as-sin twin brother who shares Prince Gunnar's love for speed, the countless magazine covers and advertising campaigns, plus social media followers in the seven figures.

I also don't know what happened with her and Kalle.

Fenella looks at me just as warily.

"Back in town tonight?" I ask her. In my mind it sounds polite, but I'm not sure because all I can think is *nahnahnah, I got Kalle.*

Childish, yes. But there's a part of me that feels good thinking it.

"Big event at the castle," Fenella says. "I thought I'd see what the town had to offer me for my last night here." She looks me up and down—that look that only women give to each other. The look is bad enough but those striking violet eyes? Who gets to have purple eyes?

Sophie leans in. "Stella's going," she whispers. "I think it's a big thing for Gunnar. And she's—" Sophie mimes her head exploding.

I can only imagine because that's exactly what I've been trying not to do—imagining myself at one of the family dinners. That seems too far off; too unbelievable.

Getting my head around me and Kalle is one thing. One thing at a time.

I make them drinks and move off to fill a pitcher with beer, Like this morning, there's not going to be enough for me to do that will keep my mind off Kalle.

Not with Fenella right in front of me, causing me to wonder and worry about what happened between the two of them.

She's beautiful, and rich. She has everything she could ever want.

Why wouldn't she want Kalle? And if she does, there's no way I could compete with her. I manage a bar. I wear jeans and T-shirts. Fenella is heir to a billion-dollar toy company. She's wearing a pair of purple flared, high-waisted pants and high heeled boots, with a gauzy shirt shot through with silver threads—most likely real silver—and tied under her breasts, leaving her belly bare.

She's gorgeous, so why wouldn't Kalle—

A shout and a crash knock me out of another Kalle-stupor. One glance shows me that once again, Jubblie Mark is in the middle of something, and once again, Coy Schmidt seems to be the instigator.

Without a word, I head over to the pool table where a beer bottle has been knocked to the floor. Thankfully, it's not broken but the puddle of beer is spreading, and Mark is doing his best to break one of the pool cues over his knee.

"They're stronger than they look," I tell him. "And if you do break it, you're paying for it. Plus, I'll kick you out of here for good."

Only a few heads turn, but Mark is one of them and he drops the cue on the table with a guilty expression.

That should have been the end of it. I know these guys, and they are all aware I don't stand for fighting or causing damage, especially when Kalle isn't around.

Unfortunately, there's a few out-of-towners in the group. Guys I don't know.

"Go away, little girl," one of the men jeers. I think I've heard someone call him Steve-o. I think it's a suitable name for a jerk.

Yes, I've already pegged him as a jerk. "Little girl?" I echo.

Jubblie Mark backs out of the crowd, Coy Schmidt right behind him. These men don't know me, and they don't know The King's Hat, and they're spoiling for a fight.

"That's what I said." Steve-o steps up to face me. He's no Kalle, but he does have a few inches on me. He's also a little unsteady on his feet and holding a nearly empty pint glass.

I make a note to add the cost of it to his bill because I have a feeling he's going to drop it in a moment.

"Why don't you toddle back off to your little hen party over there and leave us men to our business?" His sneer doesn't do anything for his level of attractiveness, which is slim to none already.

Sneers and jeers—my least favourite part of managing this bar.

"And what exactly is your business tonight?" I ask coolly.

"Smashing heads and taking names," someone behind him shouts.

"Not in my place, you aren't."

The rest of the bar has gone quiet. "Your place," Steve-o says scornfully. "You're nothing without your big, bad boyfriend here. Kalle's little princess."

"Don't you talk to her like that," someone shouts from behind me. I think it might be Ken McKibbon.

I also have a sensation there might be a wall of men lined up behind me, ready to charge if I give the word. These are men, most of whom would happily throw punches at each other if given the chance, and they've banded together to support me.

At least I think that's what is going on. And the way Steve-o looks over my shoulder suggests I may be right. It's nice they have my back, but a full-out brawl is the last thing I want, or need tonight. Or any other night.

"I think you boys have had enough tonight," I tell him in a calm voice.

"Little princess ain't telling me what to do. Go get me another beer!" And Steve-o deliberately releases the hold of his not-quite-empty glass, and it drops to the floor at my feet.

About four of them laugh.

I kneel down and pick it up. "Look, she's on her knees," one of them shouts. "She's kneeling before the king."

"What's your big, bad boyfriend going to say about that?" Another one cries.

I straighten up, glass in my hand. "He's going to tell me to throw you out of here." I flip the glass in my right hand and thrust it into the fleshy part of Steve-o's stomach. He gives a whoosh of beer-flavoured air, but no one hears it because, with my left hand, I grab a hank of his longish hair and part of his ear and smash his head down onto the pool table.

It's not exactly a smash, but it's a great move, and the cheers behind me prove it.

"Now," I say, leaning over him with my forearm pressing on his neck. It's a move Dillon practiced with me and I'm sad he's not here to see it. "My big bad boyfriend might not be here, but I'm perfectly capable of throwing your butt out of here. Or if the princess kicking you out is too much for you to handle, feel free to walk out on your own. Your choice." I release the hold on his neck and back away.

"What the—?" He scowls, and the wall behind me moves closer.

I point toward the door and then hold out my hand. "Pay up first."

There's a moment of indecision in his eyes. This is the moment it could all go sideways. I've thrown out more than a few obnoxious and intoxicated patrons, but usually, it's when Kalle is here, along with Dillon and Chase. I know no one in Battle Harbour will touch me when they're here.

These guys are from away and I might have just set the stage for a bar brawl, especially if my wall decides to attack.

Then Steve-o slaps a twenty-dollar bill—King Magnus looking wise—into my hand, and with a scowl, heads for the door.

I don't breathe a sigh of relief until the door has shut behind all five of them, and then I turn to face whoever is behind me.

There's a group of about a dozen of the regulars—Jubblie Mark, Coy Schmidt and Ken McKibbon, with Shirl Crow and

Lennie Tak and more. A nervous Tyler is behind them, with Chase off to the side.

"What are you doing here?" I demand of Chase. "I thought you were off tonight."

The second member of Kalle's security detail holds up a mop and bucket. "Just coming to help clean up the mess."

"Did Kalle ask you to babysit me?" Chase shakes his head and my expression softens.

"I had nothing going on tonight so I thought I'd hang out. You don't need me here, anyway. Your people have your back."

"Thank you," I tell the little group with a smile. Realizing that they stepped up to support me means a lot—more than I realize. That's something you would do for a leader. A friend.

They would have done it for Kalle in a second.

A general in an army. Or... maybe someone who holds a crown.

"I appreciate the backup. Drinks on me." I take the mop and bucket from Chase and thrust it at Jubblie Mark. "After you clean up your mess."

After a quick drink to settle my nerves, I pour a round for my backup. A bemused Tyler oversees Mark cleaning up the beer before giving him another bottle.

I hope he doesn't drop it.

"I've never seen anything like that." Sophie's eyes are wide and staring when I rejoin them at the bar. "Not just the way you took down that guy, but how the whole place gathered around you. That was amazing."

I can only shrug, even though the loyalty shown gives me a warm feeling. A very warm and fuzzy feeling. It would have been different if Kalle had been here—it would have been him who confronted them, and it all would have ended without my arm on someone's neck, but knowing I had others behind me...

It's a frightening thing to do, staring down a drunk, let alone physically subduing him, and if I'd had time to think about it, I wouldn't have gone that route.

But it all worked out.

"How did you learn to do that?" Sophie wants to know.

"My dad insisted on self-defence lessons when I started working here, and Dillon has shown me a few moves over the years," I tell her. "It's come in handy a few times."

Fenella still looks at me, still wary but with a hint of respect. "I had no idea you were a bouncer as well."

"That's why they pay me the big bucks," I say light-heartedly. "But I only get to do that when Kalle's not here. He always likes to jump in first."

"Like a knight in shining armour?"

"Like an alpha male looking to excrete some testosterone before he leaks all over the place."

Fenella blinks, then lets out a laugh. It's a big sound, coming from her belly. It's contagious—Sophie joins in and I do to, even though I have no idea what I'm laughing at.

It's been a weird day.

"I think you're my hero," Sophie declares, and I have to smile.

Fenella stirs her drink with a straw. "You know, I showed up for Odin and Camille's wedding because I thought I'd have to slap some sense into Gunnar and your sister," she says with a quick glance at Sophie. "It was clear there was something between them, but it turns out I didn't need to because Gunnar was smarter than

I gave him credit for. And I thought I might have to do the same for Kalle because it's clear to me he's fixated on someone else. I'm happy that there's no need to slap some sense into him." And Fenella looks pointedly at me.

"I don't really do violence," I manage.

"Says the woman who had a drunk in a wrestling hold ten minutes ago." Fenella laughs again.

26

Kalle

Two things happen at family dinner: For once, my father beats us to the table.

And Gunnar brings a date.

Stella clutches her glass of wine with a wide-eyed expression that tells me right off how nervous she is. It's still strange to see her with her natural hair colour—Stella has had funky hair for years now. The reddish brown makes her look more like her father.

Or Duncan before he went gray.

She's flanked by Gunnar and Spencer, her half-brother, both trying to ease her worries about being here. I can tell Duncan is, too, but doesn't want to push.

"So nice to have Stella with us tonight," Dad says in his heartiest of voices as plates of tenderloin atop of a bed arugula are served. Baby carrots and tiny roasted potatoes round out the meal.

I much prefer tonight's dinner to my lasagna from last night. Or maybe it was the company.

Although I did run into Fenella as she was leaving the castle. She's been staying here since the wedding as Gunnar's guest, but I don't know how much time Gunny has been spending with her. It's been Stella all the time since they got together.

I can't see Fenella wanting to be a third wheel with a new couple, but I hope she's found someone to hang out with.

There is not one bit of regret or guilt that person isn't me. All I feel for her is a mild fondness.

Edie, on the other hand... All want to do is finish dinner and call her.

I can't wait to tell her what I came up with for our date. Our very first date.

"It's about time one of us brought someone," Gunnar says under his breath, cutting into his steak.

"Got a bit of wedding fever there, little brother?" I ask. My tone is jovial; maybe too jovial because Spencer and Bo both glance over with confusion.

"No," Gunnar replies quickly and Stella gives him a look. I like Stella. She's always been a bit of a firecracker and she'll keep Gunny in line. "You could have brought someone," he accuses. "Like Fenella."

"I'm not taking Fenella anywhere." I swear a hush of relief sweeps around the table at my words. "But I'm thinking...maybe... Edie?"

There's no hush after that. "Yes," Bo says simply.

"Finally," Gunnar cheers.

"I second that." Spencer is beside me and gives me a thump on the back.

Lyra frowns. "Just to make it clear, are you asking us or telling us?"

I shrug. "Just putting it out there."

"But why?" Lyra demands, pushing back her red hair as she leans across the table. "Did something happen? I thought she was hanging around Mathias? But you did crash at her place last night..." She trails off, blue eyes widening.

"No, that's not it." I'm quick to cut that off at the knees because Lyra is like a dog with a bone when she wants to know something. "Maybe I didn't want her to hang around Mathias."

Across the table, Stella snorts and Gunnar laughs. "I suggest not getting all territorial, big brother," Lyra cautions, leaning back and reaching for her glass of wine. "It's never a good look, and knowing Edie, I doubt she'll appreciate it."

"Mathias and Dante are still here," Dad interrupts. "We had dinner last night."

"Thank you for not inviting us," Bo surprises me by saying. He's the kindest of us all at this table, and for him not to want to be around Mathias—

Actually, it might not just be Mathias. Bo doesn't like to be around many people.

"Mathias isn't that bad," Duncan corrects. "It's Dante who makes things uncomfortable."

"Mathias's friends are horrible." Lyra's eyes flash in a way that suggests the big brother in me needs to get to the bottom of that statement.

"It's not all his fault," Dad cuts in. "But we're not getting into that. Has anyone heard from Odin and Camille?"

"Are we supposed to?" Gunnar grins. "They are on their honeymoon."

"Ten bucks says there'll be a little Odin in less than a year," Dad says.

If possible, Stella's eyes widen even more. I don't know why—she's known us forever, and she definitely knows what Dad is like.

I guess being estranged from her father Duncan changes things.

"Are you betting on your son getting pregnant?" she squeaks.

"Technically, it's not Odin who would be getting pregnant," Gunnar explains.

"I know the logistics of getting pregnant," Stella snaps, squeaky voice vanishing. Gunnar gives her a chagrined look and then smiles when she turns her head.

"It only took us ten months for Kalle," Dad comments as casually as if we're talking about the wedding rather than procreating.

"What are we supposed to say—good job, Dad?" Bo asks the question with a perfectly straight face, and the rest of us crack up.

This is why I like family dinners. For once, we stop being the royal family of Laandia and just be the Ericksons.

Even though the dining room—the small one we use for less formal meals—is still set up with candles and fine china with spoons so shiny I can check my hair. Gunnar did it once and Mom was horrified, so one of us would always make a point of checking whenever we sat down.

The table is big, but there are still empty seats. No one likes to look at where Mom used to sit. And no one would dare take her chair, even after years of her being gone.

"So what's going on with Edie?" Bo asks as the others start to discuss where Gunnar should take Stella on their trip. "Last thing I saw, you looked a little besotted with Ms. Carrington."

"Fenella is fun, but not really... She's got some baggage."

He strokes his beard. "Since when has baggage bothered you? Should I start naming names, dude?"

I choke on my wine, knowing instantly who Bo is referring to. And not wanting to be reminded of her ever again. "That was not baggage, bro. She had a full set of luggage, plus a Hogwarts trunk."

Bo chuckles. "Seriously, though, why? I mean, why now? You and Edie have kept it platonic forever?" He narrows his eyes. "Or maybe you haven't."

"No, it's been just friends, but I was thinking—"

"Mathias?" Bo interrupts.

"No. Yeah. Maybe," I admit. "Him sniffing around maybe pushed me a little."

"If you're talking about bringing her to dinner, then that's a shove-in-front-of-the-train push," he warns. "Nothing little about that."

Eight years, and he's still gun-shy. Yesterday I wouldn't have hesitated to agree with Bo, but today...

"Maybe that's what I need," I tell him, my mind back on Edie. This is new; am I supposed to be thinking about her so much? Am I supposed to look for ways to bring her up in conversation?

Does this mean we're an official *thing*?

I haven't even kissed her yet.

I had no plans to say anything, but at the first opportunity—pow, verbal diarrhea about all sorts of stuff.

There's no way I'm blurting out the fact we haven't even kissed yet.

Luckily, Lyra and Gunnar's mock argument about the virtues of hostels versus hotels holds the rest of the table's attention.

"So, why, then?" Bo asks again. "If it's not Mathias."

"Dad mentioned something about it," I hedge.

"About Edie?"

"No, about getting married. I'm not getting any younger."

"No, because you're older than me."

I shake my head. "That makes no sense."

"You are older than me, and therefore getting older all the time. Do you want to marry Edie?"

I drop my voice. "I already asked her," I admit. "Totally mucked it up though, and she turned me down flat."

"Seriously?" I shrug. "Whoa. I don't blame her. We're a lot to marry into."

I stare at Bo, and find a little hope. I asked Edie to marry me, and while I was serious, I knew that wasn't the way to do it. I don't often show my romantic side but when I do, I make an effort.

Yet, I didn't make an effort with Edie. I know that now.

I knew that then, too, but I didn't think it mattered much. Now, I'm more excited about Edie and giving things a try rather than jumping into marriage, but maybe someday...

Maybe someday, because I think Edie would be really good for this family.

And even better for me. But if we're too much for her, if I'm too much for her—

"Do you think that's why she said no?" I demand. "I just thought it was because I made a mess of it."

"I have no idea what goes on in Edie's head. But they might." Bo jerks his chin across the table to where Lyra is leaning across Gunnar to talk to Stella. "Lyra said she and Kate went drinking with Edie at the pub. Speaking of that, what's this about Lyra drinking for free?" he suddenly reproaches. "You always make me pay."

I rear back at the abrupt change of subject. "Lyra pays for her drinks."

"Edie never charged her."

"What? Lyra." I raise my voice. "How much do you owe me from last night? You didn't pay Edie?"

"I didn't?" Her expression morphs into the familiar innocent waif. "I must have forgotten."

"You pulled the same thing on Tyler last time you were in town," I accuse.

Lyra, infuriating sister that she is, laughs. "Guess you better hire someone new before I come back again so I can try it with them."

I shake my head but I have to laugh. If Lyra ever took over this country, she'd have lineups of people bringing cookies and kittens and free swag. She always gets her way.

"When are you coming home again?" Spencer asks from down the table.

"Why?" she teases. "Do you miss me?"

"Definitely not."

Lyra points her wine glass at him. "You lie." And then she proceeds to hold Spencer's gaze just long enough for me to turn to Bo with a worried gaze.

Bo only shrugs.

He's so laid back, always checked out of the family drama. And Lyra and Spencer together would be nothing but drama.

But that's a discussion to have with Spencer when Lyra is far away.

Conversation moves to the storm that's finally starting to abate, and whether Gunnar will need more security on his next trip. Odin comes up more than a few times, and I doubt I'm the only one missing him.

Only Lyra is brave enough to ask Stella about her stepsister, Daphne, who almost helped hijack Odin's wedding by going to press with Camille's secrets.

"Is that the reason O picked that moment to announce he was abdicating?" I demand.

"He thought it might overshadow whatever Daulton had come up with. Kate suggested it," Dad says.

"Kate knew O was stepping down?" Lyra cries. "She never told me."

"And she wouldn't have. She's your best friend, but Kate is the epitome of professionalism," Duncan chides. "It'll be interesting to see what she decides to do."

"I don't like professional Kate," Lyra grumbles and Stella giggles.

"There!" Gunnar points his finger at her. "You do giggle."

"You used to giggle as a little girl," Duncan says with a fond smile on his face.

I think Stella blushes. "We don't have to talk about that."

"It's nice to see you all getting along again," Dad says. "When I think back to when—" He stops, an expression of surprise on his face. He presses a hand into his side. "When—"

"Dad?" Bo asks.

"Mag?" Duncan demands, fond smile replaced with an expression of concern and getting half up from his chair.

Dad seems shaky as he stands. "I think I need a Tums," he mutters. "Be right back."

He takes a step and then another. I'm on my feet, holding my breath.

Something is wrong.

Something is very wrong. "Why don't I—?"

But I don't finish, because suddenly Dad is on the floor.

27

Edie

I THINK I MAY like Fenella Carrington.

I think, maybe someday, the two of us may become friends.

Fenella and Sophie stay at the bar while I do my manager things—serving, settling a dispute over a bill, replacing the toilet paper in the men's room—and I keep coming back to them because they make me laugh.

Specifically, Fenella makes me laugh.

And instead of intimidating me or making me self-conscious, Fenella does the opposite. With every one of her stories and dropping of names, it shores up something inside of me, like she's adding her support. Because if Kalle gave up a chance with *her*, he must really think we could have something special.

And that makes me feel pretty darn good.

Until Mathias arrives.

I've been putting off texting him all day. I told Kalle that I would end things, but it seems like overkill when I don't really think there's much between us.

At least not on my side.

But if Mathias is here, looking at me with a smile on his handsome face, then maybe I've let it go on too long.

Because he's also looking around the bar. I'm so glad he arrived after Steve-o left because I have a feeling he would not be as impressed as Sophie was by my actions. "My cousin leave you on your own tonight?" he asks, watching me hold a glass under the tap. I can hear the disapproval in his tone even with a smile on his face.

"It's his night off."

"I'd never leave you to deal with this lot on your own." That should be sweet, but I think it's another shot at Kalle. I didn't like it when Mathias needled him to his face, and I certainly don't like it when he does it when Kalle's not here.

Maybe Kalle's right about Mathias.

There's no maybe—I look for the good in people, but I'm ready to stop with Mathias.

"I'm the manager," I say. "It's my job to deal with it on my own. I'm perfectly capable of dealing with anything that happens here."

A few stools down, Sophie grins at me. Both she and Fenella don't try and hide the fact they are listening to my conversation. Mathias ignores them.

"You wouldn't have to work if you were married to me."

I freeze mid-pour and catch myself just in time before the beer overflows. "Then I guess it's good that I'm not married to you because I like my job."

"Slinging beer and cleaning up throw-up in the men's room?" I stare at him in surprise but he keeps going. "I hate the thought of you serving people, especially people like her," Mathias spits out, jerking his head at Fenella and Sophie.

"What have you got against Fenella?" Fenella is listening; she holds Mathias's gaze with eyes that are as cold as amethyst and just as unforgiving.

Mathias breaks the staring contest and Fenella smirks, leaning over to whisper something to Sophie. "You don't know who she is?"

"She's a friend of Kalle and Gunnar. And of course, I know who she is."

"Then you know she absconded with my sister's former fiancé at the Met Gala a few years ago?"

Is that what's responsible for Mathias's attitude? Wounded family pride? "I suspect it's difficult to abscond with someone who doesn't want to be absconded with," I say mildly, carefully placing the pints on a tray for Bethie.

"Are you defending her?" he snaps.

Mathias snaps. At me. I can handle attitude and bad temper, and Kalle snaps more than he smiles, at least until lately. But what right does Mathias have to speak to me in that way? Even if he is defending his sister—an admirable quality—does he even know the whole story? And if his sister has another fiancé, then what's the big deal?

"I'm not defending anyone because I have no idea what happened." Bethie comes to claim the tray of beer and I wish I could wave her away and deliver them myself.

"Maybe I've misjudged you," Mathias says in a cool voice.

No serving for me—I'm staying right here to deal with this. "I'm sorry? How have you misjudged me?"

"If you're defending a woman like that." He leans an elbow on the bar. "Why do you work here, Edie?"

I suddenly wonder why I ever thought Mathias was so attractive. "Because it's my job."

"You're a barkeep. You never wanted anything more for yourself? Your father worked at the castle, didn't he?"

My mouth literally falls open. Who is this person?

"Or is it because you had hopes of snagging yourself a prince for a husband?"

"*Excuse* me?"

Mathias scoffs. "I've seen the women my cousin runs around with. He's not the marrying type, and clearly, neither are they."

There's a buzzing in my ears and I try to make sense of what Mathias is saying. Of *why* he's saying it. Because this isn't the way you speak to a woman you're interested in.

Or anyone you respect.

And then I remember what Kalle told me about how Mathias would taunt him, and I get angry all over again. "I'd like you to leave," I tell him with a voice that's as cold as the ice in the drinks.

Mathias laughs, an ugly sound. "You're not serious."

My eyes narrow, and one of the regulars sitting at the bar makes a choking sound. "Oh, I'm very serious," I say.

"I had decided to court you." I take a step back from the venom in Mathias's words. "You seemed... suitable. I had hopes of you becoming my wife. I was ready to take you away from this place, from this life."

What? Where did he idea I would ever be interested in a *life* with *him*?

"I like this place," I say automatically, because what do you say when presented with something like this? "I don't need to be rescued."

"You sure about that? Your father worked at the castle. Chasing around my cousin for your whole life while you pretend to work for him? If you wanted a prince, I was ready to give you one."

I look around the bar, at the people who were ready to stand with me. At my friends who I serve and take care of. At Kalle's place—Kalle's and mine. Because The King's Hat is as much mine as his, and everyone knows it. "Not interested," I tell him. Never in my life have I sounded so rude. "Never was, never will be. I suggest you see yourself out before you get to witness how much I enjoy certain aspects of my job." I lean closer. "The throwing out kind. What would you tell your father if you got thrown out of your cousin's bar by a simple barkeep?"

Mathias sniffs. "I expected more from you."

"What—gratitude because you thought you needed to rescue me? No, thank you. I can rescue myself, thank you very much. Now, if you don't mind, I have work to do. Good night, Mathias, and it was not good to meet you."

I watch him walk out without another word. Or a look back. That's enough of Mathias. I much prefer the Battle Harbour royal family.

Sophie and Fenella cheer and lift their glasses in a toast to me.

The door has just closed behind Mathias when my phone, jammed in my back pocket, rings.

It's Stella.

28

Kalle

SINCE MY MOTHER DIED, I've had a recurring nightmare about losing my father.

It's not pleasant, and it makes it worse that I never know how he dies in my dream.

This is worse than any dream because it's really happening.

I haven't been able to take a deep breath since Dad hit the floor.

That was an hour and thirteen minutes ago. It's a blur of faces and voices—of Spencer on the phone with Jonathan McKibbon, telling him to meet us at the bottom of the hill for a police escort. Of Dillon—who never took the night off—and Dad's head of security, Etienne carefully—ever so carefully—carrying him to the biggest SUV, with Bo hovering and trying to support Dad's back.

Minka, behind the wheel, ready to take off as soon as Gunnar is tucked in the second SUV with Dillon in charge. "It's not a heart attack," Gunnar keeps repeating. "He didn't have a heart attack."

Castle security moves in orchestrated precision, like they've planned for this.

How can you plan for your father to collapse during dinner?

I guess you have to when your father is the king.

They choose to drive him to the hospital instead of waiting for the ambulance because the castle is at the top of a cliff and we're in the middle of a storm. Etienne has the paramedics on the phone as Minka takes off with him and Duncan. Dillon takes lead on the second SUV, with Gunnar, Stella, me, and Spencer. Bo and Lyra are with the rest of the security, and the last sight of my sister is her white face crumpling as Bo takes her in his arms.

The half-hour drive to the hospital takes seventeen minutes. Seventeen minutes of my father being unconscious. Not dead. I know he's not dead because Spencer is on the phone with his father the entire trip down the hill.

When I look back on it, how Dillon careened down the hill, close behind the tail lights of the SUV that held my father, windshield wipers going double speed, and the darkness on either side threatening to swallow us whole, I will be terrified. Even Gunnar, whose top speed has been over two hundred miles an hour, hangs on tight, one hand on the strap affixed to the ceiling, the other gripping Stella's hand so hard I'm sure she loses circulation.

They meet us at the hospital; Etienne doesn't leave Dad's side as they get him on a gurney and whisk him away, while Minka and Dillon shepherd us into a private waiting room, with Duncan torn at whom to follow.

Spencer pushes him toward Stella and heads to the front desk.

It's as if a monster clutches at my chest, scrabbling for my heart, and I can barely breathe, can't speak as I pace the waiting area, the voices of my family in a haze far beyond my understanding.

What if he dies? That's the only thought that spins through my mind, and I refuse to take it any further because I know what it means.

If Dad dies, I will be king. Right then and there—Spencer and Duncan will make it so. Bo, Gunnar, and Lyra will agree, and I will become King Kalle of Laandia.

I've never known such fear.

I'm not ready. I'm not ready to lose him, so not ready to become king. I can't even bring myself to answer Minka's question on whether she can get me a cup of coffee.

She brings me one anyway, and I clutch it gratefully.

"Kalle?" I blink and Stella comes into focus, standing before me with a worried look on her face. "I called Edie. I know we're supposed to keep it quiet, but it's Edie, and I thought maybe you'd want her here. She'll be here soon."

Edie. Here. I nod, and keep nodding.

Stella drifts back to Gunnar.

Edie is coming. She'll be here soon. She's coming.

"Kalle?" Bo's voice breaks into my spiral. "Bro, you've got to chill. You're freaking us out. Lyra's a mess, and you're not help-ing."

I look at the others, at the tight group whispering together. I thought they were talking about Dad, but it looks like it was me. "I don't know what to do." My voice is unrecognizable, hoarse and raspy like I've just had my tonsils removed.

"Nothing you can do." Bo claps me on the shoulder. "He'll be okay."

"You don't know that. And if he's not—"

"Don't go there," Bo tells me. "Not yet. He'll be okay because that's what I need to believe. We'll figure it all out, whatever happens."

"How?"

"We'll figure it out," he repeats. "It's going to be okay."

"Mom..." I manage.

"I know." Bo leans forward in an awkward hug and grips the back of my head. "It's not her. It's not the same thing."

My brother holds me for a long minute until he goes back to Lyra because our little sister starts to cry when she sees us like that.

I resume my pacing, and then, suddenly Edie is there.

One moment there is no one, and then she's standing at the door, wearing the same jeans and pink T-shirt, along with her white apron still tied around her waist.

I draw in a shaky breath, and then another as I watch her from across the room.

Her gaze locks with mine, but as she takes in the room, she goes straight to Lyra, who is back to gnawing her nails, face tearstained and makeup smeared.

"How is he?" Edie asks as she pulls Lyra into her arms. My sister kind of melts into Edie, sniffling into her shoulder, and Edie looks at me.

I don't answer. I can't. It's enough that she's here and I can breathe again.

"Surgery," Duncan says in a heavy voice. "It's wait and see."

"He'll be okay," Gunnar insists like he's been saying all night.

"Stop saying that! You don't know," Lyra cries. "They took Mom into surgery and she never came out."

It's what we've all been thinking but no one was brave enough to say.

"It's not like your mom," Edie soothes, tightening her grip on Lyra.

Something she wouldn't let us do.

"What happened?" Edie mouths at Duncan but it's Bo who answers.

"It's his appendix," he says. "No one knew he was having problems and it burst. Right there at the table and he…" Bo swallows hard.

"What needs to be done?" Edie asks Duncan, but this time it's Spencer who steps up with eyes as tired and worried as the rest of us.

"Mrs. Theissen has everything under control at the castle," he tells her. "The hospital has assured us this will stay private until we give the okay to release it. I've been trying to draft a statement," he finishes, gaze tracking to Lyra.

"I'll get Kate and work on a statement with her if you like," Edie says. "We can run it by you before doing anything. You can focus on being here."

"That would be great." Spencer's shoulders sag. "Odin and Camille are flying in. They'll be here first thing in the morning."

"I'll go with Dillon to pick them up."

It's so smooth the way Edie walks in here and makes everything better.

29

Edie

I WANT TO STAY with Kalle.

I want to stay with him *so much*, just curl up with him and do what I can to make his pain and worry and fear go away.

I can tell by his eyes that he's terrified.

But I can't, because there are things to be done and I'm in a position to do them for the family.

I have to leave, but my heart stays with him.

After I give Lyra another tight hug and say goodbye, fighting the urge to throw myself into Kalle's arms, Spencer walks me to the exit by the emergency room.

There's a handful of people waiting, with injuries bad enough to make the drive in through the storm.

"Thanks for coming," Spencer says as the sliding door opens to let in a burst of cool air. "Lyra needs…" He trails off, looking too concerned for just a friend of the family.

"There are a lot of men in her life," I say. "You should get back to her."

"I wanted to ask you about Kalle."

I glance at Spencer; Spencer who is like the fifth brother, close to all and the family's main defender. Spencer is one of Kalle's best friends, but he's coming to *me* for news on him.

And I know exactly what he's about to ask me. "I don't know," I admit.

Spencer huffs. "Has he said anything about abdicating?"

"No, but he hasn't said anything about *not* abdicating either. You should know that as well as I do."

"I didn't know if he's said anything about it. He's really freaked out, Edie, and I worry this might push him over if he's sitting on the edge."

"He's freaking because he's terrified. He might be about to lose his father *and* his life as he knows it. Privacy, a personal life, probably his bar—of course he's freaking out."

"I need to make sure things are running, even with something like this."

"I know, and you're very good at your job. But you've got some time, Spencer, so go be a friend to them. And be there for your father."

He nods. "You're good for this family, you know."

I smile tightly. "Keep me posted, please."

I call Kate on the way back to the bar, driving slowly through the streets, debris from the storm making the trip more treacherous than usual. Between us, we come up with a statement for Spencer to give to the press whenever they decide to do so, vague and as positive as we can make it. Kate asks if I think we should come up with something in the event of the king's death, whispering the question like it's treason to even think about it.

Once back in the bar, I can't say anything about where I've been, what has happened, because one slip of the tongue, and the whole town will hear about King Magnus being in the hospital within hours.

Sophie and Fenella have gone; they had looked concerned when Mathias left, or at least Sophie had. Fenella had smiled.

Everything about Mathias flew out of my head when Stella called.

Mathias... he was headed back to the castle. I wonder if he knows about the king.

I wonder if he cares for the right reason.

He's no longer any concern of mine. As long as he stays away from Kalle—and now Fenella, as I've tucked her under my protection somehow—I want nothing more to do with him.

He wanted to *rescue* me? Dude— My life is better than his royal reality will ever be. Especially now that Kalle—

I keep my phone in my back pocket, waiting for the call that might change everything.

No one calls at midnight; one o'clock passes with no word. I ring the last call bell just before two, and the few diehards that are still there file out so that I close a few minutes after two.

As I clean up, I try to decide if I should go back to the hospital or wait at my apartment.

My apartment, where I woke up with Kalle this morning. And I can't help but wonder what this will mean for us.

I shouldn't think about an *us*. The king is in the hospital, Kalle's future uncertain, and I'm wondering if this means Kalle's not going to kiss me.

What is wrong with me?

My phone ringing from the back pocket of my jeans sends my heartbeat racing as I fumble for it. "Hello," I say breathlessly.

"He's okay." It's Kalle, his voice husky.

I close my eyes and lean against the closest wall. "Oh, thank god."

"Yeah. They removed his appendix. He might have sepsis—I don't know what that is—so they're giving him antibiotics."

"I'll find out for you."

"He'll be here for a couple of days, but they're sending us home. Duncan is going to stay the rest of the night with him, in case Dad wakes up."

"That's good."

"I'm going back to the castle," he says.

"You want to stay together." I nod, disappointment flooding me because I won't see him, even as I nod.

"Are you okay to drive up?"

My heart trips at the question. Not so much the words, but how he says it.

Like I'm expected to be there with him. I haven't been inside the castle since I was eighteen years old and Kalle left to play baseball.

"Are you sure?" I whisper. "Shouldn't it be—?"

"Family. That's you. Please."

I close my eyes, smiling, even with the drama of the night. "Of course. I'll see you soon."

"Drive safe."

I end the call, happy for the king and...

Happy for me.

30

Kalle

THE CARAVAN OF SUVs drives back to the castle at a much slower pace this time.

There's a sense of excitement, mixed with exhaustion. Smiles, through the tears.

Mrs. Theissen greets us at the door, her gray hair less severe, wearing a cardigan over loose pants, a far cry from her usual austere outfits.

I feel her gaze observing everything as we file into the foyer. "I'm so glad he's okay," she says. "Can I get you anything?"

"I don't want to go to bed," Lyra says. "I can't sleep."

"Why don't I fix you a snack?" Mrs. Theissen suggests. She glances at me. "I'll bring it to the big office."

Bo squeezes her arm with a tight smile. "That'll be perfect."

Silently, we head to Dad's office, which is more of a man cave/place to hang out than an office where business is conducted.

It even smells like the king.

Evidence of him is everywhere, even more than I have at the bar. Gold records and framed pictures hang on the wall; his gold medal and the shotput he uses as a paperweight. Books are everywhere because Dad loves to read.

There's still a photo of Mom on his desk, and a huge framed one of the seven of us hangs behind his desk. It's not the official family picture that hangs in one of the halls, but a casual one that Duncan took one day after dinner.

We're grouped around Dad, who is seated at the head of the table. Lyra, at fifteen, hangs over his shoulder; Mom has her arms around Bo like she's drawing him into the shot. Odin and Gunnar stand side by side with identical smiles on their faces.

I look a lot like my father.

Everyone looks at that picture when they come in.

Except for me—my attention is caught by a picture of Dad, Dante, and my grandfather, Euan.

I'm older than my father was when he became king.

Did he feel this fear? This out-of-control-ness, like a roller coaster that's about to fly off the rails? The complete certainty of knowing that I have no idea what to do now?

Euan had a heart attack; it was quick and painless. One moment he was alive, and the next my father was king.

I've been spared that—for now. But someday in the future… that's going to be me.

Gunnar and Stella sink onto the leather couch, while Lyra perches on Dad's big desk, swinging her legs, and Bo takes the chair behind the desk but pulls it around beside the couch.

Spencer hovers near Lyra and I start to pace again.

Once again, I'm having trouble breathing. But then Edie is there, sweeping into the room just as Mrs. Theissen brings a platter of sandwiches and cookies, the cook following with two pitchers of Dad's honey mead that has Bo and Gunnar cheering.

I'm happier to see Edie.

And this time, she comes right to me.

Without a word, Edie puts her arms around my waist and I pull her in close. She fits nicely there under my chin.

"It's okay now," she whispers.

Because you're here. But I don't say it. Not yet.

No one asks why Edie is here. There's no reaction save a quick intake of breath from Lyra. Stella came back with us, but Duncan is her father, Spencer her half-brother, so even without her new relationship with Gunnar, she has a reason to be there.

Since she's been estranged from Duncan and Spencer for so long, I think it's good that Stella is here.

Bur Edie doesn't have any family connections with the castle, so she's here for me.

She's mine.

The sandwiches quickly vanish, as does the mead, and Bo disappears to get a refill. I finally stop pacing and take the second couch with Bo and Lyra, with Edie tucked in beside me.

I like her close.

"This changes things, you know," Spencer finally says to me. "Legally."

"What do you mean?" Stella asks and then draws back like she spoke out of turn.

"The king will be indisposed during his recovery," Spencer continues. "We've given a statement—" He nods at Edie. "Thank you for that. But even so, appearances need to be maintained. With Odin stepping back—"

"The rest of us have to show we're still in the picture," I finish.

"We'll postpone the trip," Gunnar says to Stella, and to her credit, she doesn't even look disappointed as she nods.

"You don't have to," I tell him, the weight settling on my shoulders not as heavy as I expected. "I'll do it. I can step in for Dad. Whatever is needed."

Edie's fingers slip into mine.

Later, after Stella nods off and Lyra begins the non-stop chatter that always signals she's tired, I do the big brother thing and order everyone to bed until it's only Edie and me.

She stacks the dishes on Dad's desk in neat piles. "They're all to bed, so I'll get going," she says hesitantly, even as she gives a huge yawn.

"You're not driving home."

"How do you propose I get there then? Fly?"

"Stay here."

Her eyes are wide and wary as she looks up at me. "Kalle…"

"Stay with me. Like last night. Just… stay."

I don't want to say how much I want her to. That watching her leave will be too much for me tonight. That I was already close to breaking until she showed up, both here and in the hospital.

That she might not be my security blanket but she does make me feel safe.

Edie nods and I let out a ragged breath. "But you can't hold what I gave you to wear last night against me," she points out. "I don't keep giant-sized clothes in my apartment."

"Maybe you should start," I tell her with a smile.

I have no idea what I'm waiting for; the perfect moment is never going to come. I've gone all out as Mr. Romance before and part of me thinks Edie deserves that and more.

And then I stop myself because I wonder if she deserves me. Not me *me*, but all the baggage I've been born with.

The whole royal thing.

I know now that I never took a chance with Edie because I wasn't ready for it. It would have been good, but she would have eventually tired of my one-syllable answers and bad moods, and there where would I be? Without Edie or my friend.

It might have been Mathias's interest in her that gave me a kick in the butt, or maybe just a coincidence, but it's time to step out of the friend zone.

I'm standing in the batter's box waiting for the perfect pitch and I'm afraid if I wait too long, I'm going to talk myself out of it, like I've been doing for years.

31

Edie

AND THAT'S HOW I end up sleeping beside Kalle for the second night in a row.

We don't go to sleep right away. Kalle gets me a huge T-shirt to wear and I crawl into his equally huge bed. I haven't been in his room for years. There are sports memorabilia on every surface and posters on every wall.

It smells like him.

I lie on my back and stare at the ceiling while Kalle climbs in and turns out the light.

"I think the storm is pretty much over," he says.

"Good."

"Why are you so freaked out about them?"

No one has ever asked me that, and not a lot of people know how afraid I am of storms.

Of course Kalle knows.

"When I was ten, I was out in Dad's greenhouse and it started to rain," I tell him, stating fact and not letting my memories bubble up. "And then thunder and lightning."

"Is that the one with the glass roof?"

"The glass everything. It's all glass. I was too afraid to run back to the house. I didn't care about getting wet but I didn't want the lightning to get me. I ended up waiting it out under a table. Dad thought I was happy as a clam out there watching the storm or he would have come and got me."

"You know the chance of getting struck by lightning is like one in three million," Kalle says. He sounds amused for the first time all night.

"No, it's one in one point eight million, so that's a lot less. And you weren't around when I was ten to give me such helpful statistics."

"You were cute when you were ten," Kalle muses. "Those big eyes and the Laura Ingalls braids."

"How do you know who Laura Ingalls is?" I demand.

"I have a sister, you know."

"Yes, I know that." There's a long pause, and I know Kalle isn't trying to fall asleep. I can hear his breathing and it's not the sleepy kind.

"Mathias came in tonight," I finally say.

"Uh-huh."

"Are you trying to go to sleep?"

"Not now." He shifts and I can tell he's facing me. Waiting for me to continue.

"I guess Mathias knows about my father." I huff a breath. Pride is an interesting thing. My entire life, I lived in a country with a king and a queen and their five beautiful children. Even though I became friends with those beautiful children, I always knew that their lives were different than mine.

I was there to *help,* and I was fine with that. It's not that I thought the royal family was any better than mine, only that we existed in slightly different circles.

I was okay with that, until Mathias.

Mathias embarrassed me. He looked at my father working at the castle and me managing the bar, and he felt pity for me, like my life wasn't worthwhile.

"What did he say?" Kalle's voice is hard and just a little bit fierce. He would never embarrass me or take my family and use it against me.

"He wanted to rescue me from this life." I try to sound like it doesn't matter, only I can't quite make it. "This awful, horrible life of working for a living. Of working for your family. He wanted to whisk me away to his castle and live happily ever after, being... I don't know what he wanted me to be."

"He's an idiot."

"Maybe he meant well—"

"Maybe, but I doubt it. The man needs to realize that if you need rescuing—and you don't, because you have a great life and I'm the best boss ever—if you need to be rescued, you're going to damn well do it yourself."

"I guess."

"I know. Did you tell him I'm the best boss ever?"

"You didn't exactly make it into the conversation."

"So you didn't tell him I'm going to marry you?"

The silence is so complete that I think I might hear my own heartbeat. "I wasn't aware we had decided that," I say carefully.

"You might not have, but I have."

"Kalle..."

"What's this *Kalle*? You know that's what I want."

"Yes, but there's a huge jump between what we are and what you want," I point out.

"Yeah, and I'm not rushing into anything. I'm going to convince you because tonight just showed me that I don't want a life without you in it. I definitely don't want you to disappear into Mathias's castle, which isn't a castle by the way. It's just a big house."

"I don't need a castle."

"I know, and that's why I want to give you one."

I smile in the darkness. I can't help it. What Kalle is suggesting makes no sense. It's no more than a fairytale and I've long ago accepted that I'm the fairytale type.

But it sounds... right... when he says it here in the dark, wrapped in a blanket in a Kalle-scented room.

"Give me a couple of days to sort things out with Dad's responsibilities," he says now. "And then I'm going to start showing you that I mean what I say."

My smile grows wider. "Okay," I whisper.

Kalle shifts again, and then there's a finger tracing my lips. "You're smiling, aren't you?" he asks in a low voice. "You're smiling at the thought of all this. Of me."

"Maybe," I hedge.

I can tell by his voice that Kalle is smiling too. "I'm still not kissing you tonight," he tells me.

"What?"

"Dad was just in the hospital. It's definitely not the right time."

"I don't know what you're waiting for," I huff and flip over so my back is toward him.

"You don't have to wait," he says, the suggestion heavy in his voice. "Just because I'm showing my romantic side by waiting until the perfect moment—"

"You're showing some kind of side," I mutter. "And no, I'm not kissing you."

"Suit yourself." Kalle chuckles and then I feel his arm drape over my hip. "Just know I'll make it worth your while."

"You better."

He laughs.

32

Kalle

I'M SURPRISED I FALL asleep.

I'm not surprised I have the dream.

This time I'm back in Edie's father's truck. She's with me, and so is Dad, bleeding on the bench seat between us. Edie has her hands pressed against his stomach and there's so much blood.

Faster, faster, she says. And then suddenly it's, *watch out, watch out*. It's not the turtle on the side of the road, but a car.

Mom's car.

Mom's car is on the side of the road and I'm barreling toward it. I see Lyra in the backseat window, screaming and just before I hit—

I wake up.

I wake up gasping and shaking and also sweating, even though the blankets have been pushed down.

I sit up. Edie sleeps beside me, curled up with her hands under her chin, and just seeing her soothes me.

Or at least seeing her there tells me it was only a dream.

I slide out of bed and head to the window. The rain has finally stopped in the night and clouds scud across the sky, an inky blue.

My room looks over the ocean and the fierce waves of the last few days seem to have abated, although I can still see the whitecaps. I open the window carefully—sixteenth-century castles don't have great windows—and the sound of the wind and the waves seeps in the room.

"Kalle?"

"Sorry." I push down the window, but it screeches loudly. "Sorry."

"Is everything okay?" A creak of the bed, and Edie is beside me, wrapping her arms around my waist.

I rub her arm, feeling her soft skin still warm from being in the nest of blankets. "I'm going to be king."

"I know," Edie says, squeezing tighter.

I stare out the window. "Someday. I've always known it would be someday, but that day doesn't seem too far off now after last night. I told myself I'd give it to Odin, I'd make him do it, but deep down, I know I wouldn't have done that. Unless he asked for it. Even then, I'm not sure I could have."

"I know."

"It's real now. *I'm going to be king.* I've been running away from that my entire life."

"I know."

I give a choked laugh. "How do you know all this?"

"Because I know you." I can hear the smile in her voice. "And because it's obvious this has hit you hard."

"Really hard," I admit.

"It'll be okay. Your dad got through the night. He's strong, he'll be okay."

"But the next time? Because there is going to be a next time."

"You'll be ready," Edie promises. "Because you've stopped running."

I mull over her words as I stare out into the sea. It's always felt like I'm on the edge of the world here. The castle sits on top of a cliff; tundra and ice-capped islands lie to the north, and the most barren part of Laandia is to the west. South is Canada. To the east is the cold Atlantic Ocean.

Across the Atlantic is Great Britain and Europe. We're closer to Scotland than to the west coast of Canada.

I think about Prince William for a moment, wondering what went through his mind when his father finally became king. Knowing that his own future is set—the question is just when.

He's not much for sharing though.

I guess I'm not either.

Edie stirs beside me. "It's going to be a nice day." She points to the horizon where there's a band of pinkish purple appearing.

"It's the same colour of Fenella's eyes," I say without thinking.

"What?" Edie looks up at me with a horrified expression. But I can tell there's a smile in her eyes, so I don't think I've said something terribly wrong.

"Sorry." I spread my hands in a gesture of apology. "It just popped into my head. It wasn't thinking about her or anything."

"Must have been thinking a little bit for it to pop in so quickly. She was in the bar last night."

"Uh-oh."

"No, it was fine. We talked a bit. I think I like her."

"Uh-oh," I say again.

"No, she's... not as intimidating as I would have thought."

"No one should intimidate you."

"Especially since I stopped a bar fight between Jubblie Mark and some guys from Sandro Harbour." There's enough pride in her tone to tell me that however she stopped it, she did more than just raising her voice.

"Do I want to know how you stopped it?"

"You can ask Chase," she says primly. "But the most amazing part was that at least half the bar was standing behind me. I had so much support. It also meant that it would have turned into a real brawl if I hadn't gotten them to go."

"But you did."

"I did."

"Because you can do anything."

"Almost anything," she agrees.

"What's something that you can't do?"

"Get you to kiss me."

"Ah."

The air shifts. I've had fantasies of kissing Edie for years, and now when the reality is in front of me—literally in front of me—I haven't got the faintest idea how to begin. I've kissed... *a lot* of women, but Edie is the only one I've *longed* for. I've traced my finger along her lips countless times in my mind, teased her with my tongue in my daydreams.

I want it to be perfect and here—now—I don't know how it can be.

We're both half asleep, Dad is in the hospital and I compared the beginning of the sunrise to another woman's eyes.

But I've never left a woman wanting before.

Edie is still looking at me, so I reach down and tilt her chin just a little higher. "If it was up to me, I'd be kissing you every minute of every day. You wouldn't be able to do anything because I'd be kissing you so much. But this first one, because I've waited so long, I want to be perfect."

"Perfect is too much pressure," Edie whispers.

"Let's see what you can do, then."

Her eyes widen, and then she's up on her tiptoes, one hand fisting in my T-shirt, the other winding behind my head, pulling me down. Her lips mash against mine, missing half my mouth, and it's so far from perfect that she pulls back with a laugh.

"You're too tall," she cries.

I pick her up and set her on my dresser beside the window. "Better?"

"Much."

This time I take the lead, cupping her cheek and leaning into her slowly, so slowly that Edie has time to wet her lips and open them slightly.

Yes, I'm teasing her by making her wait, but it's fun.

I kiss her forehead, her temple, the apple of her cheek, and then move down to the corner of her mouth. Then I kiss the other side.

Edie whimpers softly.

"Are you sure?" I whisper. "Because once I kiss you, there's no going back."

"Because you think it's going to be that good?"

"Because I won't be able to let you go. Sixteen years, Edie, is a very long time." I press my lips against hers, finally kissing her properly.

And

It's

Pretty

Darn

Perfect.

Edie's lips are so soft and part under mine so sweetly.

I've kissed a lot of women but I don't do a lot of heavy kissing and now I can't understand why not. Because the way Edie kisses, she puts everything into it. Hands in my hair, legs—oh, she's wrapped her legs around my waist—and her mouth moves under mine like we've been doing this forever.

We've wasted *sixteen years.* We could have been doing this forever.

My arm wraps around her waist as I lean into her. Her skin is so soft as I grip the side of her neck to tilt her just so and make it that much better.

She moans softly as my tongue slips between her lips. My stomach does flips, tight knot undone and floating in the wind, but I still pull back for a moment.

"Is this okay?" I whisper against her mouth.

Edie kisses me in response, kisses me as soundly as any other woman has ever kissed me.

I don't want to think of any other woman, ever again. All I want to think about is Edie.

Which is why I begin to trail kisses down her throat. "I... need to know... if you can handle this," I plead between tastes of her soft skin, each a raindrop to a dying man. "Edie, please."

"Yes," she breathes, her head tipping to the side.

"Handle me. This is a lot."

She lifts her head to look at me, and as soon as I'm caught in her gaze, I know she knows I'm not talking about getting physical with her.

"As long as I have you, I can handle everything," she tells me.

The sun rises over a perfect day in Laandia and I'm kissing Edie England as it happens.

33

Edie

I DON'T KNOW WHAT Kalle says to the rest of the family about me staying the night at the castle, but I'm out of bed and into my car before any of them have made it out of their rooms. Kalle gives a grumble as I untangle myself from under his arm but I tell him to call me when he wakes up. I'm tempted to kiss him goodbye, but I don't think I would leave if I did that.

The sun is bright as I drive away and the sight of it after the intensity of last night, not to mention three days of rain, does amazing things to my mood.

Or maybe it's just Kalle.

There's a heady sense of anticipation when I think of seeing him next. And also a healthy amount of fear.

I've had relationships before, and none have really worked out. I've had my heart broken, and it wasn't pretty. Greg Kaan when I was eighteen. Kyle Dugan at twenty-four. And five years ago, Derrick Anders broke our engagement after eighteen days. He proposed to me, said he wanted to spend his life with me, and then he up and changed his mind. That was a bad one. Kalle was pretty angry about that, on my behalf. He had words with Derrick, and while I'll never know what he said because he refuses to tell me, Derrick did end up moving to Newfoundland a few months later.

I've had my heart broken, but not by Kalle. They weren't Kalle; we didn't have the connection or the history, and I didn't lose a friendship like his. If Kalle and I... if it doesn't work, then I have so much to lose, and the thought terrifies me more than any thunderstorm.

Can you handle this?

I don't have a choice now because we crossed a line last night—

Technically, early this morning, and it was several lines—

And there's no way I'm going back to holding hands.

But still, Kalle is going to be king, which means the woman he marries will be queen. And he's already asked me. If next time I see him things go as well as I think they will, I doubt that will be the last time he asks the question.

Kalle says he wants me to be queen, and if I want him, that may be a possibility.

And it's something I can't begin to process.

When I get into town, I head straight for Coffee for the Sole, only to find almost every person in town seems to have the same idea. The line up is out the door and as I take my spot I'm greeted with questions about the king.

It's like they know I just came from the castle.

It takes time for me to finally get inside and have my order taken. I see that it's all hands-on deck this morning.

Including Daphne Luute.

"Morning, Edie." Silas, the owner of Coffee for the Sole, and the best barista in the world, already looks ragged this morning. "Usual?"

"For me," I tell him. "But do you know what Odin and Camille like?" I glance at Daphne who drops her gaze.

"Are they already back? That was quick—the king." He nods. "They came back because of the king. Are you sure he's okay?"

"There will be more news today, but I think so."

Daphne moves away, adding sweetener and a pump of espresso to the coffee she's making.

"I had to hire her back," Silas says in a low voice. "But it's only for the summer."

"Poor kid." I watch Daphne and see that some of the light has disappeared from her and there's a new slump of her shoulders. "You can't pick who you fall in love with."

Silas raises his eyebrows. "That's very forgiving of you. Do you know if the castle feels the same way?"

"They will eventually. And with what the king just went through last night, making the life of one girl miserable won't be a priority. It shouldn't be anyway."

"You're right." Silas hands me a tray with three coffees. "On the house today."

"Then so is your next beer," I tell Silas to have a good day and nod to Daphne as I leave. There are many more questions before I can make my way to the door.

The air is crisp and cool, with a hint of warmth from the sun.

It's going to be a beautiful day.

Battle Harbour deserves it.

I make a quick stop in my apartment, then check the bar before I head to the airport to pick up Odin and Camille. Dillon wanted to stay with Kalle, so I said I would get them.

I'm just not sure what to tell them when they ask why *I'm* doing pickup for the royal family.

I watch the private plane taxi to a stop and try to think of an explanation that doesn't involve me giving too much information about what went on last night with me and Kalle. Even though the way I smile when I think of him is going to give it all away.

It doesn't take long for Odin and Camille to appear on the steps, and I wave. "Edie!" Odin exclaims as they cross the tarmac to my car. The surprise is evident in his voice. "Is Kalle—"

"He's busy at the castle." Or asleep, I honestly don't know. "I offered to pick you up because everyone is... a little busy."

"I'm sure." Odin loads the suitcases into my trunk and one in the backseat because I have a compact car. "Have you seen him? Heard anything else?" he demands as Camille gives me a quick hug hello.

"Duncan stayed at the hospital last night and there's been no word that I know of," I report as we get into the car, Odin in the front with me. "I think that's a good thing."

"I wish I'd been here," he frets.

I meet Camille's gaze in the rearview mirror as I pull away from the airport. "I don't think you could have done much," I tell him carefully.

"That's what I told him," Camille explodes from the backseat.

"I hate leaving all this to them. I'm the one who steps up, the face of the castle because no one else wants to."

"Odin?" Camille leans forward. "Are you changing your mind about abdicating?"

I suck in my breath. If that's true—if it's even possible—Kalle will be...

"They're doing fine," I say in a firm voice. "Spencer delegated and everyone has their roles and is preparing to step up. There's a press conference this afternoon, the statement went out..." I turn to Odin. "They're doing great, all things considered."

"Kalle?"

"Kalle," I reassure him and Odin hisses in relief. I can only imagine the guilt and worry he's gone through trying to get home as quickly as he can, not knowing what will be waiting for him when he gets here. "Everything is under control."

34

Kalle

I FEEL A BIT out of control. I wish Edie was here.

She's gone when I wake up and for a moment, I wonder if it was all a dream.

And then I know it's not because she left my T-shirt on the bed and it smells of her.

By the time I make it out of my room, Odin is back. And I'm not surprised when I find out it was Edie who picked him and Camille up at the airport, immediately dropping them off at the hospital to see Dad.

Dillon brought them back to the castle just in time for a late breakfast.

"I don't remember the last time we had breakfast together," Gunnar muses as he stabs sausages with his fork. The kitchen staff has set up a buffet for us in the dining room—eggs, bacon and sausages, toast with three different kinds of jam, and a stack of pancakes that quickly disappears thanks to Bo and Camille.

"I was thinking the same thing," Odin says, taking a seat beside me.

"I feel like I'm in some sort of regency romance with the set-up." Stella waves at the sideboard with the silver chafing dishes, the tea service at the end. "Like this is a party at the country home. Not a party, obviously, because of the king…"

"Your dad would fit right in," Bo says, taking pity on her. "With all those novels he's been on the cover of, he'd think it was another photo shoot."

"I think he should do more modelling." Camille grins at Stella. "I think the books are better when he's on the cover."

Odin raises an eyebrow. "I wasn't aware that you've read his books."

"I'm getting through them, thanks to Stella." Camille lifts her cup to Stella.

"That was good of Edie to come and get us," Odin says to me as Camille begins to talk books with Stella.

"When did she leave last night?" Lyra asks with a smirk, like she knows it was daylight when Edie made her escape.

"She crashed here," I admit. "I wasn't letting her drive down the hill in the storm."

"Isn't it convenient that it stopped storming, or we could be asking her all this," Lyra says slyly.

"Edie? What am I missing?" Camille demands. "Are you finally getting out of the friend zone?"

It feels like nothing is wrong, like Dad isn't lying in the hospital. It also feels like we're all doing everything we can not to mention what's going on. I may be relieved that Dad is out of the woods, but things need to be mentioned because things need to happen.

"Is Duncan still at the hospital?" I ask Spencer.

"Kalle really doesn't like talking about his personal life, does he?" Gunnar whispers to Camille and Stella.

I don't, but if I ease back into thinking about Edie, I'll be useless today. Plus, I'm looking at it like a reward—if I get all the king stuff done today, I can focus on Edie tonight.

She deserves my full attention.

"He is." Spencer sets his tablet on the table. "He'll stay there until one of us relieves him."

"Dad is going to hate being waited on hand and foot." Odin frowns.

"He already does. Apparently there was an issue with one of the nurses showing a bit too much respect when she started her shift and found out the king was there. Dropped a perfect curtsy right there in the hall." Spencer grins. "Your dad is already demanding to be sent home if people are going to start bowing to him."

"And he's been awake for how long?" I ask.

"About two hours," Odin puts in. "He was pretty groggy when we stopped by so we left so he could go back to sleep. I'll head back in as soon as we get settled to relieve Duncan."

"I can do that," Gunnar says.

"Let's check schedules to see who has what going on and get someone to the hospital to take over from Duncan," I say. "He's going to need some sleep."

There's a flurry of chatter while we set up who will head to the hospital and who will take over some of Dad's duties. I keep things on track, and the conversation off my personal life, and when we finish eating, Gunnar and Stella set out.

When the room empties, I stay at the table for an extra minute of quiet because I suspect I'm going to need it.

Odin pops his head back in as I finish my coffee. "Too bad you had to cut your trip short," I say as he snags the last piece of bacon on the platter.

"I'm sorry I wasn't here last night."

"Nothing you could have done." This is the first time I've been alone with my brother since he got married—and since he told the world he was abdicating. It's a little awkward.

It was a good wedding; originally, Odin and Camille had been an arranged marriage. Camille needed a husband to take over as prefect for her country of Saint Pierre, and Odin had been humiliated on reality TV, sent home before he had a chance to do much but announce to all that Camille has been *the-one-that-got-away*. Telling the world he was engaged to be married to her seemed to settle his embarrassment, plus he got the bonus of falling in love with her.

And Camille loves him. They pushed their wedding off a few months to have the time to get to know each other, and it really helped.

It's good to know the person you're going to marry.

I know Edie so well, so that's got to be a plus.

Odin must feel the awkwardness, because he doesn't waste any time. "I'm sorry I didn't tell you." He's always been truthful and real, and I hear the sincerity in his voice.

I shrug. "You don't owe me an apology. It's your life."

"But it affects your life. If anything happens to you..."

"I was surprised," I admit. "I thought you would have said something to me first."

"It was a last-minute decision." Odin sits down beside me, an earnest expression on his face. "Camille and I had talked about it because Lord Arnaud will be retiring due to health reasons and Camille really wanted to move back. And I want to help her."

"She's your wife."

"Yes, but..." He trails off and I know what he's not saying.

"And you'll get a country to run," I finish for him.

He gives a rueful shrug. "That sounds bad when you say it that way. But it's true. And I never really expected to take over here."

"Just thought you might."

He shakes his head. "Not really. When we found out about Daulton going to the press about Camille's father and how we started out as an arranged marriage, I knew Gunnar bringing over Fenella for a distraction wouldn't be enough. I went to Dad before I even talked about it with Camille—I told her about ten minutes before I announced it. I needed to do something big and I thought that might work."

"It did. You did the right thing."

"I wish I'd talked to you first."

"No, you don't, because you were afraid I'd convince you not to do it."

Odin grimaces. "You're not that good at persuading, you know."

"Really?" I lean forward. "Who convinced who to go up on the greenhouse roof?" I thrust a thumb into my chest.

"And Gunny fell off and ruined it for all of us." Odin grins.

I laugh. I love my brothers because they are my brothers, but I always like them as my friends. "Are you happy?" I ask and Odin's grin widens.

"I am. Married life is pretty good so far."

"Married life, or being married to Camille?"

"Well, Camille." He drops his head, suddenly shy.

How do you know? I really want to ask how Odin knew it would work with Camille. What gave him the courage to make such a commitment?

But I don't ask him any of that, because while Odin is married, I'm still the big brother and I'm not about to admit I don't know everything.

I've got an image to protect.

"It was good seeing Edie this morning, under the circumstances," Odin continues. "Camille really likes her."

"So do I."

Odin studies me, his expression showing a lack of emotion that I wish I could copy. "Is she on board?"

"I have no idea. I hope so."

"It's a big step," he says. "It's better to figure the personal stuff out now."

"That's what Dad said."

"Dad." Odin toys with a fork. "I really wish I'd been here. If things hadn't gone well—"

"No sense thinking about that." I get to my feet, towering over Odin still seated. "And there's no sense to apologize to me. I want you happy, little brother."

Odin stands, only a half inch or so shorter than me. "Not so little."

I slap him on the shoulder. "We should get Gunny in here then,"

Odin laughs and then he hugs me. Hard.

I let him because I could use the hug too.

35

Edie

AFTER I DROP OFF Odin and Camille at the hospital, I head home to crash for a few hours. Then it's time to open the bar.

I don't expect to see Kalle much today. From what they talked about last night, he'll be doing royal duties for the next few days while King Magnus recovers.

And he will recover.

When I unlock the door at one o'clock, I have a feeling that the rush of the last few days will ease off as people will take advantage of the post-storm summer day.

Days like this are why I told Kalle we need to have a patio.

But it will be nice to have a few minutes by myself. I'll be able to send out the beer and food orders, give Tyler a lesson on bookkeeping, and listen to Bethie tell me about the new guy she's dating.

But when I switch on one of the televisions, all of that is forgotten.

Kalle is on TV.

"...the family would like to thank all the doctors, and especially the nurses who watched over Dad, checked in with him hourly, and had to endure his attempts at humour while coming out of anesthesia," Kalle says.

I give a surprised laugh. Kalle—looking very good in a dark-coloured suit and purple tie—stands outside Battle Harbour General Hospital facing down a scrum of reporters.

This must be his worst nightmare but he's making a joke? Kalle is *smiling*, standing tall without gripping the podium. His beard has been freshly trimmed and something has been done with his hair. Styled with product, perhaps, done by someone who knows what they're doing, so not Kalle.

He looks... *hot.* So attractive that my knees weaken enough for me to need to climb onto a stool while I watch, mouth hanging open. *Sexy.* The reporters are eating up this onslaught of charm Kalle is eking out.

But it's more than that. Kalle looks...

"Like a king," I whisper.

A bubble of pride bursts and I can't stop smiling. Laughing. He can do this.

He takes questions, and it's not as smooth and polished as King Magnus, but Spencer is right beside him to bolster with information or the right word when Kalle stumbles. But it's the smile he wears that will win the country over, the ease at which he stands taking leadership.

Kalle is showing the world that he's going to be king one day, and he'll be okay in the role.

I always knew he had it in him. And now everyone will too.

36

Kalle

I TAKE A COUPLE of shaky breaths after the press conference is over and I've escaped into the hospital to see Dad.

Doctors and nurses smile and nod, keeping their distance as they watch me perform like I know what I'm doing. Those who don't work there take any opportunity to get close to me. I pose for a few pictures and wave goodbye to those in the waiting room as I duck around an older woman with a nasty cough. I jump into the elevator, holding out my hands as Chase applies sanitizer.

"That went better than I thought," I say to Spencer.

"Dude." Spencer gives me a thump on the shoulder, happiness and, yes, relief written over his face. "You did great. Like you've been doing that for years."

My first press conference was at thirty-two. Odin has been doing that for years, and even Gunnar knows how to finagle a group of crusty reporters wherever country he's in, but I've never had the need to talk to the press.

Or wanted to.

That was first on the list that Duncan and Spencer gave me this morning. Press conference, quick visit with Dad, look at the pier, talk to people at the docks to see how they fared with the storm. Be seen around town. Check out any damage. Back to the castle for a meeting with the Canadian Minister of Foreign Affairs—Duncan has yet to brief me on what that's about, but at least I know Seamus O'Regan so it won't be too bad. Then there's some dinner tonight in St. Johns that I have to take the plane for, but I can do that.

I won't get any time to see Edie.

My first instinct was to bring her along for all of this, but I knew even before I suggested it that it wouldn't work. Edie has her own responsibilities—running the bar. If I have to take over for Dad, then she's going to have to manage everything on her own. She's more than capable, but only if I let her do it. I can't drag her away for the day, as much as I want to.

And I really want to, because last night...

Last night was amazing.

Or this morning, rather. I can still feel the softness of her skin, how her lips moved under mine when we kissed.

Sixteen years of waiting and the reality more than made up for it.

Or maybe not. I would have rather been kissing her for all this time.

"What's going on?" Spencer demands. I shake my head. "You just talked to a bunch of reporters that, in the past, haven't been your biggest fans. And you look *happy* about it."

"I'm not happy about it." But then I glance at myself in the reflection in the elevator, and immediately frown. My lips had been curved in what can be called a smile, my forehead wasn't creased in my usual scowl...

I relax and realize it can be said that, yes, I look happy.

"Then why—ah." Spencer's expression transforms into understanding. "Edie?"

I shrug but can't hide the smile. "We might try... you know. Not friends."

"More than friends," Spencer says. "That's great. But Kalle, don't try. Make it happen."

Make it happen. The words echo as I follow him out of the elevator. I'm going to make it happen.

When we get to Dad's room, I can't believe how much tension rolls off me. Shoulders slump, breath out in a whoosh. I have to stop myself from rushing to the bed.

I knew he was going to be okay, but after seeing him go down like that at dinner, it's been hard to really believe it.

Still, he looks pale and a little smaller in the brand-new pyjamas. Mrs. Theissen had to order him three new pairs because Dad had been sleeping in old T-shirts and boxers for so long, he didn't have any proper pyjamas suitable for hospital rooms.

"Hey." Gripping his shoulder, I lean down and rest my forehead against the top of his head. As I pull away, Dad reaches up to grab the back of my head, and I stay put for a long moment, breathing in Dad smell. He smells a little too much like a hospital for my liking, but still—Dad.

He's going to be okay.

"You good?" Dad asks. "Looked pretty fine at that press conference." Pride shines in his eyes and despite the relief that leaves me a bit shaky, I puff up a little.

"I should be asking you that." Dillon pushes a chair closer to the bed before heading to stand outside the door with Chase.

Spencer presses Dad's hand and tells him he'll give the update when I'm done, then disappears as well.

"What good is an appendix anyway?" Dad grouses good-naturedly. "What's the point of humans having them if they don't do anything and there's a chance they will blow up?"

"That's something you can talk to your doctor about." I settle in the chair beside the bed. For the first time since he dropped to his knees in the dining room, I breathe a little easier.

He's not going to die.

Well, he will someday since even the great king of Laandia won't be able to charm his way into immortality.

"The doctors indulge me, but they don't have the time to answer all my questions," Dad grumbles.

"Or the energy?" I suggest and he chuckles.

"I know I'm high maintenance, but it's not a fun place to be. But one of the nurses is pretty amazing. And amazingly pretty." His eyes twinkle and I sit up straight.

"Seriously? Do you—?" But I'm interrupted as Bo walks in, looking more rested than I do. "Dad's interested in one of the nurses," I tell him.

Bo seems to contemplate that with his usual stoicism and nods slowly.

"I said she was pretty," Dad protests. "That's it."

"You twinkled," I point out. "I haven't seen you twinkle in…"

"In a long time," he finishes a little sadly. "But that's not what I called you both in to talk about."

"Both of us?"

"Before I call in the rest of the calvary. Gunny and Lyra," he adds at my expression of confusion. "I want to check some things with you first."

"About the line of succession," Bo says. Bo, who is now the second in line to the throne. I've never missed Odin more.

"Shoot," I tell Dad, not wanting to give words to the apprehension that's begun right in my gut.

"Do you want to be king?"

He asks without warning, without preamble. He always cuts to the chase with me, because that's how I do things too.

For once, I'd like the preamble.

He raises a hand still attached to tubes and machines and there's that pang of fear and realization that my father is not invincible. "We'll set aside the probability that you succeeding me means I'm dead, because we don't need emotion clouding things. I should have called Duncan and Spencer in for this," he muses.

"Let's just figure this out between us first," Bo says in his low voice.

"What're your thoughts?"

"Why are you asking?" I counter.

Dad heaves a breath. "Your uncle brought this up before he left. You know he was almost king," he says to Bo.

Bo nods. "I know there was talk when you were in the band. But it was your position. There was no almost with that."

Laandia is not a normal monarchy. The country wasn't taken by force, and as far as I know, we're the only monarchy who was given their throne rather than won it and proclaimed themselves king or queen.

If there are others, Bo would know.

"Some think differently. You know my father, Euan, was the second son of Leif, the first king of Laandia. His brother Bronn wanted nothing to do with being the king. He was twenty-five when he abdicated and left for Northern Canada. No idea what happened to him. He could be frozen solid in a block of ice for all I know."

"He died," Bo speaks up. "He ended up in Yellowknife for a time. Had a wife, a couple of kids. They're in Salmon Arm, British Columbia."

"Huh."

"I looked for him," Bo admits. "He wasn't that hard to track."

"I'm glad you did that. I've always wondered. These kids—"

"Probably have no idea their father should have been the king of Laandia," I say drily. And we should keep it like that because I can't imagine what it would be like if someone waltzed into my life to tell me I had a spot in the line of succession. Or that, in another reality, would have been king.

It was bad enough knowing all my life where my future lay. I had enough time to process.

But have I really? It seems to me that I've argued against the fact more than I've processed.

"I don't think he should have been king." Dad gives his head a firm shake. "From what I've heard, Bronn was brave but had a temper."

"Kings shouldn't have a temper?" I glance at Bo, who smiles and drops his head. "That rules both of us out then."

"Tempers are a sign of passion, but you need to learn to think before you act, which both of you are capable of. Bronn was not. No matter now, but I am glad he didn't end up frozen in an ice burg."

"He might be," Bo says. "I never found out how he died."

Dad grunts. "See what you can find out, will you? So we're back to the king of Laandia who wasn't supposed to be king. Second sons don't normally become king."

"King George of England," Bo supplies. "Henry the VIII, just to name two."

"I keep forgetting you're the brain of the family," Dad says admiringly.

"Just in history."

I've never been good at academics. The best part of school for me was gym class.

I remember Dante pointing out my low grades to Mathias once as an example of what not to do. But this time, instead of the surge of anger any of those memories bring about, I let it float away because this isn't the time to think about reasons why I shouldn't be king.

"Do you think Bo should be king?" I blurt out.

"No." Bo's quick response is definite.

"Bo would make a fine king, as would you. But neither of you seem very inclined."

"Is this when you give the Dune speech again?"

"No, but I hope my little health scare will give you some clarity. And my conversation with your uncle could give you an option. My father called me back from touring to ask if I could see myself being the king. I said yes, because I didn't want to disappoint him, and yes, the thought of myself with a crown was enjoyable. But when push came to shove, and my father had a heart attack that ended his life, I changed my mind. It might have been grief or fear, but just before I was crowned king, I ran."

I glance at Bo. Even with his history studies, I don't think he knows that. And Dad conveniently left out that part when we talked the other day.

"Your uncle Dante was ready to step up," Dad continues, "and he wanted to be king. Like, really wanted it. Unlike me, who let my emotions cloud my sense of duty. It was Duncan who got me back on track."

"Course he did," I mutter because Duncan has always been there for this family. And this country as well.

"Yeah, well, Dunc pointed out that I had given my word to the king and the country that I would be next. He also told me I'd be a great king, which is neither here nor there."

"I don't get the point of this," I cut in. "It's a nice story, but it's not helping."

"The point is that *I* gave my word. Not you. I answered the call to this duty, but you don't have to." His blue eyes, shadowed and tired meet mine with an intensity that pricks my skin.

"Are you saying I should step down and let Bo be next?"

"No," Bo says quickly.

"That is an option," Dad concedes. "And if Bo doesn't want it, I'll talk to Gunnar and then...Lyra."

We exhale in unison.

"Or I could appoint your uncle to be my successor, and his children after that."

"What?" Mathias in a crown? The evilness of my uncle, his cruelty and manipulation—no. No way.

"It's what he brought up at dinner, Dad continues, unaware of what is going on in my mind. "He'd still like the job, and Mathias was positively salivating at the thought of it." Dad gives a half-smile but I see the worry in his eyes. "I wasn't planning on going anywhere soon, but this little visit does bring up some worries about who is next in the line of succession. Like I said, this has never been a regular monarchy. We do things differently here."

"So what you're saying, is that if I decide I really don't want to be king, you can give it to Dante so Bo and the others don't have to deal with it?"

"It gives you an option. Something to think about."

"I don't have to think about it," I tell him.

37

Edie

I DON'T SEE KALLE for the next two days.

And I might worry that Saturday night had been too much for him. Or that he was having second thoughts about us, maybe that the emotions of the night had caused him to...

We kissed. And more. And now I haven't seen him. He hadn't even been awake when I left the castle.

I might worry—if it weren't for the texts. The constant, never-ending text string that tells me more about what Kalle is thinking than words coming out of his mouth ever could.

It's as if we're back in the nineteen hundreds and he's courting me long distance by letters.

So many texts. I reread them before I left for the day, and his observations of what his father does all day made me smile. And laugh. And it fills my heart that Kalle seems content.

He says it's because of me. I may not believe it but it's nice to hear.

I have Wednesday off; Kalle is still doing castle stuff, but I leave Leah in charge during the day and Tyler tonight, with Bethie helping out.

It's like I'm playing hooky and left the kids at home alone. I feel guilty and a little worried, but I've been working non-stop, and there have been some late hours in the last week.

I need a break, and Kalle agreed. It was him—via text—who organized Leah and Tyler to step up for me.

As much as we've texted in the last two days, Kalle hasn't said anything about the future. No talk about whether he's still game to become the next king of Laandia—or about us.

He's made absolutely no mention of the fact he asked me to marry him.

Kind of asked.

And I have no desire to bring it up because my head is swimming at the thought.

I sleep late on Wednesday, curled up with Ernie in bed. It's not often I get a lazy morning, and I take full advantage. But when I finally get up, I head to my parents', avoiding the bar like the plague, because if I go in, I'll be stuck there for the day.

I find my father in his garden. He has several—his vegetable garden is half the size of a farmer's field, with neat rows of corn and peas, beans and broccoli as well as cucumbers, squash, and pumpkins which take up the most room. Tall sunflowers separate the garden from the lawn.

As well as the vegetables, Dad has an herb garden, one for roses, and a patch in the shade with different hostas spreading out in circles. But my favourite is his flower garden. Clumps of tall echinacea mixed with black-eyed Susans and daisies, foxgloves in the early summer blend into lilies and colourful phlox rounds out the season.

When I'm at the bar and dealing with drunks more obnoxious than usual, I think of the flower garden and it makes me happy.

It's good that they have enough property. The farmhouse sits on fifty acres outside Battle Harbour, but Dad has always rented out the fields since he never had time to farm it. And now, being retired and on oxygen, my mother won't let him.

He has enough to do with his gardens.

I find him among the vegetables attacking weeds with the hoe. The scar tissue eroding his lungs makes it difficult for him to bend over, so he piles the crabgrass and dandelions into a heap to pick up later.

It's like I've forgotten how nice the sun can be in the summer. After days of rain, it feels amazing to be outside, even with the cool breeze coming in from the ocean.

Dad sees me approaching and leans on his hoe as I walk up. "Any word on the king?" he calls.

I shake my head and give him a hug. "But it's good. He went home yesterday and he'll make a full recovery."

"That's what the news says but what is the family saying?" I've never been sure what my father misses the most about no longer working at the castle—spending all the time in the gardens or having a direct line to the goings-on of the family.

He's always been more of a royal family watcher than even my mother.

"They're saying the same thing," I reassure him. "He's going to be okay. Apparently, he's not fond of the appendix though."

"Good to hear. And I'm sure Kalle thinks so too."

"They all do."

Dad attacks a dandelion with the corner of his hoe. "He knows the people would rally around him when the time comes, doesn't he?"

Does he? I have no idea because, like everything else important, he won't talk about it.

He likes to talk about me; what he'd like to do if we had time, how exactly he'd like to kiss me—

He talks about that quite a lot.

"I think he's figuring that out," I manage. "I hope."

"How are you and Mathias making out?" Dad asks, surprising me. Not only because he's never asked anything about any of the men I've dated, but because I've forgotten to tell my parents that nothing will be happening with Mathias. Not that I make a point to discuss my dating life with my family, but Mathias being part of the royal family made it a little different.

I also can't believe my sisters didn't say anything. The family grapevine works faster than 5G internet.

"We're not," I tell him.

Dad looks up with a relieved smile. "Glad to hear it. I remember him as a little kid. Poisonous, him and his brother both. His father was worse than both of them."

"I figured that out, but it might have been nice to have the inside scoop."

"You're a smart girl," he says. "Besides, I doubt you would have listened to me."

"I would have listened."

"No, you wouldn't have. And I don't blame you, since I'm only your father."

"I would have listened," I repeat with a laugh.

"I seem to recall trying to convince you that you deserve a good man."

"A man like Mathias?"

"No, I said a good man. You deserve any man you want." He looks at me steadily. "Even if he's a member of Magnus's family."

"I know I do," I say automatically, unsure what he's getting at. And feeling strange talking about *what ifs* when there's a really good chance the *what if* is reality.

"I don't know that you do." He gazes at the sky for a moment like he's collecting his thoughts. "We've got a fine spot here, me and your mother. It's no castle, but it's ours and it's home. And I think I might have tried to convince you that it wasn't enough if you were planning on moving on into the castle."

"You never did. And I never planned on moving into the castle."

"See, that's the problem. You should have been planning on that from the get-go. Because you, Edie, you are castle material. You were made to live there and rule there, and if you ask me, it's time Prince Kalle pulls his head out of his—"

"I'm really glad you feel that way," I say quickly, because I see the truck in the distance, coming up the road with plumes of dust in its wake.

There are a lot of black pickup trucks in Battle Harbour but only one who would drive like that up the road to my family's home.

Dad gives me a quizzical look. "Care to share anything with your old man?"

"Not... right... yet," I tell him slowly. As much as I want to see Kalle, it's the *why* he's here that is causing me concern.

Dad and I watch the truck pull up at the house and Kalle hops out. I see Dillon's bald head in the front seat, and after a quick conversation, he stays in the car.

My stomach flips and flops as Kalle strides up, as confident as he used to saunter up to the plate with a baseball bat on his shoulder, ready to hit a base-clearing double. I bite my lip to stop the smile from taking over my face.

I can't believe how much I've missed him.

I see him every day, all day. And when I don't see him, we talk or text.

Which is what we've been doing the last two days, but now that he's here in front of me, I realize how much I've missed the little things. The teasing. The pulling of my ponytail. Standing close enough to me so that I can breathe in his Kalle scent.

I like the Kalle scent.

I like just about everything about Kalle.

I even like that I'm in love with him.

And then Kalle walks right up to me standing among the peas and the pumpkin vines; he strokes long fingers and a big palm onto my cheek and leans down and kisses me right in front of my father.

And not just a little peck. His mouth on mine, the warm sun beating down, and the sound of birds... his lips moving in a way that makes me almost forget my father is standing there.

Almost.

Dad clears his throat just to make sure we're still aware. "Did I miss something?" he asks.

38

Kalle

I'VE ALWAYS LIKED BOB England. But having him standing there after I laid one on his daughter turns me into that twelve-year-old kid who rode his bike across a wet lawn, making skids and ruts in the grass that took the rest of the spring to fix.

"Sorry about that," I stammer after I pull back from Edie. It's only the second time I've kissed her—I consider the other night one big kiss—and I end the impromptu make-out session by giving myself a thorough kick for not getting to it sooner.

"For kissing my girl?" Bob asks. "It's not something I usually enjoy seeing, but if you explain this new development for me, I might make an exception."

I realize I'm holding Edie's hand when she gives it a squeeze. Her brown eyes are shiny, like stirring butter into melted milk chocolate.

"I'm trying to make her see that I'm a good man," I manage.

"Didn't think you need to use your tongue for that," Bob mutters and my face flames red.

Edie laughs. She gives a big belly laugh and drops my hand to give her father a hug. "We're going to try, Dad. See if we can be more than friends."

"Well, it's about time," Bob says. "Now, do me a solid and run over there and get my basket and clean up those weeds for me, would you?"

It takes a moment for me to realize he's speaking to me. But when I do, the future king of Laandia picks up the discarded weeds in the garden without a word of complaint.

I skipped out of an afternoon meeting to come here because I needed to see her. Two days was two days too long—it's like I'm an addict and I need a fix. My Edie fix.

I had no idea that I was already addicted.

Duncan said he'd take the meeting for me—something about the Sea Queen pageant at Christmas, which I thought could wait, but Duncan assured me the town takes such things very seriously. And some of the pressure was off me because Dad came home this morning.

We had thought he'd be home tomorrow, but Etienne led a security team that involved paramedics and Battle Harbour's finest back to the castle after breakfast. It was so good to see Dad up and about, even though Mrs. Theissen insisted on him retiring to his bedroom for a nap.

But he was up when I left and told me to bring Edie for dinner tonight.

So that's why I'm here—to invite my girl to family dinner at the castle.

It's been a while since I referred to a woman as my girlfriend. As a rule, I don't like the term because I always thought it gave the women I dated more of a sense of control over me.

That was before Edie.

Now I kiss my girlfriend in front of her father and help him in the garden before he leads us to the house to get a bite to eat.

Mrs. England plays it cool, but Edie points out in a whisper how her hands are shaking as she makes us grilled cheese sandwiches for lunch.

I take my sandwich with a glass of milk.

I know my family is privileged and influential. If Lyra wants something, she goes and gets it. I bought a bar without thinking twice about the price. Gunnar sponsored his own race car once to be able to get into a race. We are well-off, and that's not even considering the family jewels.

I've grown up knowing this, but I've always felt like we are a family. I know royals with dysfunctional relationships that would rival the ones on Shameless. But sitting with Edie at the kitchen table while her mother chats with us as she makes us lunch, I think we might have missed a bit of the family-ing of being a family.

I've known Edie's parents most of my life, but I've never sat down and had a conversation with them as a man who is dating their daughter, rather than a prince of Laandia.

It's nice.

After we eat, Bob shows me his gardens, pointing out each rose. And when we get to the striking yellow rose with the red edges, he tells me it's called Double Happiness and it was my mother's favourite.

He clips a flower, the bloom tucked in like a shy kid meeting someone new, and hands it to me.

There's still a lump in my throat when we drive away.

"Where are we going?" Edie wants to know. She's holding the rose for me, lightly brushing a finger over the soft petals.

"I wanted this to be our date day, but there's not enough time to do everything I planned," I tell her. I made Chase and Dillon drive Edie's car back into town so she could ride with me.

"What did you have planned?" She has a bemused smile on her face, just another smile that makes me want to kiss her.

"I wanted to spend some time with your parents, and we got to do that," I say, tapping my fingers along with the music Edie selected from her phone. I may not always appreciate her choices, but I've always let her play deejay and I'm not about to stop now. "I thought I'd take you to the curling club and see about renting some ice time, but the storm knocked down a tree and it went through one of the windows, so they're not letting anyone in there until it's fixed."

"You've been planning this for a while?"

"I had a meeting with the deputy mayor yesterday. It was pretty boring."

She laughs. "You planned a date while you were meeting with the mayor?"

"Deputy," I correct. "And why not? Dad says he tunes out a lot. His assistant is pretty amazing, and Duncan was there too. I doubt I would be able to do much without having a babysitter."

"Dunc's a pretty cool babysitter."

"That he is."

Edie turns to look out the window, her hand still resting on mine. "So you wanted to take me curling?"

The way she asks makes me reconsider. "I thought it would be fun."

"Maybe for you," she mutters under her breath.

"I heard that. No curling then."

"I don't need a big deal made over me," Edie protests.

I pick up her hand and press my lips to her knuckles. "Maybe I want to."

She lets out a soft sigh and I kiss her fingers again. "Is it supposed to be like this?"

"Like what?" Reluctantly, I let go of her hand and grip the steering wheel because there is a tree brought down by the storm and the branches lie on the road.

I'm not sure if I'm supposed to do something about that.

I've always had a sense of responsibility for the citizens of Laandia, but it's ramped up since Dad was in the hospital. Now, it's all I can think about—them and Edie.

I want to make things better for them. I want to make sure they're happy and content in my country.

My country.

My girl.

My girl, who is currently talking, so I need to pay attention. No tuning out with her, except if it's during one of those reality shows she watches.

"It's so easy," Edie says. "This feels like we've been together forever."

"We've been friends for a long time," I point out. "It's not much different. Only I get to kiss you whenever I want now."

"Technically, you could have been kissing me for a long time."

"*You* could have been kissing *me*."

But Edie shakes her head. "I'm not sure if I would have been brave enough to say anything. And even if I did, I honestly don't know if we'd still be together."

"Why?"

"Because you're in a very different headspace now."

She's right, but then again, she usually is. I can feel the change in me—my well of anger seems to have slipped away.

It feels good.

"You think you know me so well," I scoff.

"I think we established that I do know you very well." She smiles at me, eyes shining. "But I have to admit, I didn't see this coming. You got me there."

"Surprises are a good thing."

"Most of the time."

"All of the time with me." And then I take her hand again and hold tight.

This all feels good.

39

Edie

S O THIS IS WHAT it's like to date Prince Kalle.

Countless other women have gotten to experience it and finally, it's my turn.

I already know I'm not going to want to let anyone else have a chance at this. Because this is comfortable. Sweet. Sexy. Outside the grumbly bear mode, Kalle is warm and funny; he doesn't say much but he makes me laugh.

It's a lot like hanging out with my friend Kalle.

Only now I can touch him whenever I like. I can thread my fingers through his, pat his backside when there's no one looking. When he pulls me under his arm, I turn into his chest and kiss his shoulder, or as close to it as I can reach.

Boyfriend Kalle likes to touch me as much as possible. I don't mind one bit.

We stop at the high school where there is a baseball practice going on. I knew Kalle helped out with the school team, but I had no idea he acted as a mentor to some of the players.

Riley, in grade ten, has to show him the split-fingered fastball he mastered. Kalle thinks it was upward of eighty miles an hour, and tells him to keep working on his speed and he'll get there.

He'll get to the major leagues, Kalle tells me under his breath. He's convinced this kid will be the fourth Laandian to make it to the big leagues.

Then there's Conor, who plays centre field and can hit well past the fences, and David who sits on the bench for most of the game but is keen and so determined to get better. Amy, the only girl on the team. At six feet, she can run like the wind and lay down the most perfect bunt Kalle has ever seen.

He tells her that—twice—and I think she might drop to the ground in hero worship.

And then there's Caleb, his dark hair cut in the mohawk fade that Kalle sported before it grew out, playing second base with a number eleven on his shirt, same as Kalle wore. I know Kalle sees himself in the sixteen-year-old.

I remember sixteen-year-old Kalle, and I see him in Caleb too.

After the practice, Kalle hangs out with the kids for a bit and then we take off. I expect him to stop at the bar to check things, but he drives straight through town without stopping.

"Where are we going?" I finally ask.

"Castle. Dad thinks he's ready for dinner," Kalle says casually, but everything inside me snaps to attention.

"Family dinner?"

He glances over with surprise because even I can hear that my voice has a touch of hysteria in it. "Everyone's home, so he wants us together."

"But I'm not—"

"What aren't you?" Kalle interrupts. "I don't know what you're not. Welcome? Expected? Allowed to come? You're all of those."

"I can't go wearing this," I protest, plucking at the fabric of my T-shirt. There's no way I can dine with King Magnus in jeans and a T-shirt that I've worn helping my father in his garden.

"My father will probably still be in his pyjamas. You can wear whatever you want."

King Magnus in pajamas... I'm not ready for that.

I'm not ready for this.

I've been in a dream world today, pretending Kalle is just Kalle and we're just friends becoming lovers.

I'm not thinking about the future. About what will happen if this works.

And I think it's going to work. Unless, of course, I continue with this freakout, this spiral of fears, of doubts, of thinking that I'm only—

"Edie?"

I look over at Kalle, but I'm not focusing because I'm stuck on this image of *me* in my pyjamas with the king and the rest of the family in beautiful clothes and jewelry *laughing* at me.

"Edie. Stop."

"Stop what?" I ask breathlessly. "I'm not doing anything."

"Stop whatever is going on in your head. I can see it, because I know you pretty well, too."

"I'm not... This is a bad—"

"It's not a bad idea. It's a great idea, and something I should have done years ago. You're coming to dinner with my family, and you should have been doing that for a long time now. I'm trying to make up for lost time."

"By throwing this at me at the last minute. We're almost there..."

We go around the bend and I see the castle. Even though I was only here a few days ago, and I've driven this road countless times, today, my breath catches like the first time I saw it as a little girl.

Four stories of not-quite-white stone that shines like the moon in the dark and has a golden glow when the setting sun hits it. It's a fairytale castle come to life with turrets and towers and even a portcullis, always raised in welcome. There are dungeons and secret passages, and behind, overlooking the ocean at the bottom of the cliff, are the gardens that my father took such good care of.

He first brought me here when I was five. Now all these years later, I'm arriving with Kalle. Not as a friend Kalle, but *Kalle*. My Kalle.

"You done freaking out now?" Kalle asks as we round another curve and the castle disappears from sight.

"Maybe."

"So, no."

"You don't understand, because this is where you live," I protest.

"You're right. I live in a castle and I'm pretty lucky about that. But this is where my family lives. You're coming for dinner with my family, just like I ate lunch with your mom and dad."

"She made grilled cheeses," I mutter.

"They were pretty good. And now you're going to have burgers with Dad and my brothers and Lyra. And sure, that might freak you out if you didn't *already know them*."

"Yeah," I concede. "You might have a point."

"I have many points," he says as we round another bend and the castle reappears, closer than ever. "It's all good."

40

Kalle

I T MIGHT BE, IF *I* can stop freaking out.

I managed to calm down Edie—because I could tell she was about to bolt—but I can't expect her to do the same to me, because she has no idea that tonight is the first time I've ever brought a woman to dinner with my family.

Both Mom and Dad were open to us bringing significant others, but the unspoken consensus among my brothers and Lyra is that the person who comes has to be someone really special to be included in our inner circle. So much of our life has been shared with the public, and these family dinners are where the little pockets of normal take place.

Duncan and Spencer were always included because they are family and always have been.

Bo brought someone one time, but Camille and Stella were the first for Odin and Gunnar.

Lyra has never brought anyone, same as me. There's never been anyone I ever considered bringing.

Edie was the first one to ever stay the night as well.

And I can't tell her any of that because what thirty-two-year-old man hasn't brought a girlfriend to meet his family?

Red flag right there.

There are enough flags of every colour warning Edie away from me.

I manage to keep it together as I pull up to the castle. Dillon and Chase are still driving Edie's car and park it right behind me.

"Maj," Dillon calls to me. "You good?"

The man never misses a mark. "Yeah. We'll head back after we eat."

"Sounds good. We're off to bug Mrs. Theissen."

"Dillon?" Edie calls after him. "I need to ask you something."

"Anything, m'lady," he drawls.

"Why *Maj*?" she asks. "I've always wanted to ask, because the official way of addressing Kalle is Your Highness and—"

"I know all that," Dillon interrupts. "But he'll be Your Majesty someday, so he best get used to it."

Edie nods and Dillon tips an imaginary cap to her.

I take Edie's hand and we walk into the castle, Dillon and Chase veering off to make trouble with the staff. The wedding decorations have been taken down but there are still flowers on every surface, the heady smell of lilacs and lilies drifting about. And then we're in the dining room, the last to arrive.

Dad is already there, seated at the head of the table, looking tired but with a smile on his face. He seems... thinner. He's not wearing pajamas but old jeans and one of his concert T-shirts. I told Edie she didn't have to worry.

Now, if only I could take my own advice.

Edie is welcomed by everyone, even more than I am. Camille, Stella, and even Lyra give her a hug.

"Thanks for letting me... thanks for the invitation," she stumbles as she greets Dad.

"Anytime," he says and asks about her father.

I have no idea what they say, as I pour two glasses of wine.

"It's good to see Edie," Odin tells me as he drifts over, holding his glass out for a refill.

"Yeah. I know this is for family, but it's time everyone realizes she's family."

Odin slaps me on the back. "We realized that a long time ago. We've been waiting for you to get it."

I get it now.

41

Edie

I MANAGE TO CALM my breathing while I talk to the king, but it's hard to feel comfortable here, with everyone.

Kalle's right—I do know them all, but this is the inner sanctum. It might take a while to get used to it. Because who would have thought a family dinner with the royal family of Laandia would be burgers and French fries? Or that two-hundred-dollar bottles of wine would be drank like it came from a box. Or that Gunnar would keep teasing his brothers, with Lyra joining in, until Bo laughs so hard he spits out a mouthful of the very nice wine, spewing it over Odin's shirt.

It's like a normal family, but in a castle.

That settles me down a bit, but I'm still tense, especially when Kalle stands up as soon as the dinner plates are cleared.

I look up at him with wide eyes, but he only smiles. "I'm going to take a minute here," he says to the table.

Gunnar leans forward to clink his glass with a spoon. "You're supposed to do that if you want to make a speech," he calls from across the table.

"I'm not making a speech. I just want you all here for this."

"Sounds like you're going to make a speech," Bo points out. "Is it going to be a long one?"

"I don't like long speeches," Lyra complains. "I want dessert."

"Leave him alone," Odin orders. "It's no wonder he never says anything with you lot."

Kalle holds up his hand. "Gimme a minute." He looks stressed, and I touch his arm, smiling up at him with reassurance.

"You can have all the minutes you want as long as Lyra gets dessert," Gunnar says.

Kalle finally turns his back on them as Gunnar and Lyra continue their remarks… but they quiet quickly as Kalle begins to speak.

"I know you like fairytales," he says to me. "All those books you have. I might be a prince, but my life isn't a fairytale."

"I know that," I murmur.

"I'm not trying to scare you off," he adds.

"Kind of sounds like it," Lyra says sarcastically. The king shushes her.

"In the fairy tales, they get married after only a few days—I've known you practically all my life. I could take the time to court you and woo you, as Odin calls it, but honestly, I don't want to waste any more time. I want to get to the good stuff with you," Kalle says, speaking slowly like he's been rehearsing.

That's when my heart starts to beat double time. It's beating so fast that I press my hand against my chest because I think maybe… I think Kalle…

"What good stuff are we talking about?" Gunnar guffaws.

Kalle ignores him. "I spoke to your father when I was there, and he gave me his blessing. He said you'd be the queen of all queens."

Queen.

Kalle gives me his lopsided smile, the one no one else gets to see. "Afraid it's a package deal."

I didn't even realize I spoke. "You're going to be king?" I whisper.

"Did you have any doubt?"

I shake my head. "Never."

"Neither did I, when it came right down to it. But it's not just that—that I'll be the next king." He glances at his father and there is so much pride in his face, so much joy shining through that it hurts.

Something is wrong with my eyes. My face is wet and I can't stop smiling.

"This," Kalle says, gesturing to me. "I never see you cry. I want to. I want to see you cry when you're so angry that you could spit, just before you forgive me and we make up. I want to see you cry when you hold our babies in your arms—if not our babies, then our nieces and nephews. I want to take you to watch the sunrise and see every sunset with you. I want to share my life with you, Edwina England—and my throne, when the time comes. Which hopefully won't be for a while."

Kalle pushes out his chair and drops to one knee beside me. "Oh, my god," Lyra cries.

I clap my hands over my mouth as Duncan hands Kalle a little box.

I don't even glance at it. I only have eyes for Kalle... down on one knee...

"I've known for a long time that you're the only one I want standing beside me," he continues, his voice strong and solid. "I'm sorry I forgot to tell you all that, but I won't make that mistake again. I will tell you every day how much I love you, that taking those driving lessons with you all those years ago was the best thing that ever happened to me."

My throat chokes and I can't say a word. What am I supposed to say to that? To hear Kalle tell me he loves me, that he wants to spend—what exactly is he saying?

But he's not finished. "Edwina England, will you do me great honour and privilege of becoming my wife and the next queen of Laandia?" Kalle asks sounding as formal as a king should.

Are you serious? Are you sure you want me? *How do we do this? It's so* fast*!*

But I don't say any of that because there is only one word that fits this moment.

"Yes," I whisper.

"Say it again," Kalle orders as a smile creases his face, as spectacular as the sun crossing the horizon in the morning. "Say it so they can hear."

"Yes," I say. "Yes," I cry. "Yes, I'll marry you."

I keep going but my words are muffled as Kalle stands and pulls me up from my chair so that he can hug me.

And then he's kissing me. I hear cheers and clapping in the distance, but I keep kissing him until my face is buried into his chest. "That's how you propose," I manage to get out and Kalle sweeps me off my feet with a laugh.

This might be the best kind of fairytale.

42

Kalle

IT'S BEEN A WEEK since Edie has been wearing my grandmother's ring—Odin got our mother's since he was the first to get married. If I had known that, I might have done this earlier.

She went back to work the next afternoon like nothing had happened.

Only, a lot had happened.

We announced to the world that we're getting married. That, officially, I will be the next king and Edie will be my queen.

There's been a bit of a reaction about that—so much that Edie hired Mabel Crow to help out with managing the bar because she wasn't getting much done with all the requests for interviews and random people popping in to take pictures with her.

I think she's handling it okay. I put Dillon on her security detail, and today was the first time I've been away from her for more than an hour without checking in.

I might have asked Edie to marry me—properly this time—but there was still one more thing to do.

"What is that?" Edie demands, hands on hips. I just passed a group of tourists leaving the bar clutching their phones so I know she's been doing more selfies.

"This?" I lift it up. "This is a cat box." A soft *meow* validates my words.

"A cat? I have a cat."

"And I think Ernie needs a friend." I've been staying with Edie every night, and I don't think her cat likes me. I've tried everything, but he's pretty possessive about Edie.

I don't blame him. I'm kind of possessive about her too.

Last night I had an epiphany when I was trying to cuddle Edie and the cat kept getting in the way.

Ernie needs someone of his own to cuddle. "It's the cat from the alley," I say sheepishly. "Stella said she hadn't been adopted yet, so I thought..." I check how she's doing in the cage and the little tortoiseshell bundle of fur blinks yellow eyes at me. "This is Bertie."

"Bertie?" Edie asks with a laugh.

"Bertie and Ernie,"

"But I don't know if I have space in my apartment for Bertie and Ernie. Two cats is a lot and it's not a big space."

"That's the other thing. I thought it might be time to move to a bigger place."

"But you like my apartment better than yours."

"True, but maybe we'd like the castle better than both." I give her my best smile. "Want to move home with me? Since we'll be doing all the wedding planning from there."

Edie smiles and crosses to me, taking a moment to check on the cat before she reaches up and kisses me. "And there isn't much time to plan the wedding, is there?"

No, there is not. Now that I've found what I wanted, I'm not waiting around.

Prince and Edie have their HEA, but what about Prince Bo?

Find out who he has been waiting for when you sign up for my newsletter and receive this BONUS EPILOGUE!

In the meantime, keep reading for a sneak peek of this sweet romcom spin-off of my Love in Laandia series, **Coffee Break with the Billionaire**—part of Cinnamon Rolls and Pumpkin Spice!

Acknowledgements

Thanks so much for reading Royal Rising, the third book in my Love in Laandia series. Bo's book is up next – Royal Reluctance!

And I gave Fenella Carrington a book! Check out Coffee Break with the Billionaire, part of the Cinnamon Rolls and Pumpkin Spice series!

I dedicated this one to the dads, because there are a few father-child relationships going on. We've got King Magnus and Kalle, Magnus and his father, and Edie and her dad. Who knows—maybe we'll have Kalle have a father-son/daughter relationship of his own!! Bo would love that!

Plus, I've never dedicated a book to my dad and it's about time I do. Edie's father Bob is based on my own father, except that he's never cut the lawns for a castle and I don't think he's ever done a crossword in his life. I'm sure he would be very good at both though! My father is also hooked up to oxygen full-time, thanks to a little something called idiopathic pulmonary fibrosis. It's a lot nasty, but Dad's attitude is amazing, just like Bob England.

A huge thank you goes out to you, my readers. I'm living the dream because of you!! Thanks to the IG Booksgrammer community for being so welcoming and helpful; to Regina, and Blu, and Dylan for my people!

And always, thanks to Mom and Dad, E, and my kids.

Fun Facts:
I made Kalle take up curling because I just started to curl. It's a lot harder than it looks!
I have my daughter to thank for the shared bed scenes!
For a very long moment, I was going to kill off King Magnus.
I know! Aahhh!!!

Thanks so much for spending your time with me and my books!

Holly

Coffee Break with the Billionaire

A Cinnamon Roll and Pumpkin Spice Sweet Rom-com

T HE MAN WHO DESIGNED these shoes was a sadist.

And I know it was a man because a woman would not do it to another woman—make the baby toes squash beyond recognition, add no padding in the sole and even less grip on the bottom, causing me to skid along the damp pavement as I dash across the street.

A taxi screeches to a halt as I cross against the light, resulting in a long, drawn-out honk. A Maserati slides by, the driver shouting something incomprehensible out the window, along with a finger gestures. I ignore them and continue to cross because cars will stop for me because I'm Fenella Carrington and things always happen for me.

Except for this. This does not happen to me.

The music from THE CLB pounds after me, as does my very latest ex-boyfriend, Tiger Brannon. "Fenella—wait!"

"For what?" Forgetting I'm in the middle of a busy street at midnight, I whirl around to face Tiger panting after me.

You'd think a rock star would have better cardio but in reality, Tiger is in horrible shape, skinny to the point of scrawny with no visible muscle tone. He's the lead singer for Opium and a fairly boring one at that. He never moves, just hangs onto the microphone like my friend Gigi when you give her a bottle of Dom Perignon, and wails into it.

"What should I be waiting for?" I shout at Tiger. Okay, it's more like a shriek than a shout, but I'm an emotional woman and this has been a very bad night. "For you to make out with another woman?" I hold up three fingers. "In one night? Did you think I wouldn't find out?"

There were a lot of things I'm only now finding out about Tiger.

The sprinkle of rain has picked up, adding to the general crappiness of the night. The shoes are not meant for this weather, a surprise for Los Angeles, but neither is what I'm wearing—my Stella McCartney purple velvet flares and brand-new vest, which isn't really a vest but mesh covered in Swarovski crystals. It sparkles prettily in the light of the headlight, but also molds to my torso when it's wet.

Of course I didn't bring a jacket because that's what drivers are for, to keep you out of the rain.

More cars are stopping and there are many arms, with phones, hanging out of cars as Tiger is recognized.

Which makes it worse because no one is recognizing me. I'm famous too. Granted it's more for my father's money, but I've been on the cover of forty-six magazines and have over seventeen million followers, so hello—look at me!

That makes me sound vain, and I'm not that self-absorbed. I'm just really mad at Tiger.

Tiger reaches out a tattooed-covered hand to me. "Babe."

I jerk away, stepping back into the path of an oncoming car, which swerves around me. There is more shouting and a scream of excitement. Another fan. "Don't *babe* me. Three girls? What are you thinking?"

"Fenella!" A woman shrieks from across the street. "I love you!"

I smile and wave but turn back to Tiger with a frown.

"I didn't think we were exclusive." Tiger holds out his hands with an appealing smile. And he is appealing if you like the gaunt frame covered in tattoos and piercings. His eyes are a strange sil-ver-green, full lips—albeit with a double hoop—and the shock of platinum hair suits him.

He's the lead singer of the band with the most downloaded song on Spotify this month. Tiger is appealing.

At least he was.

I hold up my hand with the three-karat, square-cut pink dia-mond ring that Tiger presented me with nine days ago. Nine days! "Not exclusive?" I parrot. "What do you think this means?"

I shriek the last part, like a hyper fangirl. But it's still not enough, so I take off the ring and throw it at him. It bounces off his cheek. And leaves a scratch.

"Jesus!" Tiger slaps a hand on his cheek before scrambling for the ring. It's so big that it's not hard to find on the street.

"Babe. Fenella. You're making a scene," he pleads.

"Yes, and I'm very good at it."

Want more? Coffee Break with the Billionaire is ready for you to enjoy with your pumpkin spice latte!

READING LIST

Love in Laandia

Royal Rumble
Royal Retelling
Royal Rising
Royal Reluctance
Royal Rebel

Suitor Science

Hating the Chemistry Teacher
Falling for The Suitor
Fraternizing with the Ex
Marrying the Billionaire Best Friend
Loving the Wrong Guy
Finding the One

Don't

Don't Tell Me You Love Me
Don't Want to Be Friends
Don't Stop Me Now
Don't They Know It's Christmas

Love & Alliteration

Perfectly Played
Beautifully Baked
Pleasantly Popped

Charlotte Dodd

The Secret Life of Charlotte Dodd
The Missing Files of Charlotte Dodd
The Best Worst First Date Ever
The Hidden Past of Pippa McGovern
The Last Stand of Charlotte Dodd

Sisters in a Small Town

Coming Home
Hanging On
Stepping Up

Unexpecting
Unexpectingly Happily Ever After

STANDALONES

Cinnamon Rolls and Pumpkin Spice – Coffee Break with the Billionaire

Oceanic Dreams – I Saw Him Standing There

Absinthe Doesn't Make the Heart Grow Fonder